ADRIENNE
ELLIS REEVES

BITTER WATER,
BLESSED
HEARTS

ARABESQUE®

BITTER WATER, BLESSED HEARTS

An Arabesque novel

ISBN 1-58314-675-X

© 2006 by Adrienne Ellis Reeves

www.kimanipress.com

Printed in U.S.A.

This book is dedicated to
Lauren, Ellis and Ernest Johnson.
Faith, trust and love always bring healing.

ACKNOWLEDGMENTS

Salutations and gratitude to Judy Watts, Kieran
Kramer, Nina Bruhns, Stan Yeager and Vicki
Sweatman, my Summerville critique group, for their
unfailing support and inspiration, and to Debbie
Reeves whose computer skills carried me through.
Thanks, also, to L. Caswell and Gwen Ellis for being
an attentive audience, and for their patience. I am
also appreciative of the perfect writing environment
extended me by Wilma and Firuz in their home.

Prologue

In the midsummer heat, no breath of wind stirred the trees bending over the pond that neighborhood boys splashed in trying to catch minnows in their hands. When a boy grew tall enough, it was a rite of passage for him to grab the longest branch he could find and try to swing across the pond to the other side.

"I saw my brother Scott swing across," seven-year-old Mikey Phillips bragged, slapping mud on one side of the fort he was building as he crouched at the edge of the pond.

"That's what I'm gonna do," Adam Mayes said, taking a glob of mud from his pail to make a tower on his fort.

"You can't. You're only six." Mikey wiped his hands on his blue shorts. "Your family's not gonna let you do it anyway, 'cause you're their only boy." His hands dry, he began sticking small stones in his fort.

"I'll do it. You'll see." Adam pressed his full lips shut as he emptied his pail and flung it behind him. "Nothing's gonna stop me!"

Mikey selected another stone and glanced at his best friend. He knew Adam meant what he said when his mouth looked like he'd eaten a lemon.

"Okay. I'll come with you."

Mikey was six months older than Adam, who lived next door, but they rode their bikes, climbed trees, explored woods, and sneaked away to the pond, always together.

"What're you doing?" Adam saw Mikey scooting around on the ground picking up stones.

"I'm making a stone fort 'cause it's stronger." Intent on finding stones to fill the pocket of his shorts, Mikey didn't look up.

"I'm putting another tower on mine." Adam patted his tower, rubbed his fingers on his red shorts, and reached for his pail to mix more mud. It wasn't there.

He looked around. It had landed in the pond when he'd tossed it behind him. He ran down the short slope to the pond and waded out to the bright yellow pail bobbing in the water.

It moved just out of reach of his stubby fingers.

He took two more steps.

Suddenly, the firm bottom his toes had been clutching disappeared. Panic-stricken, Adam kicked his legs and beat at the water with his arms.

"Mikey!" he yelled, and swallowed gulps of water that seemed to fill him up. Then something grabbed his legs and the more he kicked, the tighter it held.

His arms and legs grew weaker.

Adam felt his mother pick him up and lull him into peaceful sleep in her rocking chair, as the quiet motion of the water carried him away.

Chapter 1

The soft swish of rain dancing on the window awakened Jenny Cannon in the ebb of darkness. This was her first night back home in Brentwood, South Carolina. Lying now in her narrow bed at the top of the house, worn out by all that had happened in the past week, she let herself be swept back into the flow of slumber. Morning would be time enough to worry about what was ahead of her.

When six o'clock came the rain was still falling, but intermittently now, and Jenny stood at the angled dormer window dreading the hours ahead. Maybe if she stood here long enough she'd receive some sign of comfort and reassurance.

The scene from this house her parents had bought a few years ago was so different from the house Jenny and her sisters and brother had been born in. It had been a dear and familiar home until Jenny was thirteen.

This house, set among similar ones, two and a half stories

high, with a modest yard planted with shrubs and a few trees as part of the package, hadn't been built then. As Brentwood had grown, developers had bought wooded lots, laid out streets, and built these homes not only for the new people coming south to escape harsh winters, but also to entice long-time residents to move up to a better location.

Jenny heard the door open and turned to see Nicky, sleepy-eyed and hair-tousled, coming toward her.

"Hi, darlin'." She picked him up. At six, he was getting almost too heavy for her to hold, but she knew he was also feeling disoriented in this new setting.

He leaned his head against her neck. "Why're you up so early?" she asked.

"I couldn't sleep 'cause I'm not in my own bed." His voice was still drowsy and he rubbed his eyes as he snuggled closer in her arms.

"It's your bed now. Gramma and Grandad bought it just for you," she reminded him. "Remember they told you that yesterday?" Things were bad enough without Nicky feeling bereft of his own bed. Mom and Dad had gone to great pains to furnish the bedroom half a flight down for this grandson they hadn't seen for a year.

Jenny shifted him to a more comfortable position. "Pretty soon it'll feel just like the bed you've been sleeping in," she promised.

Nicky opened his eyes. "What're you looking at, Mommy?"

"When I was your age, I lived in another house and I was trying to see if I could find it."

"Can I see it?" Nicky leaned forward, straining Jenny's back. She pulled up a straightback chair and stood him on it next to her.

"I can't find it," she said almost to herself. There were so many things she hadn't been able to find in her life, and now she wondered if she ever would.

"You sound sad, Mommy." Nicky's soft brown eyes met hers. "I'll help you find it. What does it look like?"

"It was an old house, Nicky, painted white, with a big porch and a big yard with lots of trees in it. We had a little garden in the back, some flowers in the front, and one year Grandad made us a swing from the biggest tree on the side of the house."

Opposite the tree with the swing was the house that had been like a second home to her all those years ago. She felt the muscles in her throat tighten. She couldn't afford to think about that. Not now. Not ever.

"I have to get ready to go to my new job but it's still early, sugar. You want to go back to bed for awhile? You can have breakfast with Gramma and Grandad later." She hoped he'd say yes. It was going to be hard enough to get herself ready for the day, which she dreaded more and more. She didn't want to have to pretend that all was well if Nicky was at the breakfast table along with Mom and her sharp eye.

"When you coming home?" Nicky asked, as if he was ready to be persuaded to go back to bed.

"This afternoon, just like I did when we were in Chicago. I heard Grandad say something about a surprise for you later on, so maybe you need to go back to sleep for awhile so you'll be good and ready." As she spoke she carried him back to his bed and tucked him in.

"Have a good day, Mommy," Nicky said as he kissed her goodbye. He'd heard the phrase so often that lately he'd started saying it every time his mother went off to work.

"You too." Jenny brushed his cheek wondering what she'd have done these past four years if she hadn't had her precious son. Her second thought was that having a good day was the most unlikely event in the next twelve hours. But she could bear anything as long as Nicky was safe and secure, as long as nothing happened to him. She'd dedicated her life to keeping him safe.

Her dormer space had its own tiny shower, and as she stood under the soothing hot water, her muscles began to relax and some of the tension drained away. She chose an emerald knit dress that she knew followed every line of her figure and emphasized her long legs. Today she needed every advantage she could get. Sheer hose, black pumps and silver earrings also helped. She brushed her thick, shoulder-length hair until it gleamed, applied a subtle makeup that highlighted her brown eyes and smooth-skinned cheeks. No point in using lipstick until later—after coffee.

As she dressed, she looked around the room, thankful once more that she hadn't had to go to the house she'd told Nicky about. That she couldn't have borne. When Mom and Dad had returned to Brentwood, they, too, had closed the door on what had happened there by selling the old house.

"Jenny?" Her mother's soft voice came through the closed door. "Breakfast is ready."

"Come in, Mom." Jenny smiled at her through the mirror as her mother entered the room.

Rebecca Mayes was a small woman who kept herself in shape with rigorous exercise and careful diet. Her face had not wrinkled and her skin was smooth. Jenny had her wide-spaced brown eyes and small nose, but the tilt of her head and jaw and her wide mouth had come straight from Albert Mayes, her father. The milk chocolate skin color ran through the family.

"Did you sleep well, honey?" Rebecca automatically

smoothed the spread on the single bed. "I wish you'd taken the other guest room and given yourself more space."

"There's enough space here. I like it." She couldn't tell her mom that she'd chosen it because nothing about it reminded her of her bedroom in the old house.

"I peeked in on Nicky. He's fast asleep," her mother said proudly as they went downstairs. She was proud of everything her grandson did.

"I got him back to bed by reminding him that his grandad said he'd have a surprise for him later and he needed to be rested for it."

The golden pine table sat in a nook with three bay windows that looked out at a yard with shrubs against a fence, a fountain, and a covered patio.

"While Nicky's here, we're going to the nursery for some plants and flowers. I want him to help us put in them in the ground. Has he ever done that?" Rebecca brought the toasted bagels, sliced melon, scrambled eggs, and coffee to the table and sat down.

"No, he hasn't. The apartments we've lived in were taken care of by the gardeners."

She took a long sip of coffee. "You still make the best coffee, Mom. I think Nicky might like digging in the ground and planting something."

"It's wonderful having him here, Jenny. Thank you for coming." Jenny felt the emotion in her mother's voice and the love in her eyes, conveying all the unsaid things between them.

"Your dad and I will take the best care of him while you're at work," Rebecca promised.

"I'm certain you will." Knowing that had made it possible for her to return to Brentwood, even though her mind had told her not to come.

"I'll go to the school and get the information about transferring his records from Chicago," Rebecca said.

"That'll be a help." Jenny stood up. "Thanks for the breakfast."

"You didn't eat much," her mother protested.

"I'll try to do better at dinner," Jenny promised.

"You remember how to get to the school from here?" Rebecca followed her to the door.

Jenny slipped on a light coat and took an umbrella from the closet.

"I wish you could have had a bright sunny day for your first day at your new job," Rebecca said.

"Bye, Mom." Jenny hurried to the car and, as she drove away, she thought how appropriate it was that the day was not bright and sunny.

She was glad these streets were unfamiliar, but Brentwood wasn't so big that she could get lost, and eventually she came to the side of town where she'd used to live. Despite herself she drove slower and slower as she turned onto Green Street, then a short two blocks on Danville, and finally onto Springview Avenue. Her heart started beating faster and faster. By the time she pulled into the parking lot of Springview School, there was a knot in her stomach.

She locked the car after she got out and made her way around to the front entrance.

A thin sheen of perspiration covered her face and the knot in her stomach grew tighter. Instead of announcing herself to the secretary, she made a familiar turn to the right where the ladies' restroom had always been. She had barely made it when all of her breakfast came up.

When the retching was over and she'd washed her mouth out, she examined her dress. Not a spot had gotten on it.

She took time to put cold water on her face and neck, then did her makeup all over again. By the time she was finished, her stomach had settled down and she felt a little more in control for what she had to face.

If only she was a woman of faith, so she could pray for strength and courage and believe it would be granted. But she had only herself to rely on. *You can do this. You've done harder things in your life.*

That was true, but nothing went as far back as those times that were the foundation of her life.

She took a final look in the mirror, decided to deepen the crimson on her lips to offset the washed-out look that came from losing her breakfast, straightened her shoulders, and left the restroom.

The secretary's chair was vacant. Jenny waited a moment or two then marched down the hall to the principal's office. The door was open. She took a deep breath and walked in.

The man at the desk glanced up. Shock washed over his features and his eyes almost went blank. Slowly he rose to his feet. His mouth worked but no words came out. "Hello, Scott." Jenny hoped her voice was calm even though she was shaking inside.

"Jenny Mayes?" His voice was disbelieving. "What are you doing here?"

Dr. Scott Phillips had been at his desk since six o'clock trying to clear more folders from his in box pile. Sometimes he thought he'd never catch up with the position he'd been called to, literally, out of the blue. There he'd been at the end of his vacation in England, getting ready to resume his job as vice-principal at King Elementary in upstate Connecticut.

He'd hated going back to that job, especially after the stimulating two weeks he'd spent in London. His goal was to become a principal at a school where he could put into practice the educational concepts he'd come to believe in, instead of kowtowing to out-of-date practices that kept running kids out of classes, unprepared for what lay ahead of them.

Then, out of the blue, a call had come from Joe Alston, school board chairman for a school district that had a vacancy because of the principal's fatal heart attack just as the school year was about to begin.

"I remember talking to you the last time you were home, Scott," Joe had said. "The board needs someone immediately and I have your résumé here on my desk. Can you come?"

Come home to Brentwood, South Carolina, to be principal of the school he'd gone to from the fourth through the sixth grades? Scott's head was reeling.

"What about the vice principal, Mr. Alston?"

"Confidentially, we had to let him go after he roughed up a student. We're bringing in another one this week, but he can't handle the top job. You know Perry Freeman had been principal here for the past ten years, but we haven't made much advancement in test scores. I need to warn you that we're categorized as an at-risk school, Scott. You think you can handle that?"

Joe Alston had known the Phillips family for years in Brentwood. He'd been friends with Scott's father, Ward, a local attorney, and kept an eye on Scott, whose growing skills and reputation as a rising educator had garnered publicity. Joe wanted that talent put to use in Brentwood, which was sorely in need of ways to pull the young people out of a background where a dropout mentality began in the early grades. He felt that Scott Phillips could turn that around.

Scott believed Joe Alston had figured out his secret desire.

Changing at-risk student populations to one of confidence and courage that laid the foundation for good grades, success in passing state-mandated exams, and developing the desire to finish their education was what he'd wanted to do, professionally above all else.

"Yes, Mr. Alston. I'm sure I can handle it."

"There's just one thing, Scott."

"What is it?"

"We can only offer you the job as interim principal while we conduct a search for a permanent candidate."

Scott wasn't deterred. "My name will be on the list for permanent principal if I do a good job, won't it?"

"Of course."

"That's all I want, a chance to show the board what I can do as principal."

"Great! You'll have the help of a lot of good teachers, and the vice principal, Ed Boyd, will be useful. He doesn't want the responsibility of the top job. Of course, you know there are always some staff who will have a hard time making the change from Freeman, who didn't always require that they really hard work. You'll also be getting the services of an educational consultant because of Springview's at-risk category. Now, how soon can you be here?"

It had taken Scott two weeks to put his affairs in order. The Connecticut school district had penalized him for breaking his contract. He paid the fine gladly, left everything in order for the next vice principal, closed his apartment, told his friends and colleagues goodbye, and turned his car toward home.

Arriving in Brentwood, he made short work of renting an apartment and not so short work of explaining to his mother why he couldn't take a bedroom in their house.

"Mom, I can't. I'm going to be up to my eyeballs in work,

keeping very irregular hours, and I'm not going to disturb you and Dad."

"He knows what he wants to do, Elly," his dad said, not looking up from his magazine.

"We'll expect you to come to dinner often, Scott, because I know how you'll get caught up in your work and forget to eat. You're too thin now. Isn't he, Ward?"

Scott was six feet, two inches and had always been trim. He didn't think he'd lost weight, and apparently for once his dad agreed with him as he glanced up from his magazine. "Looks the same to me," he said dryly.

Scott wished he could say the same about his father. In the past year his diabetes had become more severe, and it showed in the gray tinge under his brown skin, the way he sat in his leather chair reading instead of working in his yard or playing golf, and the way he had to go to the doctor every other month, if not sooner. His flagging energy was apparent to Scott's mother, and she confided to him that she was very worried.

"He's just the not the same man I used to know," she'd said wearily a few months ago when Scott had come down for a weekend.

He wasn't to Scott, either. Hadn't been for years. What had started out as a feeling of subtle disappointment from his dad when he was fifteen, became an estrangement as Scott pursued his chosen career in education, despite his father's wish for him to follow in his footsteps and practice law.

The last time he'd been home, his dad's appearance and his mother's words had hit Scott hard. He'd vowed then to do what he could do to sweeten the relationship between his dad and himself.

Thus, when Mr. Alston had offered him the job in Brentwood, it had the advantage of making it possible for Scott to be near his parents on a continuing basis so that he could put an end to the estrangement with his father before it was too late.

He knew his father thought more of Richard and Michael, his younger brothers, and of Alnetta, his older sister. But perhaps now that he was here at least for a year, they could meet for the holidays and come together as the close-knit family they used to be when they lived in the old house.

He hadn't been by the old house or the woods or the pond. He'd avoided going in that neighborhood. He didn't even know if the woods and pond were still there. His previous visits home had been brief, and he'd never gone to see if it was the same. He had enough on his plate with his job; he had neither need nor time to deal with past history and emotions. Better to let them stay where they'd been for the past eighteen years.

Thank God for Mr. Joe Alston. He'd made Scott's introduction to the entire staff as positive and friendly as it could be.

Scott had exuded calm and control from the beginning. He had made a phenomenal effort to learn the names and tasks each staff member was responsible for.

"I have an open door policy," he'd said. "My door will be open unless something confidential is being discussed. Feel free to come in. What we want to build here at Springview is a family—a community of learners who are dedicated to helping each other. I know that's the idea some of you already have, and we're going to do all we can to support it. Thank you for welcoming me, and I'll be visiting you in your classrooms."

He'd jumped into the work with enthusiasm. Finally, he had his own program to develop and run. He didn't need anyone else's authority. But first he had to determine exactly where the school was in relation to South Carolina test scores. When he found out, he saw how far he had to go to bring the students up to par. He didn't fool himself that it could be done in the single year he had to prove himself. But he had to make the kind of beginning that would let the students know that in another year they could be at the level they were supposed to be. Then the school board would surely be willing to give him the permanent position so he could finish what he'd started.

In order to do that, the whole environment of the school needed changing. That was the key. In the six weeks since arriving, he'd been working until midnight most nights, learning how the school had been operating, and laying out his plans of action.

He'd been informed that the educational consultant, a Mrs. Mattie Stokes, would be arriving on Monday. He was looking forward to having her assistance in the many projects and assessments that needed to be done.

He heard the tap of heels coming toward his door and thought it might be Mrs. Stokes.

He looked up to welcome her and there stood Jenny Mayes! At first, it seemed impossible, yet every cell in his body recognized her.

Chapter 2

The tone of her voice had deepened but the intonation was the same and the way she said his name. No one else had ever said it quite that way.

"Jenny Mayes! What are you doing here?" He was finally able to get it out through his dry throat.

"It's Jenny Cannon and I'm your new educational consultant," she said. "May I sit down?"

"Of course." He rushed around the desk to pull up the cushioned visitor's chair. He closed the door and then returned to his seat.

"I was expecting a Mattie Stokes."

"She had an illness in her family and couldn't leave. So they called me at a moment's notice and asked if I could fill in."

"Fill in?" Was that good or bad?

"Actually, they gave me the job. Over the phone on Friday. They said someone should already have been here, so it was urgent. I'd just finished a teaching job in Chicago, so I closed the apartment, packed some clothes and drove down. Got to my parents' house yesterday so I could report for work today."

Jenny hardly knew what she was saying, and she doubted if Scott was listening. His deepest brown eyes were fixed on her with an intensity as if she'd come from another planet. As if he'd never seen her before.

He was strange to her as well. He'd been a tall boy, but now he was well over six feet. His face had grown into his aquiline nose and large mouth. Now he could be described as a man with strong features that sat well with his broad shoulders and trim waistline. He'd loved to run and jump as a boy. Probably he still did.

She suddenly saw him as a boy, fifteen years old, standing in front of her house talking and teasing. They were about to go through the woods to find their brothers, Adam and Mikey, when fifteen-year-old Tiffany rode up on her bike, her hair loose around her face and wearing a pale rose lip color.

"What're you doing, Scott? Why don't you get your bike and come riding with me?" She fluttered her long eyelashes, which Jenny knew for a fact were fake, because Tiffany had been with Jenny's sister Helena when she'd bought them.

"Ride where?" Scott hadn't said he'd go but he was looking at Tiffany pretty hard. Jenny wanted to tip the bike over.

"We could go to the park," Tiffany cooed. She acted like Jenny wasn't standing there.

"Jenny and Scott. Go find the boys like I told you to," Jenny's mother called from the porch.

"Guess I'll see you later, Scott." Tiffany rode off with a wave.

"Come on," Scott said as he darted off, his long legs taking big steps.

Jenny, mad and jealous, poked along, not even trying to

keep up. Scott had disappeared into the woods and Jenny followed. It was hot, as usual on a Saturday afternoon in July. Maybe when they got back home, she'd make a pitcher of lemonade and see if Scott wanted some. She was feeling better as she came out of the woods where the pond began.

At first she didn't understand what she was seeing as she looked at the three figures farther down the pond. Then she started running, passing Mikey who was standing as if frozen, and into the water where Scott was holding Adam in his arms.

"What happened to Adam?" she screamed, trying to get him out of Scott's arms.

"He was in the water and I couldn't find him." Scott's face was ashen. "Go for help." He pushed past her to the bank where he laid Adam down and began to try to draw the water out of his lungs.

Jenny ran, screaming "Mama" all the way until her mother heard her. Everyone in Jenny's house and in Scott's house next door heard the screaming and ran back to the pond. Firemen came from the station two blocks away, but it was too late. Adam had drowned.

Between them, Jenny's dad and mom cradled Adam in their arms. "What happened?" her dad asked.

"When I came to look for them, Mikey was in the water, thrashing around," Scott said.

Mikey said, "I was trying to find Adam. He was looking for his bucket that had gone in the water." Mikey was leaning against his mother, shaking so hard she bent down and took him in her arms.

"Did you see him go in the water?" his mother asked.

Mikey shook his head. "I was looking for stones for my fort. Adam was mixing more mud to put on his fort. That's why he needed the pail. But it was in the water." His words ended in a sob and he buried himself against his mother.

"Adam must have gotten in over his head and struggled. In trying to find his way up, he got tangled in that underwater weed. That's why I couldn't find him right away." Scott got the words out between swallows.

Jenny wanted to die. Never in her whole life had she seen such deep sorrow in her mother and daddy's faces, as they held Adam and cried.

Adam was the son they'd waited for so long after having three girls. He was a lovable boy with a big smile and the center of the household. Her dad was always saying what he and Adam would do as soon as Adam got a little older. They spent a lot of time together, and Jenny knew how much they loved each other.

Her mother was bent over Adam, crying with guttural noises Jenny had never heard before. Everyone in both families was crying, and when she looked at Scott she could hardly stand it. He looked like she felt, like his world had come to an end.

Her sister Patty put her arm around Jenny when they all left the pond. Scott was walking with his mom on one side and Richard on the other. Mr. Phillips carried Mikey.

If she had gone to find Adam and Mikey when her mother first told them to, none of this would have happened. But she'd stood with Scott, her best friend in the world, laughing and liking the way he was teasing her about her braided hair. Then that Tiffany had come up, and Jenny sure wasn't going to walk away leaving her and Scott together. She'd forgotten for a few minutes that they were supposed to be looking for Adam and Mikey. Even after her mom had reminded her, she'd been slow and let Scott go ahead because of Tiffany.

Now Adam was dead. Her precious little brother and her

parents' only son. The weight of grief, shame and guilt was so heavy she didn't know how she could stand it. Or if she would ever be free of it. All she knew was that her life would never be the same.

Scott was stunned. He felt as if he'd sustained a tremendous body blow. The most tragic event in his thirty-two years came roaring back to him. He was once again the fifteen-year-old boy, carefree, on a sunny afternoon teasing Jenny, the girl next door who'd begun following him around as soon as she could walk. She was thirteen now and he was beginning to think of her in a different way.

Flirty Tiffany had tried to get him to go riding with her, but he wasn't about to leave Jenny. They were going to walk through the woods to the pond to see if their brothers were playing there. The little boys knew they weren't supposed to go without someone older, but once in a while they tried to sneak away, just like Scott and Richard used to do.

When Jenny's mom told them to go find the boys, he ran on ahead just in case the boys were there. The pond was too deep for them in certain places. When he saw his brother Mikey in the water splashing around and crying, his heart sank. Something terrible had happened!

He scooped Mikey up and took him to the bank.

"Where's Adam?" He looked around but could see no one else.

Mikey pointed to the water. "In there. I was trying to find him."

Scott plunged into the deepest part of the pond but the water was so dark he couldn't see anything. He kept swimming around, frantically feeling with his hands and feet for Adam. After what seemed a long time, his hand touched Adam who was caught in the thick fronds of weed.

By the time Scott had pulled Adam free of the weed, his lungs were near to bursting. He caught the boy under his arm and shot through the surface of the brackish water just as he heard a scream.

Jenny came running. All he could think was to send her for help while he laid Adam on the ground, pumping his little chest and blowing breath into his mouth. Adam's face, usually so rosy and filled with life, was pale and lifeless. His bright eyes were closed and bits of weed clung to his wet hair.

Deep in his heart Scott knew his efforts were useless, but nothing in the world could keep him from trying and praying for a miracle that would bring Jenny's brother and Mikey's best friend back to life.

"I'll take over, son," someone said. He looked up as Adam's dad gently pushed him aside. Adam's mom knelt on the other side. "My baby," she moaned. "Don't let him die, please, God. Bring him back to us."

But Adam was gone and Scott knew it was partly his fault. He hadn't come soon enough to check on the boys, and when he got to the pond, he hadn't been able to find Adam fast enough to save him.

He'd felt terrible when his friend Joey had been in an accident that put him in the hospital for a week. Scott had been allowed to see him when Joey was all bandaged up with tubes to help him breathe. He'd felt sick to his stomach, and tried to understand how Joey must feel when he could only whisper, "Hi, Scott."

But the way he felt now was like being on another planet compared to that. Joey had healed and was now walking and talking and running again. Which Adam would never do. Ever.

Mikey would, but Adam wouldn't be with him as he'd

always been. He looked around for Mikey. There he was holding on to Mom. They came over to him and he stood up.

"Scotty," his mom said, and hugged him tight. She hardly ever called him that now that he was so tall. She only used that nickname when she wanted to show him she was pleased or when she felt he needed to be comforted.

There was nothing for her to be pleased about. Adam was dead. But being a mom, she guessed he needed to be comforted and he let himself be held close against her while he hugged her back as strong as he could. He wanted to cry, and he let himself bring up a few sobs, then swallowed the rest. "It's all right, Scotty," his mom whispered, her teary cheek against his. But nothing even she could say would ever make it all right.

Jenny was looking at him across the desk. He came back to the present still rattled, but aware that the onus was on him to conduct this interview. He had to put his professional face on, and he was thankful for the many times he'd had to repress any personal feelings in order to deal with the person on the other side of the desk.

What was it Jenny had said? That her name was Cannon. "You're married now?"

"Widowed. Douglas died four years ago in a skiing accident."

"I'm sorry." Immediately he wondered what kind of guy Cannon had been. Was she still grieving? The Jenny he knew had been a sensitive girl.

"How about you?" Jenny asked.

"Still single." Wedded to your career was the taunt he'd heard from the women he'd dated these past few years.

"Tell me something about your academic background, Jenny. Has it always been in education?" Scott sat back in his chair, one part of his mind on what she was saying, the other part still marveling that Jenny Mayes was the person answering the question.

"I had a double major at San Jose State University, psychology and education. I was fascinated with why people behave the way they do, and also with the part education plays in making us who we are." She pulled a slick black folder from her briefcase and slid it across the desk.

"The packet of information they sent you was about Mattie Stokes. Here's mine."

"Thank you. I'll look at it later, if you don't mind. Please go on."

"I decided to focus on education and got my master's at Stanford. Since then I've done a little bit of everything—teaching, writing curriculum, counseling, administration, published articles, and am presently seeking a grant for my doctoral degree."

A gadfly or an exceptionally curious mind harnessed to creative energy? Scott wondered.

"I'm sure that with your experience you've developed some principles about what education should be, or what you'd like it to be."

He laid out the bait quietly and watched Jenny's eyes brighten with awareness.

"As you well know, Dr. Phillips, there are as many ideas about education as there are practitioners, not to mention parents and even students. I can only tell you that I believe the school should be the heart of the community. I also believe that if we can find out why the student behaves as he or she does, why he or she won't study, and why they fail tests, that we can build on that knowledge and eventually overcome these negatives."

Scott could see that Jenny expected him to argue, or at

least state some different ideas, but why should he? Plenty of other educational leaders had espoused the same theories that Jenny held.

His experience was broad enough to know that it wasn't the theories so much as how they were practiced that made the difference. For that he'd have to wait and see.

"I don't know if you were told what happened here. Perry Freeman had been principal for the past ten years and he died of a massive heart attack one week before school was to open in August. I came in on an interim basis while a search is being made for a permanent candidate, of which I will be one. In the six weeks I've been here, the workload has been very heavy, as you might imagine." Jenny nodded, her eyes fixed on him. "Test scores have gone down in the past few years, and many of the students are from families on the lower economic scale. We have only this school year to turn the school around. That's my goal and the one I've told the staff."

"What was their response?"

"Mostly a wait-and-see at the initial meetings but there seems to be a little more hopefulness that it can happen. I see the school as a family. A family of learners, with helping each other as the credo. Not competition."

"But a little..." Jenny began.

A knock on the door was followed by its opening after Scott said, "Come in."

"Excuse me, Dr. Phillips, but I need the paper orders I left yesterday for your signature," said a brown-haired, cheerful-looking woman with an armful of books.

"Miss Fellows, this is our new educational consultant, Mrs. Jenny Cannon. Mrs. Cannon, Gladys Fellows is our media specialist." As the women acknowledged the introduction,

Scott took a sheaf of papers from his top basket and handed them to Miss Fellows.

"Thanks. Sorry to interrupt. Welcome to Springview, Mrs. Cannon."

"I think you'll like her library, it's one of the most welcoming I've seen," Scott said after the door closed.

Scott had a suspicion later that Gladys Fellows had spread the word about Jenny, since three other teachers had tested his open door policy with requests and matters that didn't seem urgent to him.

He showed Jenny to her office after introducing her to Ed Boyd, the vice principal.

Back at his desk he moved piles of paper around trying to find what he'd been working on earlier. Jenny Mayes Cannon had driven it all from his mind. He couldn't afford that distraction.

Returning to Brentwood had been difficult enough on his emotions. How could he possibly deal with what the job required and also face Jenny Mayes every day?

Chapter 3

Jenny waited until Scott showed her to the small room that would for now serve as her office.

"Sorry this is so small, but we're pushed for space. The vice principal is looking for a more suitable space."

"This will do. Thanks." She wanted him out of the room and the door closed before she shattered.

She sat in the chair, put her head down between her knees until the desire to faint subsided.

She couldn't do this.

She couldn't face Scott Phillips day after day and be constantly reminded of the guilt she'd repressed so she could make something of her life.

When she got home from the pond that awful day she'd been so overcome with grief and guilt that she'd huddled in her bed, inconsolable for the rest of the day. She'd been numb, unable to eat during the funeral preparations. It seemed to her that she moved in a cloud, through which she saw her family as they talked to her and tried to shake her out of her trauma.

"You're just being selfish," her sister Patty yelled at her. "Don't you think we all cared about Adam? You aren't the only one missing him!"

In a part of her mind, Jenny knew that was what it seemed to Patty and the others. But they didn't understand that she was the one who should have been at the pond minutes before, and then it wouldn't have happened.

One night her mother had come to her room and taken her in her arms. "Don't blame yourself, Jenny. It was an accident. Maybe we were only supposed to have Adam with us for this time. He was so special. His spirit was so bright. We can't always understand God's ways." She stroked Jenny tenderly. "All we have to do is try to accept them and have faith."

Did Mom really believe that? Jenny knew her mother wasn't eating or sleeping well, either. Dad disappeared for long periods of time and came back with red eyes, and he looked years older. Patty and Helena, the oldest sister, were quiet and the whole house seemed like a mausoleum. So how could Mom think it was okay that Adam had died like that?

People came to say they were sorry and ask was there anything they could do. They brought so much food there was hardly any more room in the refrigerator, because at mealtimes no one had an appetite.

Dad's brother, Uncle Trevor, and his wife, Aunt Delia, had come right away from San Jose, California.

Uncle Trevor was a man who made things happen and he sort of took charge but in a nice way, arranging the funeral at their church and then seeing what Mom and Dad wanted in the service.

He hadn't tried too much to talk to her, just sat with her

for a while with his arm around her. Jenny heard him talking into the night with Dad.

Patty came into her room with a note. "Scott wants to see you," she said. "You haven't said a word to him, Jenny. Are you mad at him?"

Jenny shook her head no.

"Then why won't you talk to him?"

"I can't. It reminds me too much."

She couldn't tell Patty about the nightmares she had of Scott standing in the water holding Adam's lifeless body and walking toward her. How sometimes Adam would open his eyes and look at her although he was dead.

"How do you think he's getting along, Jenny? You don't feel any worse than he does!"

"Yes, I do. He still has his brother," Jenny said.

Later that day Patty held out a note. "Scott sent you this." Jenny paid no attention so Patty put it on her dresser.

On the day of the funeral Jenny saw everything through a veil. Mama's sister Margaret and her family had arrived from Nashville, and it took two big cars from the funeral home to take all the family to church. They were ushered into a side room so they didn't have to face the rest of the congregation. The church was packed with people.

Mom sat next to Dad. He had his arm around her shoulder and she laid her head on him, holding a handkerchief to her eyes. Jenny sat between Patty and Helena. The three sisters held hands. Jenny felt those hands were her anchor to the world as the ceremony went on. Then they were led out of the church to the cemetery where Grandpa and Grandma were buried.

The family sat in the row of chairs under the marquee. When the small coffin was brought and lowered into the grave, Jenny dug her fingernails into Helena's hand. All around her she could hear people crying. The pastor said some words then that came to Jenny like a faraway sound.

The next thing she knew she was lying on the couch inside the church with two deaconesses in their uniforms talking to her and wiping her face with a damp cloth.

When Uncle Trevor and Aunt Delia had returned to San Jose a few days later, it had been decided that they'd take Jenny with them. She needs a change, they'd said, and her two cousins would love to have her with them. Uncle Trevor had been wanting Dad to come into his architectural firm for some time. This time his offer was accepted, and four months later, Jenny's whole family moved to San Jose.

Now I'm back here in Brentwood, she thought, sitting up in her chair once the faintness had passed. *What was I thinking of coming here?* When the job had been offered, they'd told her about the interim principal and that his name was Scott Phillips. That was the final bit of information. They'd already described the school, and it had interested her, because she knew that with her background she could do the first-rate job she needed as the last part of her application for a grant that would pay for her doctoral degree.

She had to have the degree in order to provide for herself and Nicky in the years to come.

Also, having the job in Brentwood made it possible for Mom and Dad to have Nicky with them for a year. She owed them that.

So when, as an afterthought, the person telling her about the job had mentioned the principal's name, Jenny had been startled, but she'd thought she could handle seeing him again. After all, they were no longer thirteen and fifteen. They were grown, mature professionals brought together to fix up a failing school and give the students a better chance in life. She could do this, she thought, and took the job.

She hadn't counted on what seeing Scott would bring forth. Waves of emotion that she had no control over had assaulted her. The guilt and loss she had felt eighteen years ago came back as if it had happened yesterday. It seemed like the effort she'd put into coming to terms with her failure meant nothing as soon as she saw Scott.

She gazed blindly at the part of the playground her window overlooked. She and her sisters had played there, as had Scott and his brothers and sister. It was the neighborhood school to which they'd all gone. Working here now at this school could be a pleasure. If only she could put behind her that Adam should have gone here, too.

Gladys Fellows opened Jenny's door a crack. "May we come in?" She pushed the door wide. "Louise Jordan and Yvonne Mitchell wanted to meet you. Louise is in social studies and Yvonne is in math."

Yvonne had a wide face and a gap between her upper middle teeth. "I wanted to see if you were the Jenny I knew the year I came to this school in the third grade." Her bright eyes were curious and friendly. "I think my desk was across from yours."

Jenny suddenly remembered the little girl with a gap-tooth smile who got the best grades in arithmetic. "You were good in arithmetic then," she smiled. "But your family moved away, didn't they?"

"My daddy got moved to Atlanta that summer, so I was only here for that year."

Jenny felt a flash of security. Yvonne hadn't been here to know about Adam.

"Come have coffee with us before the next bell rings."

Gladys led the way to a room with tables and chairs, a coffee machine and a microwave. Louise opened a small refrigerator. "Anyone else want juice? Those of us who don't drink coffee can have juice now, a gift from our new principal," she explained to Jenny who also opted for juice.

"You mean Dr. Phillips bought it himself?" Jenny asked.

"That's what I mean." Louise smiled.

Before Jenny had finished her can of cranberry juice, three other people came in. Her heart dropped when she recognized Dave Young.

Still stocky, with a shock of dark hair, long face, and a slightly off-center nose he'd acquired playing football with Scott and their group. He came over, a surprised look on his face and said just what Scott had said.

"Jenny Mayes? What are you doing here?"

"Hello to you too, Dave," Jenny said. "I just arrived an hour ago."

"You're a teacher?"

"I'm the new educational consultant," Jenny said.

He bent down and hugged her. "Gosh, it's good to see you again." To the others he said, "We grew up together, until the Mayes family moved to California. You been out there all this time?" he asked Jenny.

The bell rang. "We'll catch up later, Dave," Jenny said, and made her escape back to her office.

Dave Young was the last person she'd have thought would turn out to be a teacher. If he was the kind of man that he'd been as a boy—steady, industrious, fair-minded and excellent in athletics—then he'd be an asset to the school. But not to her. He knew all about Adam. Had been one of Scott's bunch, which meant that if he wanted to he could satisfy the curiosity of anyone who wanted to know about the new person on the staff. As with any institution, she knew full well about the gossip and rumors, the small feuds and jealousies that schools bred.

Dave was one more reason against her staying here. The agency would have to search for another replacement Mattie Stokes.

Chapter 4

Wednesdays classroom visits were one of the highlights of Scott's week. It didn't matter to him that teachers and students knew he might pop in, sit quietly in the back for ten minutes, then leave. If they were on their best or worst behavior, he wanted to see it all. He was also liable to slip into a classroom anytime he had a few moments to spare. He'd made an effort to learn the names of all the staff and most of the students quickly. People deserved to be called by their names, he felt. In the six weeks since his arrival he had seen how some of the students seemed to feel more comfortable when he addressed them by name. If you wanted the school to feel like a family, knowing names was important.

In Louise Jordan's fifth grade social studies the subject was the capital cities of the United States. As he quietly took a seat in the last row he paid attention as Dan said that Trenton was the capital of New Jersey.

"New Hampshire, Annette?"

"I think it's Concord," Annette said.

"Good. How about New York, Keisha?"

"I know that because my aunt lives there. It's Albany."

"Correct. New Mexico, Pete?"

"Is it Santa Clara?" he asked uncertainly.

"You have the first word right. What's the second one, class?"

"Fe."

"North Dakota, Ruby?"

"Bismarck."

"Next is our neighbor state, North Carolina. Steve?"

Steve sat with his head down, looking at his desk. Scott wondered if he'd heard the teacher. Some of these kids had hearing problems. In the silence there were one or two snickers, followed immediately by a repeat of the question by the teacher.

"Don't know," Steve muttered. This time the snickers were louder and Scott could see the flush creeping up Steve's face.

Louise Jordan passed the question on, and, as Scott slipped out of the room a little later, he was pleased with the teacher for not dwelling on Steve's failure. The boy was already embarrassed and the snickers had humiliated him further. Scott made a mental note to check tomorrow to be sure Steve had come to school because incidents like this were how dropping out of school began.

It was Professor Hill at university who'd first given him insight into what was to become his defining concepts about society's influence on young boys and girls.

"Young people, especially young boys, think that what they have to do is be better and get more attention than someone else. The older they get, the more they compare girlfriends and athletic ability and sexual conquests. Think about yourself and your male friends, Scott. Isn't that true?" His keen eyes held Scott's attention.

Scott, remembering the long discussions among guys in his dorm rooms that featured exactly these topics, blushed. "I guess you're right."

"That's because you've been taught that's what makes a man. Grown men do the same with jobs, titles, cars and everything else because they represent power and security."

"That's not good?"

"It leaves men feeling isolated because it destroys any concept of working together, of community. We have to begin with children, teach them that what is important is relationships. And working on something beyond self-interest."

Hours of discussion with Hill and further study had brought Scott to the understanding that these students he was dealing with now must buy into helping instead of aggressively competing, caring instead of comparing. See other kids as likable. Accepting responsibility instead of putting it on another student. The most difficult was to take the lead in helping and building good relationships, even if other students laughed at you.

He knew this was a big job. Changing long-held attitudes would not be easy, but he wanted to set these youngsters on a path of success, being able to stay in school and getting the most from it.

Proving this concept could work was one of the main reasons he needed the authority of the principalship.

As he walked toward his office, he passed Jenny's door. What would she advise about Steve's behavior? He doubted that her approach would be the same as his. From the conversations they'd had, he'd observed an edginess, a sharpness that disturbed him. A few of the teachers had the same tone with the students, probably formed over many years of unsatisfactory interaction with them. He already had his eye on them as possible rebels against his concept of a helping family. But he didn't have to put up with incompatibility in the services that the educational consultant was being paid to provide toward taking the students from the at-risk category.

Jenny invited him in and offered him a chair.

"I'll only take a minute," Scott said, standing. "I've just come from a social studies class where the students were being given an oral quiz on the state capitals. One student didn't answer when asked about North Carolina. There were a couple of snickers. When asked a second time, he muttered, 'I don't know.' This time there were several snickers and the boy flushed red from embarrassment. The teacher went on to another student. What's your take on the situation?"

"First, a demerit for the students who snickered. Next, talk to the student to see why he wasn't prepared. No textbook? No quiet place at home to study? Does he need a tutor? The teacher should have controlled the students who snickered. Laxity in the classroom encourages that kind of behavior," she pronounced.

Scott winced inside. As he had anticipated, Jenny was dogmatic and sharp. Totally at odds with the way Scott approached such problems. With him, it was always the student first, and how could the school be of help in providing the family atmosphere and habit of helping so that the students would feel comfortable that this wouldn't happen again. Confidence and self-worth would become a part of the student's attitude as a result.

Jenny, rolling a pen in her hand, reminded him of when she'd come over for him to help her with algebra. Sitting at the kitchen table she'd fidget with her pencil while he was explaining the problem.

"You explain it better than the teacher does," she'd said. The admiration in her voice made him feel ten feet tall even while he'd said, "It's easy, Jenny. You'll get it some day."

The admiration had been replaced by a challenge so definite it made him wonder if she'd decided to fight him at every turn. If so, it was better that they end the job now. He could do without a consultant, especially if it continued to be Jenny Mayes who kept him in a turmoil of unwanted memories.

Jenny's phone rang. "The secretary said Dr. Phillips is with you. Tell him there's a fight in the girl's restroom," the breathless voice said.

"Fight in girl's restroom," Jenny relayed, getting to her feet and heading down the hall with Scott.

Only the two girls were in the restroom, so Scott went in with Jenny. He recognized Amanda, a tall fourth-grader and Rhonda, a stout fifth-grader, pulling hair and kicking at each other.

Jenny took hold of Amanda while he grabbed Rhonda. "Stop this, now," he commanded in his sternest voice.

Rhonda, who seemed to be getting the worst of it, sniffled. "She started it," she accused and tried to kick out at Amanda.

"No, I didn't. You're the one who called my brother bad names," Amanda yelled. She lunged for Rhonda again. Scott could see Jenny had experience in this area as she held Amanda firmly against her, her arms locked to her side.

"The bell is going to ring in a few minutes," Jenny said, "and this place will be full. Why don't I stay here and help you get cleaned up while Dr. Phillips goes back to the office? Then I'll go with you to see him."

"I'll expect you in five minutes," Scott said. Jenny handled that well, he thought, and prepared himself for another confrontation between Amanda and Rhonda, but by the time they were seated in his office, they had stopped calling each other names.

"Tell me what happened. Amanda, you first, and Rhonda, while she's talking you can't say anything. Then it's your turn and Amanda can't say a word while you're talking. Okay?"

Both young faces looked at him, then nodded.

"I was in the restroom when she came in and said, 'You've got a dumb brother,' and laughed. I told her Steve wasn't dumb. 'He is, too,' she said. 'He didn't even know the capital of North Carolina after the teacher asked him twice. He's dumb.' You better take that back, I told her. 'Why should I,' she said. 'He knows he's dumb and the whole class knows it.' That made me so mad that I went for her and hit her in the nose. She pulled my hair and kicked me, so I kicked her back. Then the teacher came in, and I guess she called you." Her eyes were bright with anger and she didn't look at all remorseful, Scott thought.

"Rhonda, it's your turn," he said.

"I was just telling her what happened in class," she said defensively. "You were there, Dr. Phillips. You saw how Steve couldn't answer the question. Amanda didn't have to get so wild about it. When I pulled her hair and kicked her I was just defending myself. I didn't start the fight. Amanda did," she ended self-righteously.

Scott glanced at Jenny and saw the concern in her eyes. He looked at her reassuringly then let a few moments of silence go by. He found that this was one way to lower the emotional temperature in such instances. Jenny, sitting between Amanda and Rhonda, touched each one's hands while they waited for what the principal had to say.

"Rhonda, do you ever miss the answer to the teacher's question?" Scott asked.

"No, sir. I'm smart," she said smugly.

"I see. Then you get A's on all of your exams and quizzes?"

"Well, no, not all the time."

"That means that sometimes you don't know the answer to a question?"

"Yes, sir. I guess you're right." The smugness was gone from her voice. Amanda was looking triumphant.

"How would you feel if people called you dumb or some other name you didn't like?" Scott had a suspicion that other students called her fat.

"I'd be mad," she said so swiftly that it confirmed Scott's idea. He turned his attention to Amanda and let Rhonda think of what he'd said to her.

"Amanda, Rhonda isn't the only one at fault here. While your loyalty to your brother is a good thing, you have to find a way to express it without fighting or saying bad things to people that will just get you in trouble."

"I don't like no one dissing my brother," Amanda muttered.

"Of course not," Scott said, "but you also know the rule at this school about fighting. You both know it, don't you?"

"Yessir," the girls said in unison.

"Springview has a no fighting rule. What are we supposed to do instead?"

"Work out our differences by talking to each other," Amanda muttered.

"You both will get a demerit for fighting, and Mrs. Cannon will take you to her office and help you to talk over your differences so you won't have to fight again."

Jenny gave him a look that said she knew he was throwing this in her lap as a test.

Jenny came in an hour later. "How'd it go?" he asked.

"Surprisingly well after they got over being scared that I

would lecture them. Amanda and Steve stick together pretty tightly, especially since their dad left the family to move in with a young woman and their mom works two jobs to support the household. Amanda didn't come out and say it, but it's clear she's the articulate, fast-thinking and acting sibling while Steve is slower in school but a good athlete and protective towards her. I gather this isn't the first time she's been in trouble for acting before thinking."

Scott agreed that several teachers had mentioned Amanda.

"Rhonda is conscious of her weight and works hard in school to be smart instead of pretty. Her friends are two other big girls, and they have a hard time getting along with a kid like Amanda, who is slim and lively. After they told me about home and school, I had them look at each other and tell the other person at least one thing they liked about her."

"That was smart," Scott said. "What'd they say after they stopped giggling?"

"I see you've done this before," Jenny said. " I was surprised that it was Rhonda who spoke first. Said she liked the way Amanda looked and dressed. I wish you could have seen the shock on Amanda's face. I know she didn't expect that. Rhonda was serious and Amanda had to come up with something serious and good. Finally she told Rhonda that she didn't like what Rhonda said about Steve, but at least it wasn't behind her back. She told Amanda to her face."

"Honesty," Scott murmured.

"Exactly," Jenny said.

"I asked if they thought they could get along better now that they understood each other more, and they said probably."

"What's your conclusion, Jenny?" Scott asked.

"They may never be best friends, and I liked the fact that they acknowledged that, but I feel they'll respect each other and that's a good beginning." Her statement was confident and she met his eyes calmly. "I feel they'll think twice before they do anything next time."

"I agree and I think you did a good job. The change in attitude is crucial."

The words resounded in his head. Could he get Jenny to change her attitude about staying? She hadn't put it in words yet but it didn't take a rocket scientist to see she was ambivalent about staying. In the five days she'd been here, her office was still bare except for the briefcase she brought every morning. In meetings it was clear that she was holding back, assessing every situation, and when they were together, her reserve was several layers deep.

This was the first time she'd broken through it, as she dealt with the two students and made a difference with them. To be fair, his attitude had to change. He couldn't honestly say that he was comfortable working with her.

Jenny Mayes had been such an integral part of his life. She'd begun to follow him around as soon as she could walk, and when she was three or four sometimes he was the only one who could comfort her when she got hurt. Just as he'd begun to think of her in an entirely different way, the accident had occurred. After that she refused to see him or speak to him. He could only think that she hated him. That suspicion, plus guilt, plus the fact they'd never had a chance to talk about it made for significant emotional baggage that he'd been carrying for years.

However, Springview School had to come first. That meant putting it ahead of any problem he or Jenny might have.

"Jenny, Springview had one of the worst records for fights last year. I made a vow to do everything in my power to change that, not for myself, but for the sake of the kids themselves. They must have a safe learning environment. Seeing how well you handled this fight, I know that we could work well together for these kids. You've seen all the posters around the school about making this a family environment where we work together and help each other."

His voice deepened as he leaned across the desk toward Jenny, who was gazing at him as if mesmerized. Little Jenny Mayes had looked at him like that.

Scott took a deep breath. "I know you've been trying to decide if you should stay or go, Jenny, and I admit that I've thought the same thing." He saw the surprise in her eyes.

"But I'm asking you to stay and help rescue these kids, so that next year they won't be in the at-risk category and will be on their way to a healthier learning climate."

This wasn't what Jenny had expected. Working with Amanda and Rhonda had been the most satisfying thing she'd done in a long time, and she'd expected appreciation from Scott. But how had he known that she'd nearly made up her mind to tell him she was leaving? Surely the old connection between them was not that strong? Then to be asked, almost begged, to stay!

She dropped her head so she couldn't see his face and pondered his plea. She agreed that the students at Springview were important, but she had nothing to sustain her when it came to facing the guilt Scott reminded her of every day. Faith had deserted her, and hope. Without faith, prayer was empty of meaning, although sometimes in desperation she said the words. But not often, because she only felt worse afterwards.

"I don't know if I can do this," she said quietly.

"I don't know either, Jenny." Jenny lifted her head to meet his eyes, somber and steady. The lines around his mouth showed. "But there's too much at stake and I have to try." He stretched out his hand. "Will you try with me, Jenny, please? For the sake of the children?"

She dared not put her hand in his, so she touched it with her fingertips and said, "I'll try, Scott."

On her way home a little later, she wondered what she had agreed to. Back with Scott after eighteen years—was she still foolish enough to follow him as she used to do when she thought he hung the moon? Surely she wasn't that weak-minded.

It was when he'd said for the sake of the children that she felt a response in her.

For the children. If she could keep that as a mantra, maybe she'd be able to make it through this assignment, achieve a fine recommendation from Scott, get her grant for the doctoral work, and get on with a life far away from Brentwood and Scott.

Chapter 5

Scott pulled his black Lexus into the parking lot at his apartment complex, backed into slot G-10, and turned off the ignition. His arms piled with papers and folders, he took the elevator to the third floor. Mr. and Mrs. Wallace were making their way slowly toward him, her cane making no noise on the carpeted hall floor.

"More work on the weekend, Dr. Phillips?" she said in a sweet high voice that had lost most of its power.

"Just catching up. I hope you're both well." Scott liked his neighbors, who treated him with a genteel courtesy.

"Young man like you ought to be outside on a fine Saturday like this," Mr. Wallace said, his eyes twinkling.

"As soon as I do some of this I'll be out," Scott assured him as he went down to door ten.

He was lucky to find this place, he always thought when he opened the door. Besides the kitchen and laundry room, it had a large dining area furnished with comfortable chairs and table. The living room had a couch and chairs in gold and bronze, with adequate lamps. The only thing he'd brought were his bookcases, books and entertainment center. Two bedrooms and a large bath gave him space to use one bedroom as a study. He dumped the load he was carrying onto the bed and headed for the refrigerator.

He mixed cranberry juice and ginger ale in a large glass, filled a plate with a sandwich of sliced ham and chips, turned on the television and watched a college football game. He thought with nostalgia of the earlier years when he could play football, run, swim, play basketball, and one summer he'd even learned to ride horseback. All that physical exercise had sharpened his reflexes and kept his body in shape. Now he could hardly find the time to run, but soon he had to get back to a regular routine. He had to be at his physical and mental best for the months ahead if he wanted to be successful in making his deal with Jenny Mayes a victory.

Yesterday he sensed her reluctance in agreeing to stay and work with him for the good of the Springview students. He wanted to believe that she would keep to her promise. He wanted to have faith that she would stay the course, but faith had been almost impossible to come by since Adam.

That was one reason he'd sought a cause and put all of his energies into it. Faith didn't come into it, just persistence and unflagging work. He turned off the game, put his dishes in the dishwasher and settled down to the paperwork he'd brought home.

A few hours later he heard the phone ring.

"I'm glad I caught you at home," his mother said. "I was afraid you'd still be at school. I'm getting ready to fry the chicken, so your dad and I expect to see you in another hour. Okay, son?" The words sounded like a demand but the voice was persuasive. Scott chuckled. This was how his mom had successfully raised three boys and a girl.

"I'll be there. Just make sure there's plenty of mashed potatoes."

Eleanor Phillips, tall and gray, possessed the feminine version of the strong features she'd passed on to her oldest son. She welcomed Scott at the door.

He wasn't surprised by the critical look she gave him. "You're working too hard, Scott. But I know my telling you doesn't mean you'll stop. Your dad's already at the table, and so is the food, so sit right down."

"Hi, Dad." Scott pulled out the chair for his mom and brushed his dad's shoulder as he passed by his chair. "Hope you're feeling better today."

His father nodded in return. "A little better today. Got an appetite too."

"He shouldn't be having this fried chicken and he knows it," Elly Phillips scolded, "but he promised to have just one piece."

"We're all going to die sometime and one piece won't hurt me."

Scott felt right at home hearing the familiar give-and-take. The diabetes his dad had kept under control in earlier years had become a serious matter. Ward Phillips had married a young wife after he was well established as a lawyer. Now, at seventy, he'd retired due to the ravages of the disease and arthritis. One of the benefits of getting the position at Springview for Scott had been the fact that he could be closer to his dad.

Not only closer physically, but he hoped they could heal the estrangement that had existed for so many years.

"You have a fine mind, one meant for the law. Why don't

you go to law school and then come into partnership with me, Scott? Phillips and Phillips, Attorneys at Law. It would make me so proud to have that lettering on the door." His dad had said this to him in several ways through high school and college. Scott had been pleased that his dad wanted him as a partner and thought he had the makings of a good attorney, and for a while he was tempted. Then his brother, Michael, eight years his junior and known as Mikey to his family, began having serious problems in high school. He became sullen, displayed no interest in school activities, and occasionally disappeared from home.

Alarmed at what his mother relayed about Mikey, Scott began to make frequent trips home on weekends to see what he could do. Mikey avoided him, which made Scott even more worried. Despite their age difference, they'd always been good friends and able to talk to each other.

Early one Sunday morning, Scott went into Mikey's room, intent on catching him before he could disappear.

"What d'ya want?" Mikey grumbled, still half asleep.

"I want you to talk straight with me. How come you can't stand school anymore? Girl trouble?" Scott didn't think that was it, but it was a good place to begin the conversation.

Mikey made a face of disgust.

"Teachers you don't like?"

Mikey looked straight ahead expressionless, yet Scott sensed there was something Mikey wanted to tell him. He tried to remember himself at eleven, but he'd liked school, athletics, and roaming around with his brother Richard, his pal Joey, and sometimes with Jenny tagging along.

"Who you hanging out with now?" Maybe there'd been a falling out with his friends.

"No one. They're all jerks." This said with such tension that Scott knew he'd hit a sore spot.

"They said something bad about you, Mikey?" He knew that was it.

"Kenny said he heard that I'd let a boy drown when I was seven. I said I didn't. He said his dad was one of the firemen who was there and that's what he saw. I said I didn't care what his dad told him, it wasn't true." There was such hurt in his eyes and anguish in his voice that Scott went over to the bed and put his arm around him.

"Of course it isn't true. We all know that."

"Sometimes I feel it's true." The words were so soft that Scott could barely hear them.

A lump came up in Scott's throat. How could his dear little brother feel that way when it was Scott who was responsible?

"Why should I be here when Adam isn't?" Mikey asked, his eyes fixed on Scott.

"You're here because you didn't go into the water to get your pail and Adam did. It was just an accident, Mikey. Did you throw Adam's pail into the water?" Scott was horrified at Mikey's question and was reaching for anything he could bring to mind.

"No."

"Then it wasn't your fault. It was just a tragic accident, Mikey. We don't know why some things happen. That's why they're called accidents."

Shaken to the core to learn the depths of his brother's emotion, Scott urged his parents to get counseling for Mikey. He was better for a while, but when he got to high school he went to pieces again. He dropped out of school in his senior year, went from job to job, got into drugs, and had some trouble with the law.

Scott had helped as best he could. Talking with Mikey when Mikey wanted to be in touch, but he felt unable to give his brother what he needed most.

He couldn't find it for himself, so how could he tell Mikey how to find it? He could do something for other young people like Mikey and the law wasn't it. He changed his major to education and resolved to turn all of his energies to developing and implementing concepts in early childhood education. He wanted classrooms that were proactive, concerned, productive and watchful of the students.

Telling his dad of the change had been difficult. His father's deep disappointment had led to feelings of alienation between them, and although it caused Scott some distress, his goal in life was set.

"You're looking a little thin to me, Scott, " Elly said, piling his plate with two pieces of chicken, a mound of potatoes, some green beans, and two rolls.

"Enough, Mom," Scott protested as she considered another small piece of chicken.

"I know you only eat right when you come here," she said.

Time to change the subject to get her off what he ought to be eating "You'll never guess who showed up in my office on Monday."

"I heard it was Jenny Mayes." His mom looked at him inquiringly.

"What's she doing here?" His dad neglected his chicken to fix his sharp gaze on Scot. "Were you expecting her?"

"Not at all. I'd been told a Mattie Stokes was coming, but it turned out that there was an illness in her family so she couldn't leave. At the last minute they sent Jenny Mayes. I mean Cannon."

"What is her job?"

"She's our educational consultant, sent by a federal agency to help at-risk schools."

"I saw her mother in the store last week. She didn't mention it," Elly said.

"She probably didn't know about it. Jenny said she only learned Friday morning that she was to report here on Monday."

He'd been wanting to ask if they saw much of the Mayeses now that they were back in Brentwood. Once upon a time when the families lived next door to each other, his mom and dad were best friends with Jenny's mom and dad. The threads of their lives were closely entwined. The children were in and out of each other's houses; the families went on picnics together, made pilgrimages to the nearest beach for days in the sun and water. After Adam died and the Mayeses moved to California, the tie had been broken except for occasional letters.

Both families had suffered, and, over the years when he came home from college, Scott sometimes asked had they heard anything from the Mayeses. Sometimes there would be news, yet he'd missed the fact that Jenny had married. He was curious about the guy, but he wasn't going to ask his parents. Maybe Jenny would tell him when she became comfortable enough with him.

Maybe his mom, the purveyor of news among the family, hadn't mentioned it out of concern for his feelings.

The air was fresh and sparkling as Jenny and Nicky set out for their usual Sunday walk and run. This was a ritual Jenny held sacred. Even in Chicago, when the weather didn't cooperate, they went out either bundled up to their noses or wearing the briefest of shorts and shirts in the summer heat. Today was a perfect fall day for Brentwood. Here the air rarely had the sharp edge you could count on in Chicago. It was more like San Jose, she thought, with trees in color which—though not as brilliant as in New England—still gave you the joy of nature's palette.

"Ready to run?" Jenny asked.

"I'll beat ya to that big tree." Nicky flashed a smile and set off, his thin legs pumping hard. He hadn't been able to beat her yet, and Jenny didn't want to let him win. He needed to keep striving so that his win would be truly earned and real. Still, she managed to slow enough that she touched the big tree in the middle of the park only a few seconds before he did.

"Can I go on the swings, Mom?" Nicky was skipping with energy as he pulled at Jenny's arm

Since the swings were in sight and no one else was round, Jenny said, "Run ahead and I'll follow you."

In his red sweater and jeans he was the epitome of what healthy little boys should be, and Jenny's heart ached with joy that she had him, and pain that Adam hadn't had the chance to go beyond that point.

From a path on the right angle to hers, a tall man appeared. He was closer to Nicky than she was and in a panic she began to run toward Nicky.

"Jenny." The man called, and she suddenly realized it was Scott.

Embarrassed that Scott saw her running to protect Nicky from him, she flushed. "Hi, Scott. Do you run here often?"

"As often as I can, but I haven't seen you here before."

"Mom. Is that a friend of yours?" Nicky asked, his face alive with interest as he stood by the swing.

Scott was utterly surprised, and Jenny was embarrassed again that she hadn't mentioned her son earlier.

"Scott, this is my son Nicky Cannon. Dr. Phillips is the man I work for at the school."

Nicky stepped forward, hand outstretched. "Hi, Dr. Phillips."

"Hello, Nicky. I'm pleased to meet you," Scott said, shaking hands.

Jenny held her breath. It was not her habit to let Nicky mingle with her adult friends, consequently she was uncertain of Nicky's response. He and Scott examined each other gravely, as if she weren't standing there. Then Scott looked at the swings.

"How about a push?"

Nicky broke into a smile and scrambled up into the nearest one.

"Okay?" Scott asked Jenny.

"Not too high," was all she could say, as Nicky held on tight and Scott pushed him gently, then a little higher.

"This is quite a surprise," Scott remarked "Why didn't you mention it earlier?"

Having no other answer, Jenny shrugged. "It never came up."

She was interrupted by Nicky who cried out excitedly, "Look how high I'm going, Mom."

The involuntary step she took must have registered with Scott who immediately slowed the swing. "Don't want to get too high, son," he said. "Are you still holding on tight?"

"Yessir, I am. Really tight," Nicky promised.

"Three more pushes. Okay?" Scott said.

"Okay," Nicky reluctantly agreed.

Jenny relaxed, thankful for Scott's sensitivity. She knew she needn't worry, but keeping Nicky safe was the prime objective of her life.

Scott slowed the swing and was in the front to lift Nicky out at once. "Thanks, Dr. Phillips," he said, relaxed in Scott's arms. "Are you my mama's boss?" Candid eyes looked into Scott's.

"Yes. Why?"

Not knowing what Nicky might say next, Jenny wanted to snatch him away from Scott, but she couldn't help noticing how tenderly Scott held her son.

"She's really tired sometimes when she gets home." His unblinking stare was on Scott.

"I know. It's a hard job. But I bet she feels better when she sees you."

Jenny's heart was trembling. She had to put a stop to this. "I certainly do," she moved toward them. "We have to let Dr. Phillips go on with his running, Nicky, so tell him goodbye." It wasn't very graceful but she had to put a stop to this lovefest between Scott and her son.

She avoided Scott's glance as he set Nicky down.

It was clear he got her message as he said, "See you around, Nicky," and turned away.

"Wait," Nicky said. "When will you see me around?" He was being held by Jenny's hand, but his whole attention was on Scott who looked at Jenny for her answer.

Jenny, treading water, looked at him helplessly. "I don't know, Nicky. He's very busy, you know."

Nicky's face took on the mutinous expression that Jenny hated to see. He knew when he was being put off.

Scott bent down to Nicky. "We both live here, sport, so we're bound to run into each other." He ran his knuckles lightly over Nicky's head. "See you at work, Jenny," he said, and took off running.

Scott had managed to spoil her Sunday walk. Not only had

he distracted her from the peacefulness she'd come to find, but he'd mesmerized her son just as he'd mesmerized her when she was a child, to the extent that she'd never been able to forget him.

Chapter 6

Scott ran down the path that circled around and brought him out to the parking lot. Why hadn't he taken the path that cut across the park as he'd started to do?

Then he wouldn't have seen Jenny and met Nicky, and wouldn't be so mad he could bite nails. Why hadn't Jenny told him she had a son when she mentioned that she'd married and been widowed? What was the big deal? It wasn't like there was anything to hide about Nicky.

In fact, he was a great kid as far as Scott could see. Friendly, inquisitive. Could talk to adults. A fine boy all around.

They'd sure gotten along from the first moment. He hadn't missed that she was running to protect Nicky until he'd called her name and she'd recognized him. Then she'd been embarrassed, and rightly so. He swerved to avoid the brown terrier straining at the leash held by a young woman on inline skates.

"Sorry," she said with an appreciative look as she resumed her conversation on the cellphone sprouting out of her ear.

The good weather had brought out skaters, children pushing and playing on the carousel that had been empty the last time he ran, and people throwing balls wherever there was a space. Did Nicky get to go on the carousel or the slides scattered around the park? The way Jenny acted, he doubted it.

How could she have changed so drastically from the young girl who hadn't wanted anyone but him to hold her until she could get her balance on her first two-wheel bike. When they all went to the pool at the Y, she wouldn't let anyone teach her to swim except him. "I want Scott," she always said, and Scott got his share of teasing about it from his brothers and her sisters. But he didn't care. He complained a lot, but he always taught her what she wanted to learn and was secretly pleased that she trusted him.

Did she even know the word trust now? She probably wouldn't have let him give Nicky a couple of pushes in the swing if he hadn't set it up.

Where was that Jenny? There'd been a bond between them even at that early age that he took for granted. It had just begun to take on a different aspect when he was fifteen and in high school. Girls were mysterious creatures with their short dresses, lipstick and perfume, winking at him and giggling in groups as they passed in the hallway or lingered near his locker.

But Jenny was as familiar as the face he saw in the mirror. She'd told him her thoughts and fears. She told him stories she made up, and dreams she had. Sometimes they sat in silence, looking at the pond or trees, listening to the way the wind sounded when it was getting ready to rain. With Jenny he knew he didn't have to be anyone but who he was.

Now who he was couldn't be told she had a son!

He reached his car, wiped his sweaty face, and vowed that the next time he could find a solitary, private moment with her, he'd find out why.

The moment came Tuesday morning. He was in his office, as usual, at six-thirty. A little later, making his usual trip down the hall checking to see that nothing had happened during the night, he smelled coffee as he passed Jenny's office.

"May I come in?" He pushed her door open.

"Morning, Jenny. Serving breakfast?"

Her first look of surprise and pleasure made the years between them vanish. This was the way she used to look at him, but before he could respond her expression changed to the impersonal one he usually saw.

"Hi, Scott. Have some." She gestured toward the hot coffee and the toasted bagel. "Mama insisted on feeding me even though I wasn't home."

Scott sat opposite her and accepted a cup of coffee. "Thanks. How are your mother and dad? I haven't had a chance to see them yet."

"Mama's busy as usual with her women's club and church work." Jenny laid a half bagel on a napkin and pushed it across the desk to Scott. "Want to share?" As Scott watched, a soft blush rose under her skin at her unthinking use of their old way of communication.

He waited until she glanced up to see his awareness. "Is it any good?" That had always been his response.

"Eat it and see." She lobbed the ball back to him.

Scott swallowed a small bite of bagel and grabbed the opportunity to ask the question that had been bothering him since Sunday.

"This is how it used to be, Jenny. What's happened?"

"What do you mean?"

"You know what I mean. We knew each other so well, you and I. Maybe better than we knew anyone else, even though we were young."

"That was a long time ago, Scott."

"Not such a long time that you couldn't even tell me you had a son!"

The flush deepened in her face and her voice became defensive.

"It just didn't come up." It was the same answer she'd given him Sunday.

Scott sipped his coffee after another bite of bagel and wondered if the defensiveness in her voice meant that at some point Nicky had been at risk, causing Jenny to be overprotective. Might as well leave the subject for now, he decided, but he'd come back to it.

He liked the way her rose-colored suit reflected the flush in her skin. Her hair was so shining he wondered if she brushed it a hundred times every night. Better not ask. Find a safe subject.

"What's Mr. Mayes doing since he and your mother moved back?"

"He takes on an architectural design project now and then, whenever he wants to. Plays golf, works in the yard."

Scott rose, set his empty cup down. "And enjoys Nicky, I know. Thanks for breakfast." He closed the door firmly behind him.

Scott hadn't actually slammed the door, Jenny thought, but that's what he'd wanted to do. When they were growing up he'd sometimes get impatient with her. Especially when her short legs couldn't keep up with his long ones.

"Hurry up, Jen. You're so slow," he'd complained. As her legs grew longer she had no problems keeping up with him.

She could do that now but she'd have to guard herself. She'd been thinking of him when he popped in half an hour ago. That's why she'd been startled out of her professional facade. For a few moments he'd been Scott, her best friend in the world, the one every other boy had been measured by, and she'd instinctively fallen into their old pattern.

She paused in cleaning off the breakfast remains, remembering his instant participation. The routine had started when she'd bring whatever she could find in her mother's kitchen to their rendezvous—cookies, muffins, leftover cold biscuits, fruit. He was always hungry. She was always eager to share.

But he'd tease her, pretending he wasn't sure it was okay to eat. "Eat it and see," had been her challenge, because sometimes she wasn't sure herself.

With the last crumb off the desk, she looked in her compact to repair her lipstick. Her face still felt a little warm from the blush she hadn't been able to control under Scott's questioning.

What upset her was his awareness of her confusion. So why had he continued, asking her the reason they weren't like they used to be when each had known the other so very well?

He knew as well as she did. Did he ask it to torment her, as if he hadn't been there that terrible day and witnessed all that occurred?

It was a double curse, hitting each of them as well as both of their families.

She didn't carry the guilt alone. It had been Scott's bedfellow as well as hers. They hadn't needed to discuss it for her to have that certainty. For his own sake, she hoped he still retained his faith. Hers had vanished along with her brother's body. Over the years, she'd hoped for a miracle. Logic told her Adam couldn't be restored, but years of going to church had taught that faith could be renewed.

All you had to do was believe. Belief was a simple matter if one had a clear conscience. The stain of guilt on hers was so deep she despaired of ever purifying it.

She shivered. What was she doing? Rarely did she let herself dwell on such bitter thoughts. It was only happening now because of Scott Phillips. If there was any way to get out of this job, she would, because as long as they were in contact, the past was bound to intrude. She had to do a better job of handling it.

She picked up her folders and went down the hall as the first bell rang. Lynn Bartlett was straightening the chairs and tables in her homeroom. "Come in, Jenny. I'll be with you in a minute," she called. She twitched two blinds to correspond with the other three, put several books in place as she came down the room, and set out a chair for Jenny.

She was a study in black and white, Jenny thought. White skin, short black hair, mid-calf black skirt and starched white blouse. Her blazing red lipstick suggested that there was more to Lynn than first met the eye.

"I've been the teacher in charge of this homeroom at this school for a long time," she began, sitting straight at her desk. I understand you lived here before. Did you know Mr. Freeman, the former principal?"

"No, I didn't. I've been gone eighteen years." She was eager to hear what this teacher had to say about Perry Freeman. The more direct information she had, the better she could assess what she needed to do.

"Mr. Freeman knew everyone in town of any importance. That's why he kept his job so long. They knew he wouldn't try anything too new or different that might cause controversy. But the school has fallen more and more behind, until now we're in the at-risk category." Her lips thinned and she shook her head as if she hated saying the words.

"That's why I'm here, as you know. To help fix the elements that put Springview at risk." Jenny sensed that Lynn Bartlett was committed to an idea that might cause an uproar and Jenny wanted to hear it.

"Dr. Phillips told us at his first meeting that he wanted to turn the school around this year, and he'd be willing to listen to anything we had to offer. I told him what I wanted to do and he was interested. Now I'm telling you, so you can help make it happen, Jenny," Lynn said.

"This space and the hours the students spend here are a waste of time. No one wants to come here, and they can't wait for the bell to ring. No learning takes place. I want to change this into an activity room where the time is spent in arts, crafts, music activities, role play—but all of it as learning tools for the students. What do you think?" Her large eyes searched Jenny's anxiously.

"Who would teach these subjects?" Jenny asked. "And are you proposing they all be covered in one year?"

"I would teach them all. I've had training and experience in my earlier teaching experience, but these subjects are the first to go when money is tight. I've made out a detailed plan that schedules different segments week by week." She pulled a black notebook from her desk drawer and handed it to Jenny. "It's all in there."

Leafing through the thick volume, Jenny was impressed by the meticulous layout of hours, with the names of the activities, its methodology, and desired outcome. "You must have worked on this for months," she said.

"Actually a couple of years. It's been my dream for these students," she said simply. "Their imagination needs to be developed and disciplined for their future. Too often, they use their talents for a disservice."

Jenny nodded in agreement, remembering the confrontation between Amanda and Rhonda.

"There's one other matter before you go, Jenny. Dr. Phillips said what I personally have been wanting to hear from a principal, but there're some people who didn't like it."

"I'm sure he knows that," Jenny replied. "Change is hard."

"Especially if you're going to be held accountable. Perhaps you could let him know to watch his back."

Jenny had been in only one school where the entire staff got along with the administration, so she was accustomed to the gossip, rivalries and occasional bad blood within the school community. Surely Scott had the same experience, but it was distressing to find it here at Springview, where his tenure was so brief and his hopes so high.

She'd been at the school a week, and she didn't want to go running to him with the first piece of gossip she heard, even if it was well-intentioned. She would give Lynn's plan a serious look, and then discuss it with Scott.

"Mama! I wanta go on a hayride!" Excitement had Nicky jumping up and down in his chair at the dinner table.

"Sit down, Nicky," Jenny straightened his legs and pulled him down to a sitting position.

"Can I, Mama?"

"What hayride are you talking about?" Jenny asked.

"My friend Tod said he goes every year and it's lot of fun. You get to ride on a wagon full of hay that is pulled by horses. Then you have cider and donuts." The more he talked, the more enthusiastic he became. He even forgot he was eating his favorite macaroni and cheese.

"It's organized by the community youth club," Jenny's dad explained. "They're very careful, and they only keep them out for about an hour." Nicky's bright eyes and wide smile touched Albert's heart. What a joy it was to have this child close to him at last.

"We're not going to decide yet, Nicky. So finish your dinner now." Jenny's voice was firm. Albert saw her get that protective expression, and glanced at his wife. They both knew that meant making an effort to get through Jenny's obsessive need to keep Nicky from any situation that might bring him harm.

When Jenny came down from putting Nicky to bed, she brought it up. "I've never let Nicky go out to something like that, Dad, and I'm not ready to let him go now." She sat down and opened a thick black notebook as if to bring the subject to a close.

Albert wasn't going to allow that. "The boy's nearly seven, Jenny. You mean he's never had anything to do with harvest activities?"

"When he was in preschool, they had something at the school and he participated." She resumed reading.

"He's old enough and big enough to go on a hayride just around this neighborhood. Why don't you want him to go?"

My poor Jenny, he thought with an inward sigh. So brilliant intellectually, but so damaged emotionally since Adam. He'd do anything to get her past that day's trauma. He and Rebecca had talked about it many times, but now to see how it was affecting Nicky's life—that was where he had to step in.

"I don't know the people in this neighborhood." Her mouth was set in stubborn lines and she avoided his eyes.

"Your mother and I do. It's a safe place, Jenny." He spoke gently. "You were telling us about Nicky's father the other day. You described Doug Cannon as a man who loved physical activities and that he was killed in a skiing accident. You said he was adventurous and fearless. Wouldn't he want his son raised the same way?"

"He's not here to raise Nicky. I am, and it's up to me to keep him safe."

"He'll be safe with me. I'll take him and never let him out of my sight," Albert promised.

Jenny got up, clutching the notebook against her. At the door, without looking around, she said, "You don't understand. I can't lose him, too."

Jenny tucked in the blanket Nicky had kicked off, smoothed his hair, and kissed his cheek.

She showered, selected her clothes for the next day, then slipped into bed to study Lynn's notebook.

Through it all, one thought played over and over in her head.

How can Dad not understand? He lost his only son, so how can he be so brave with my only son and his grandson?

Chapter 7

The morning dew lay heavily on the grass, dampening the smart navy pumps that went with Jenny's long navy skirt and sky-blue sweater. The confrontation with her father had troubled her sleep, and this morning she'd put on some favorite clothes to make herself feel better.

The shoes would dry, she thought, as she adjusted the long blue and silver scarf that set off the ensemble.

She cracked the car window to let in the breeze that no longer held the summer lushness. The tinge of fall was a welcome sign, even though it came late to Brentwood. In Chicago, by now the leaves would reflect their October coats of reds, oranges, and yellows. She missed that. On the other hand she didn't miss the icy streets that would follow in the winter.

She parked the car at the school, picked up the briefcase and Lynn's notebook. As she passed Scott's open door, he looked up from his desk.

"Jenny. Good morning. Come in, please." He came toward her, his lips curved in a smile.

He closed the door after her. "I like what you're wearing. How are you, Jenny?"

He was standing so close and looking at her so intently that Jenny felt a little tremble inside.

"I'm fine, Scott. How are you?" She didn't meet his glance.

Scott took her chin in his hand and angled her face so that he could search her eyes. She didn't know what he saw in them, but a frown knit his brows.

"What's wrong, Jenny?" he asked.

"Nothing," she said, moving back, afraid that if she didn't, she'd lay her face in his large, comforting hands.

"Yes, there is. You know you can tell me," he said softly, stroking her hands.

The temptation was so strong. There was no one else she could talk to about her dad, and yet how could she tell Scott when he already felt hurt that she hadn't told him about Nicky? Her head was abuzz with confusing thoughts as her senses took in Scott's closeness and warmth.

"Let me help, Jenny." His arms came around her, notebook and all. It was an awkward position because of the notebook between them, but Jenny managed to lay her head on Scott's chest with a deep sigh of contentment. It lasted only a second.

Footsteps came down the hall. Scott was behind his desk and Jenny was in the chair with the notebook open by the time a brief knock sounded.

"Come," Scott said.

"Morning, Scott, Jenny." Ed Boyd, vice principal, came in, desk calendar in his hand. A portly man with a short haircut and rimless glasses, he relieved Scott of the endless detail of schedules and textbook procurement, among other things.

"That staff meeting is all arranged for tomorrow afternoon. The agenda is the harvest festival activities, and a progress report. Satisfactory?" He looked over his glasses at Scott, and, at his nod of approval, made a checkmark on his calendar and left, closing the door behind him.

"Have you had an opportunity to study Lynn Bartlett's idea for changing her homeroom into an activity room? She asked me to look it over also, and I think it has a lot of merit. Since she's trained in the activities, it wouldn't take long to begin to implement the plan. It should entice a lot of students to involve themselves in arts and crafts. What do you think?" Jenny was grateful to have Lynn's notebook at hand to act as an antidote to the unexpected emotional scene that had taken place a few moments ago.

It couldn't happen again and it was up to her to see that it didn't. Ed Boyd probably hadn't suspected anything, but the call was too close for comfort. She and Scott should make a vow to be only Dr. Phillips, principal, and Jenny Cannon, educational consultant, as long as they were in this building together. Be strictly professional and nothing else. Otherwise there could be a scandal, and what would that do to his chances of being appointed permanent principal? Or hers for obtaining a doctoral grant?

"I studied Lynn's notebook and I'm glad she had you look at it," he said. "I haven't gotten back to her because I have to be sure how many hours of homeroom we're mandated for."

"That's an item I can research for you," she offered.

"It's all yours then, and thanks. Let me know as soon as you find it."

Courteous yet brisk, his tone let Jenny know their conversation was over. At the door, she turned. "Thanks, Scott," she said softly, intimately.

* * *

Scott dropped his head in his hands. What was he going to do about this grown-up Jenny who'd begun to haunt him? When the young girl Jenny had gone away to San Jose, he'd thought about her every day at first. But she no longer lived next door, and as high school, football and college with all its joys and sorrows intruded, his Jenny-next-door had retreated in his memories.

It was only when he began to get serious about a girl that he found himself remembering Jenny. Did the girl have Jenny's steady gaze that made him feel he could climb mountains and swim oceans? Was she sincere and honest? Eager to share her ideas, dreams and silences with him?

The girls he went out with were leggy, attractive, vivacious and fun. When they got serious and competitive for his time and began playing games, he lost interest. Jenny hadn't played games.

The weirdest thing was that occasionally he'd see a grownup Jenny ahead of him on the street. With heart beating fast, he'd sprint to catch up, only to find it was a stranger to whom he'd have to apologize.

He sat up, looked at his desk calendar. She hadn't been here two weeks, and already he was caught in a dilemma he wasn't sure he could solve.

There was the gap to bridge between Jenny the girl and Jenny the grown-up who was desirable to him in ways no other woman had ever been or could ever be.

Then there was Jenny Cannon the educational consultant with whom he had a professional relationship. She was under his supervision. He was pledged to observe her work objectively and write a report on it.

He was no babe in the woods, and he could handle this

just as he'd handled other difficult situations. He'd broken up fights, fired people who then made his life miserable, stood toe to toe with furious parents as well as stubborn administrators.

But there'd been no one involved who was anything like Jenny. His emotions had never been present as they were now.

He hadn't meant to touch her when she came into his office. He'd only meant to pass the time of day, but the faintly bruised look in her eyes said she'd had a bad night and something was wrong. She denied it, but he always knew when she was keeping something from him. Before he realized it, he'd taken her in his arms to comfort her. She laid her head on his chest, and, for a split second, it seemed the girl Jenny Mayes and the woman Jenny Cannon became one. Before he could take it in, he heard footsteps and she slipped away from him.

No way could he let this happen again. He was a grown man, not a sixteen-year-old kid with no control. From now on, any contact between them would be strictly professional. He would see to that!

Jenny waited in front of the school at twelve, watching for Patty's dark green Ford. When it arrived, she found that the lunch date her sister had made turned out to be sandwiches, fruit and coffee in the gazebo at the park.

"You don't mind, do you, Jen?"

Patty had their dad's oval face, thoughtful air and dark eyes. As Jenny accepted the paper plate holding a ham sandwich, grapes, and a cookie, she saw the shadow in Patty's usually clear eyes.

"This is okay, Patty. How are my nieces, and when will you bring them down to play with Nicky?"

"At eight and six they run me off my feet but they're fine.

We'll come down when they don't have ballet or soccer." She played with some grapes.

"Sterling still busy?" Jenny sensed that Patty's husband was the reason for her sister's hurried trip from Lexington to spend a lunch hour with her.

"His contracting business is so successful we hardly see him. Last year he said I didn't need to work, and he'd like me home with the girls. That sounded wonderful, and it was for a while." She put aside the half sandwich she'd been trying to eat.

"Why isn't it still good?" Jenny asked.

Tears welled in Patty's eyes. "I think he's seeing another woman, Jen." Her voice wobbled but she swallowed hard and shook the water from her eyes.

Surely Patty's marriage couldn't be unraveling. It had been solid and stable from the beginning, with the birth of each daughter making it even more so. As far as Jenny knew, Sterling had always been a loving and responsible husband and father.

"What evidence do you have, Patty? Maybe you're misunderstanding what you see?"

"I don't think so, Jen. He's been going out on night appointments several times a week. When I asked how come he had to see clients after dinner, he said these were out-of-town developers, and he had to see them when they made themselves available."

"You don't think that's true?"

"I guess it could be, because he has seen other people sometimes at night. But not this often. Then one night he came home smelling of perfume."

Although her voice was steady, the unhappiness in her eyes made Jenny reach over to hug her for a long moment.

"What did he say when you asked him about it?"

"That the men had their wives with them and they went to

a café after the business was finished. They had some food, and he danced with one of the wives. He got defensive and asked why I was always questioning him, when all he was doing was trying to make a good living for his family." She sniffed and dabbed at her eyes.

"I said he never takes me dancing, and then we had sort of a fight and he moved out of the bedroom. We hardly talk anymore, and the girls know something's wrong. I don't know if I can trust him now, Jen. What should I do?"

"What do you want to do, Patty?" She didn't think her sister was ready to break up what had been a loving family and to separate Alicia and Katy from their father.

"I can't keep on living like this. Wondering every day if he's with another woman and how will the girls feel if we break up. What if I'm wrong? Maybe it is all business and I'm letting my suspicions ruin what we have?"

She looked up from the tissue she'd been shredding. "I'd feel so guilty. I'd never be able to forgive myself."

No, Jenny thought. *Not Patty, too.* She didn't know what that kind of guilt could do to your life, how it played havoc with relationships. She had to divert Patty from that path.

"You still love Sterling, don't you?" she asked.

"I'm not feeling very kindly toward him these days, but yes, I still love him. That's why this hurts so much."

"Try to build on that love you've had all these years, Patty. Let yourself trust him. Trust is a part of love. I'm sure your heart knows that. You have so much invested in him and in your marriage. Don't let suspicion ruin it."

She didn't know how Patty would respond. Her face was somber, her eyes dull. Jenny took Patty's hand in hers as she waited. They were chilly so she blew her warm breath on them and rubbed them gently.

"I knew you could help me, Jen," Patty said. Her face had brightened and hope was in her eyes. "I'm going to believe what Sterling tells me. My love is big enough to give him the benefit of the doubt, and I know trust can develop from that."

She gathered her sister in a fierce hug. "Thanks, Jen."

What a hypocrite I am, Jenny mused later. *I know the right words to say to help others. When it comes to Jenny Cannon, the words don't work.*

Jenny Mayes had had absolute trust in Scott Phillips. Even when he made a mistake, which wasn't often as far as she was concerned, her trust had been unbroken.

But guilt, like an insidious poison, had destroyed her ability to trust. That's why she hadn't told Scott she had a son. He was bound to find out, so it had been a useless action, and eventually embarrassing to her and hurtful to him.

Before Adam she would never have thought of such a trick.

If only she could find her way through this before it took a more serious toll.

Chapter 8

Scott had to admit that while Perry Freeman might not have been a dynamic principal, he had one accomplishment that would be a lasting legacy, the Brentwood Room.

The spacious room where staff meetings and other events were held had ivory walls adorned with paintings by South Carolina artists. Light poured in through windows on both sides of the rectangular space. Even the dark blue chairs, arranged this afternoon in neat rows, had well-padded seats.

"We had to hold a contest to select the name," Joe Alston had told Scott with a chuckle. "Perry wanted to name it for Larry Gordon who'd been the most influential board member in pushing the bond through, but that was too political."

"Would that be Lawrence T. Gordon?" Scott asked in surprise.

"Sure would. You know him?"

"We were on opposing football teams all through high

chool. I was never his favorite person. If he's on the board, guess I better watch my step."

Joe laughed. "Larry's okay as long as you stay on his right ide. Another name people wanted for his room was Martin uther King, Junior, but Brentwood won out."

Scott watched his staff come in by twos and threes. They elped themselves to the beverages and cookies he always rovided for staff meetings, with the idea that a sip of coffee r tea and a bite of cookie helped to keep the energy flowing nd lessened the boredom.

This was only his second full meeting. If you made an ffort to know your staff, talked with them and kept yourself vailable, you needn't afflict yourself or them with frequent neetings. When you did have one, people were more likely o attend and be interested. Or at least curious.

"We have only two subjects to discuss this afternoon," he egan when he saw that people had stopped coming in. "First s to plan the Harvest Festival for this year. Any suggestions?"

Games and a silent auction were the first ideas, followed by ix or seven more. A few generated mild catcalls and laughter.

Sherman Boone, a fourth grade math teacher, interrupted he laughter.

"I don't see why we have to do anything. It's not our re-ponsibility."

"That's right," another teacher near Boone said. "We never lid anything before. I don't see why we have to change now."

Scott noticed a small group near Boone nodding their eads in agreement.

"Because we're trying to show our students that the school ares about them, and change the way they feel about the school y letting them plan the festival. We're trying to stop fighting, bsenteeism, and bring up the grades," Lynn Bartlett said.

"Let me tell you what I have in mind." Scott felt it was time to intervene. "Each homeroom can select something to do for the festival and the principal's office will give out prizes. Lynn Bartlett, David Young, and Gladys Fellows will be the supervisory committee."

"Can parents come?"

"Of course. This festival is open to the community. All in favor?"

The majority of the hands went up, and that was enough for Scott. The rest would grumble but would fall in line.

Scott used the rest of the hour to describe the progress they'd made in improving Springview's environment, and the influence it was having on the students.

"We have a long way to go before the end of the school year, but there's already a difference in the classrooms I visit. I know this will begin to show up on report cards. I congratulate you on your hard work, and I thank you."

Jenny thought he was looking directly at her when he said his thanks. All good speakers made the audience members feel that way, and he was good. She'd give him that. This was the first time she'd heard him. The boy who had always held her attention now was able to hold the attention of a roomful of people, even when some opposed him, like Boone and his coterie, who must be the troublemakers Lynn had said Scott should be warned about. After today he didn't need warning; he could see it clearly for himself.

She started to go to the front to tell him she'd enjoyed the meeting, but he was surrounded by people, and maybe that would be more personal than professional, so she left the room.

Several teachers came up to Scott with more questions, then Dave Young walked back to the office with him. Dave had lived two blocks from Scott when they were growing up.

Almost as tall as Scott, broad-shouldered and agile, they'd played sports together throughout school.

"Devon and I are having a spur-of-the-moment get together tomorrow night, Scott," Dave said, "and we want you to come. Just food and talk. Wear jeans. Okay?"

Scott didn't hesitate. "I could use a night off. Thanks."

"One other thing I've been wanting to mention. You've got some people here who resent you, so watch out." Dave's usually pleasant face was serious as he issued the warning. "See you tomorrow about seven."

Scott laid his notes on his desk and wondered why Jenny hadn't spoken to him. He'd spied her in the third row from the back as soon as he stood. She hadn't been at the initial staff meeting so she had no basis for comparison about his presentation. Still he'd like to know her opinion about how it went. What she thought about him.

From a purely professional standpoint, of course. Nothing personal.

"Come on in, Jenny. I was hoping you hadn't forgotten." Dave ushered her into a room that seemed filled with people, music, and the fragrance of good food. "Devon, Jenny's here," he called.

Devon's pixie-like face broke into a welcoming smile as she surprised Jenny with a hug instead of a handshake.

"I'm so glad to meet you, Jenny. Dave'll see you meet everyone while I put the food on, and we'll talk later."

"You know everyone except Roger. He came here after your folks moved," Dave said comfortingly as he hung her jacket in the closet.

Jenny had been uncertain about accepting Dave's invitation, and had dawdled until the last moment. She dreaded meeting old friends and having to wonder if they remembered her as the girl whose brother Adam drowned.

"It's time you got here, Jenny." Suddenly Scott was beside her. He slung an arm carelessly about her shoulder. "I thought I might have to come get you."

Jenny's relief was instant and involuntary. Of course he would have sensed her anxiety, and had come to give her the support she needed.

"Since you're here, Scott, I'll go help Devon," Dave said.

"You okay?" Scott asked quietly.

"I am now. Thanks." The small smile she gave him was meant to be reassuring, but he saw the shadow of uneasiness in her eyes.

"Clare Smith's dying to see you. I don't know if you'd heard that she married Harry Minor," he said, giving her the information she'd need as he walked her over to the first couple waiting to greet her.

"Jenny Mayes! I'd know you anywhere, girl. You haven't changed a bit," Clare declared, her face, square and ruddy, breaking into a wide smile as she grabbed Jenny and kissed her on both cheeks.

This was so typical of Clare, who Jenny recalled as getting in trouble with teachers because of her tendency to exaggerate. She had to smile as she returned the greeting.

"I try my best to keep her in check," Harry said, "but this time she's right. Great to see you, Jenny. You're looking good."

Roger Watson, tall, dark, and suave was introduced, and in the general conversation Jenny felt her tension leave. Maybe she'd enjoy the evening after all.

A sultry voice spoke from behind her. "Hi, Jenny. Remember me?"

She turned to see Tiffany, the girl whose flirtation with Scott had made them too late to save Adam.

It was only the pressure of Scott's hand on her shoulder and the strength emanating from him that halted the dizziness she felt. With a tremendous effort she kept her legs from trembling and her voice steady.

"Hello, Tiffany. How are you?"

The long brown curls Tiffany used to fling over her shoulders for the boys to admire had become a fall of shining blond hair. Her makeup was flawless and her designer jeans emphasized her long legs. Her beautifully cut red knit top was enhanced by a gold necklace that ended at her cleavage. Matching studs shone from her ears.

Tiffany, Jenny thought, was the kind of woman who made every other female feel underdressed.

She'd taken time with her own outfit, discarding several tops before deciding on the apricot knit. She knew she looked adequate, but the Tiffanys of this world always got a second or third look from men.

She had Harry and Roger's attention, and even Scott was bantering with her while keeping his arm on Jenny's shoulder. Tiffany glowed with the attention, but it seemed to Jenny that Scott was the center of her interest.

Was she single? Married? Divorced? There was no band on the third finger of her left hand, she noted. Maybe she and Roger were connected. He seemed the type of man to hold her interest.

When Devon and Dave announced dinner, buffet style, Jenny held back. She was curious to see which of the two unattached males Tiffany would snare as a dinner companion.

"Jenny, come sit with me so I can tell you about my children," Clare said, taking Jenny with her to the table. Their plates filled with meat loaf, mashed potatoes, baked beans, green salad and crunchy rolls; they settled on the love seat with their plates on tray tables.

"How many children do you and Harry have?" Jenny asked.

"Four," Clare beamed. Jenny was handed pictures and a complete description of each child. "I love children," Clare said. "We have story hour every night, and as soon as they get older, I've decided to put my stories into a book."

"That's wonderful, Clare. Will the book be just for your children?"

"I'd like to publish it for other children. Put my yen for exaggeration to good use. You think I could do it, Jenny?" Uncertainty crept into her usual confident air.

"I think you can, and when you have it more clearly in mind, I know some people in Chicago who could help you," Jenny said.

Tiffany's sultry voice murmured on the air, causing Jenny to look up. The blond had scored a double whammy. She sat in a chair with Roger on one side and Scott on the other.

"Are the mashed potatoes good?" she asked Scott.

"Very good. Want me to get you some?"

"No. I just want to taste some of yours. Please." She leaned closer to him and waited, red lips parted slightly, while Scott piled his fork with potatoes and lifted it to her mouth.

"Mmm. They are good," she purred.

Jenny turned to Clare. "Let me show you a picture of my son, Nicky."

When her plate was empty, she left Clare to talk to Devon, who was at the other end of the room.

"Do you like being home again?" Devon asked.

"It's taking some adjusting," Jenny said. "Especially as it happened so quickly." She explained about being asked to substitute for Mattie Stokes.

"I'm glad you're at Springview." Devon's face was animated. "Dave says it could be such a good school, and he's hoping the board will keep Scott on, because he's the best thing that's happened there for a long time."

"I hope so too. He's one of the best principals I've ever worked with." Jenny picked up a framed photograph on the nearby table of an engaging Asian girl who seemed to be about eight years old. "Cute girl. Who is she?"

"Our daughter Lily," Devon said. "Come see her."

She led Jenny to a bedroom in the back of the house and turned on a shaded lamp. Jenny recognized the sleeping girl.

"I've seen her once or twice at school, but no one mentioned she was your daughter." The bangs across Lily's forehead and the long black hair on either side framed her delicate golden face.

"We'd been married three years, and I miscarried twice. I wanted to try to get pregnant again. Dave said not to, but I knew how much he wanted a child and I felt guilty at not being able to give him one. Then we had the opportunity to adopt Lily and I knew my prayers had been answered." She tucked in a corner of the bottom quilt.

"She's the joy of our hearts and I thank God for her every day," Devon said softly.

As Nicky is the joy of my heart, Jenny thought. "How old is Lily?"

"She came to us when she was three, but she'd been malnourished. Although she's nearly nine, she still has some growing to do." Devon turned the lamp off. "She loves to run and play hard. She's strong for her size."

The pride in her voice was clear as they walked back down the hall. Would Devon let Lily go on a hayride with a group of other children? Of course, Lily was older than Nicky, but she wasn't much taller. Still, maybe it wasn't a fair comparison. Yet the maternal emotion which came across as Devon spoke of Lily was the same as Jenny felt for Nicky. She wished she'd thought to discuss the hayride with Devon, but the appropriate moment had passed.

Later, as she was driving home, she thought of the home Dave and Devon had created. You felt good being there, because it was welcoming and filled with a feeling of harmony. What was it Devon had said about thanking God every day for Lily? The house Jenny and Doug had lived in for the two years of their marriage hadn't felt like that. It had been well-furnished and colorful but it lacked the atmosphere that Dave and Devon's house had. Could it have been the absence of daily thanks?

She found it hard to go to sleep as scenes from the evening kept playing in her mind. Her last thought was of Scott's physical and moral support when Tiffany appeared. Had she told him she was grateful?

For those moments, she and Scott had been as they used to be. Totally attuned to each other.

She could never have that with anyone else, and she could never have it with Scott again.

Adam stood between them.

Chapter 9

The day was bright and sunny. Jenny was excited and happy because Scott had promised to show her something special, and she couldn't wait to see him. His surprises were always unusual, like the perfectly woven bird's nest with one tiny blue egg in it that he'd found on the ground.

She'd been walking, but now she started running down the path from her house. Soon it turned and went through the woods. The sun on the leaves made a dappled pattern. A bird's song rose in the air, and Jenny thought she'd burst from sheer happiness.

The woods ended and she came out by the pond. At first she didn't see Scott; then in the distance he suddenly appeared.

Jenny's steps slowed, then stopped. That couldn't be Scott. The person coming toward her was dripping wet and he was carrying something strange.

He came closer and closer. Jenny wanted to move, but couldn't.

"I found him for you, Jenny," Scott said. He stood in front of her and held out his arms to hand Jenny her dead brother, Adam.

Jenny backed away.

Adam opened his eyes and looked at her accusingly.

"Why didn't you come for me, Jenny?"

A strangled sound of horror shot Jenny straight up in bed. What was that awful noise? Belatedly she realized the sound had come from her own throat.

The nightmare had returned.

Shaking, she left the bed, got a glass of water and went to stand by the window. She had dealt with this nightmare in various ways during the years when it had come frequently. It hadn't bothered her for some time, but she supposed the stress of coming home and meeting Scott had produced it. Each time it came, it took all of her willpower to make it go away. To refuse its terrifying effect.

So she stood by the window, drank the water in slow sips, and took deep breaths. She forced her mind to focus on what was outside the window. The way the roofs slanted. The three different makes of cars in the driveway across the street. The light downstairs in the back of the house two doors to the right. The twinkling of the stars in the clear night sky. She named to herself the constellations she recognized.

It took nearly thirty minutes before she felt calm enough to get back in the bed. She held the images of what she'd seen from her window until her eyes drooped in tiredness, and she slept.

Sunday morning breakfast had always been special in the Mayes house when Jenny was growing up. Although getting up time was later, everyone had to be at the table to eat a big breakfast and still get to church on time. The children took turns in asking for a favorite meal.

Jenny was both touched and amused the first Sunday she was home to have her mother explain this to Nicky and ask what he'd like to have.

"I can have whatever I want?" Nicky's eyes widened as he glanced at his grandmother and mother, because even if he wanted it would his mom let him have it?

When reassured that he could, he didn't hesitate. "Four big pieces of French toast with lots of butter and syrup and four pieces of bacon!"

This Sunday as Jenny went downstairs, Nicky bounced ahead from step to step.

"Grandma said last night it's your turn today, Mom." He jumped the last two steps. "What'd you say you wanted?"

"Don't jump the steps, Nicky. You can fall and break your ankle or leg. I've told you that before," she said automatically, knowing that he might or might not remember her command the next time. As he got older it became harder to keep him safe, protected from harm. This was a fact her rational-side knew, but getting her emotions to accept it was another matter.

"I bet I know what you want for breakfast." Nicky came to a halt by the kitchen door.

Her mother took a dish from the stove to the table where her dad was having coffee.

"I can tell you what I've just cooked," her mom told Nicky.

"No, Grandma. I'm gonna guess. If I'm right I get to ask you for something, Mom. Okay?" He grabbed her hand and shook it. "Okay?"

"Okay, Nicky."

She and Nicky always played guessing games but this time he had a plan in his mind that excited him and she was curious to learn what it was.

"You asked for biscuits, eggs, sausage, and that stuff I don't like, grits." He ran to the table. "See, I was right."

The food went around the table, and Grandma, looking fondly at Nicky, asked, "How did you know?"

"Because sometimes Mom'd cook this in Chicago and say it was her favorite breakfast." Busily cutting his sausage, Nicky looked up. "Now can I ask you something?"

Jenny nodded as she buttered her biscuit and wondered what was coming. She wasn't always prepared for Nicky's questions.

"Can you take me to church this morning? I told my friend Tod I'd meet him there. He said they have a class for kids our age and they do some fun things."

Go to church? Jenny was so startled she took a big swallow of hot coffee. It burned going down, making her gag. She flew to the bathroom coughing and wiping her eyes. When she returned to the table Nicky asked, "What happened?"

"The coffee was too hot for my throat," she explained, wishing she could give as simple an explanation about why she didn't want to attend church.

It hadn't been a regular part of Nicky's upbringing. Sunday had been for sleeping late, enjoying a breakfast that was different from hurried weekday meals, then finding whatever the city had to offer for the entertainment and education of a young child.

If occasionally she was bothered by how far she was straying from how she and her sisters had been raised with regard to the church, she reasoned that when her son was older, she would think about it again.

Meanwhile, she taught him honesty, truthfulness, kindness and consideration of others. And when he asked questions about God and how the world was made, she answered them as best she could.

She wasn't ready to go to church but once her son's curiosity was aroused, Nicky was very persistent.

An hour later, Jenny walked up the familiar steps holding Nicky's hand to keep him from running in his excitement.

The first person she saw was Deacon Grant, minding the door from the entrance hall into the sanctuary. His hair was now gray and there might be a line or two on his face that hadn't been there eighteen years ago, but he had the same wide smile and hearty handshake.

"Jenny Mayes," he boomed. "I heard you were in Brentwood, and I'm mighty glad to welcome you back to your church home. Who is this young lad?" He included Nicky in his smile.

"I'm Jenny Cannon now, Deacon Grant, and this is my son Nicholas."

"You're going to like the service, Nicholas, and I want to see you coming back," Deacon Grant said as he opened the door.

An usher handed Jenny a program and directed her to a seat in the third row from the back, after Jenny declined a seat toward the front. As the congregation gathered, people tended to look around each time someone new came in. Jenny saw the surprise on faces as they recognized her with nods and smiles, which she returned.

"What're we going to do now?" Nicky asked.

She was glad to show him the program and explain the service in hushed tones. It helped to repress the memories of the last time she'd been in this place and had had to sit in the front with the rest of her grieving family.

The minister came to the podium, the choir marched in singing, and the preliminary service began. Then an usher came to take Nicky to the children's class.

Jenny settled back in the corner of the pew and tried to keep at bay the memories of Adam's funeral. But she couldn't. He had been baptized here, and a few years later, buried here.

When she was still young and hopeful of forgiveness, she'd gone to a counseling center in college. Eager to regain her faith she'd listened to a counselor who was also a lay minister.

"You weren't to blame," he'd said earnestly. "You were young, unformed, and you made a mistake in judgment by not instantly obeying your mother. For all you know, Adam might have been in the water even before your mother told you to go look for him. Forgive yourself, Jenny, and then your guilt will gradually go away and you will find your faith again."

It had sounded so good. Surely she could do that. For a few days she began to feel relief from the burden of guilt. It didn't last. She had been taught responsibility and she'd shirked hers so that she could stay with Scott and prevent Tiffany from being alone with him.

Caught up in self-loathing for her failure, she stopped going to the counseling center.

Every time she was with her parents she felt the weight of her guilt. They'd yearned for a son and Jenny remembered the great joy in their faces when they first held Adam and looked at each other. He was their golden child.

Yet they'd never blamed her. In fact, their loving support during her inconsolable grief and shame had made her feel doubly unworthy.

One day when she was feeling depressed and lonely, she went into the college chapel and tried to pray. She knew the words, had heard them over and over in church as she said them. Nothing happened. They were just words.

There was only emptiness around her. She left the chapel in tears, convinced she was undeserving of forgiveness.

Hard school work and community service were what kept

er on an even keel and made life worthwhile. It was while she was getting her master's degree that she met Douglas Cannon.

She was instantly attracted to him because he was tall, athletic, kind, and reminded her of Scott Phillips.

She'd decided immediately not to tell him about Adam. When he proposed, she felt that perhaps she was being given a step on the path to redemption. They were married in a church and once more she tentatively allowed herself to hope.

At the end of the first happy year she'd gotten pregnant. Nicky was born nine months into the second year of their marriage.

Jenny was rapturous, not only because she wanted a child of her own, but also because for the first time she felt positively about the possibility of forgiveness and the regeneration of faith.

Three months later Doug was killed in a skiing accident. Their infant son never had a chance to know his father.

Jenny knew then that she hadn't been forgiven.

The presence of Nicky in her life pulled her through. She dedicated herself to him with a fierce sense of responsibility.

He must be protected from all harm. He must not die prematurely as Adam had because of her carelessness. She was aware that some people thought her obsessive, but they hadn't lost a little brother.

A slight stir in the congregation brought Jenny back to the present. Listening for the first time to the minister's words, she realized that he was winding up his sermon.

"These are troubled times, not only overseas, but right here in our own country. You have only to look around you to see it. Many people have serious, tragic problems. Although we live in a relatively small town, we have them, too."

His thin face was set in sober lines and his voice resonated throughout the church. He leaned forward, holding his flock with an authoritative eye.

"People are not obeying God, brothers and sisters!" He paused for emphasis.

"We must take to heart what the psalmist said in chapter five. 'Make them bear their guilt, O God; let them fall by their own counsels; because of their many transgressions cast them out, for they have rebelled against Thee.' "

Jenny's heart beat rapidly. She felt flushed, and dug her nails into her hands to hold herself together until she could leave.

She was bearing her guilt at great cost to herself, but the thought of being "cast out" chilled her very soul. Surely it wouldn't come to that.

She hadn't rebelled against God. She wouldn't dare.

It was more that she couldn't find a way to make the connection, the same connection she'd always had—before Adam.

Clad in black shorts and sleeveless T-shirt lettered in black with University of Michigan across the front, Scott ran at a steady pace all around the city park. Instinctively he avoided people and dogs, his mind fixed on how Jenny had acted last night at the get-together.

The professional demeanor they had to maintain at school was one of the reasons he'd been looking forward to the two of them being off campus.

Maybe they could have a private talk and finally clear up the reason for their long separation. He wanted to ask her face-to-face if she'd hated him after Adam. Was that why she wouldn't see him or answer his note?

If not, why hadn't she let him come over? She was the person he'd most wanted to talk to, even while they were all still at the pond. He knew she'd understand how he felt

nd the anguish that ate at him when he couldn't find her
rother alive.

Jenny knew so much about him that no one else knew. She
vould have understood, even if he hadn't been able to put it
ll in words.

The same way he'd known last night when Tiffany showed
p that seeing her would be a blow to Jenny. He'd made sure
o be there, even to put his arm around her when Tiffany
poke to Jenny. They hadn't needed words. His intuition had
een confirmed when Jenny had almost sagged against him.

He hadn't been too surprised to find that grown-up Tiffany
vas as self-indulgent and flirtatious as the high-school Tiffany
ad been. Her maneuvers hadn't bothered him until he realized
hat she was watching Jenny as well as him for a reaction.

Immediately, he'd excused himself. He strolled to the
essert table where Harry was hanging out waiting for replen-
shments. Harry was now a top salesman with the local
General Motors dealer, and soon they were discussing the
uture of the auto industry.

"We're getting into the European market, you know. You
rive one of our cars, Scott?" Harry munched on a handful
f cashews.

"My first car was a Chevy," Scott recalled nostalgically.
About third- or fourth-hand when I got it, but I worked on
, kept it polished, and thought I was hot stuff."

"Stick shift, right?" Harry remembered his first car in
etail, and Scott listened while wondering when Devon and
enny would reappear.

"Here's some fresh coffee," Dave said. He was followed a
noment later by Devon with a plate of brownies, and Jenny
vith an apple pie.

"That's what I was waiting for." Scott held a plate out to

Jenny, who was cutting the pie. "Two slices, please." He figured that would get her attention.

Jenny raised her eyebrows. "And the second piece would be for—?" She was interrupted.

"You, Jenny." She looked at him in surprise. "Want to share?" he asked quietly. "We haven't had a chance to talk all evening. Join me."

She hesitated for a second then followed him.

When they were seated she said, "Devon took me to see Lily. I was so surprised because I'd noticed her at school but no one had mentioned she was Dave's daughter." She took the fork Scott handed her and began eating a slice of the pie. "You wouldn't know by looking, since she's of Asian background."

Scott dismissed the subject, for every moment alone with Jenny was precious. "How are you, Jenny? I know you didn't expect to see Tiffany, and it upset you." Concern shone in his eyes.

"It was a shock, but it helped that you were next to me. Thanks. Is she still single?"

"Presently, yes. Said she's been divorced since last year." He suspected that news wouldn't sit well with Jenny.

"So that's why she's on the hunt, again with both you and Roger in her sights," she said giving him a direct glance.

"I don't think so, Jenny. She's an incurable flirt, that's all, who never has and never will mean anything to me." His eyes held hers. "I don't want to talk about Tiffany. I want to talk about us."

Jenny's eyes flickered. "What about us?"

"I want to know what has happened to you since I saw you. How did you get through those eighteen years?"

Jenny looked down at the remains of the pie. Scott could sense her reluctance and withdrawal.

"Talk to me, Jen," he whispered compellingly.

"I got through those years the same way you did." He could scarcely hear her. "You make each day the best you can."

"Excuse the interruption, Jenny, but we have to go." Clare came up and gave Jenny a hug. "Don't forget to call me."

"You can count on it, Clare." Jenny stood up as the party began to break up and people said goodbye.

Roger and Tiffany involved Scott in a lengthy farewell and by the time he turned around, Jenny had slipped away.

Frustration at their time together being cut short had stayed with him during a restless night. As he ran this Sunday morning, he wondered when he'd have a second chance, especially now that it seemed Jenny wasn't anxious to pursue the matter.

He set his lips firmly. Whether she wanted to or not, he would make it happen. Maybe she didn't realize how important it was that they discuss Adam and how his death had affected each of them.

"Hi, Dr. Phillips."

Scott thought he heard someone call his name. He slowed his steps and listened.

"Dr. Phillips. I'm over here."

The voice came from the carousel. There was Nicky waving wildly as he went slowly around and around with a bunch of other kids.

Scott's heartbeat accelerated. With Nicky here, Jenny had to be close by. He spotted her sitting on a bench with several other people, and nodded to her before going over to speak with Nicky.

"I saw you running," Nicky said when he came around to where Scott was standing. "That's why I called you. I wanted to tell you I went to church this morning." He smiled up at Scott. "I liked it."

"I'll be sitting with your mom when you get off and you can tell me all about it," Scott said. He grinned at the thought that Nicky had probably sat in the same little chairs he'd sat in when he was six.

The bench was full, and Jenny led him to another seat on the other side of the carousel.

"Why did you run off last night, Jenny?" Scott leaned back against the wooden slats of the bench.

"It was getting late." Jenny had Nicky's denim jacket on her lap and began to straighten out the sleeves.

"Too late to say good-bye, when we'd been talking before Clare interrupted us?" He regarded her skeptically. "Mrs. Mayes raised you better than that."

She made no reply but kept smoothing the jacket with short jerky movements.

The curve of her slender neck, its vulnerability and fragility clutched at Scott. There was a melting warmth within him.

She seemed almost breakable this morning. Maybe she was upset about something and he should leave her alone.

On the other hand all he wanted was some honest talk between them. He didn't see how that was too much to ask.

"Jenny, why won't you talk to me?" He sat forward, trying to see her face.

Again there was no reply. Then she said slowly, "I can't see how it will help." The words were spoken to the air.

"How can you say that?" Scott was indignant. "Talking always helped us before."

"We were children then," she said so sorrowfully it scared Scott.

"We might have been young but we were still Jenny and Scott," he protested. "There was always a bond between us. You can't deny that, Jenny." In an effort to keep her from becoming more remote, he laid his hand on her arm and squeezed it.

Jenny sighed. Scott's hand felt so warm and comforting. She wished she could talk to him, but she couldn't.

If only she'd let her parents take Nicky to church this morning she wouldn't have the minister's warning still ringing in her mind.

The guilt she bore for the transgression that resulted in Adam's death had never been equated with the enormity of being a rebel against God.

If she could have found a way to dispel that guilt she would have done so long ago. She was worried, but she couldn't make it a topic for conversation with Scott now.

She wasn't sure where he stood and she didn't want to infect him with what she was struggling with. He might have been able to eradicate the guilt he felt.

She knew he'd carried a great sorrow. While they were all still at the pond she'd been able to sense it. But he was a strong-willed person even at fifteen, and had probably been able to put it all behind him as the years went by.

"Nicky and I have to go," she said quietly. She slipped her hand out from under his as she stood. "I'll see you at school."

She met his eyes for the first time. The suffering she thought she saw there tightened her throat, and she quelled the instinctive desire to take his hand.

She turned away quickly and bit her lip to keep the tears from falling.

Chapter 10

Carol Gordon debated whether to use gold or orange candles to complement the bowl of bronze mums as a centerpiece for the dining room table.

Her husband Larry was very demanding, always reminding her in various ways that when they were entertaining, everything had to be just right in order to reflect their status in the community. After all, he was the manager of the successful savings and loan, as well as vice chairman of the Brentwood district school board. He ought to be the chairman but Joe Alston kept beating him out by two or three votes. He was confident that by hook or crook he would get the coveted position.

Carol decided she liked the gold candles, and besides they were almost the same flattering color as the silk top she wore with her slim black skirt and dangling earrings.

The doorbell sounded. She took a final look at the table,

touched her hair in the mirror, and hurried through the hall. Larry liked her to answer the bell on its first ring.

As she greeted Larry's cousin, Sherman Boone, and his wife, Eloise, she thought Larry must want something special to have gone to the trouble of such formality for Sherman, with whom he was often in touch. He looked quite nice tonight in his dark suit, his hair brushed neatly back, his fleshy cheeks newly shaven.

Then she remembered another couple was coming, someone she didn't know, but Larry had wanted them here with Sherman and Eloise. She no longer tried to keep up with all of his schemes and stratagems.

"Turned a little cooler this evening," Eloise observed. A thin woman who bragged about her ability to find beautifully tailored knits and silks at discount prices, she slid into a chair, smoothing her Empire-waist ivory dress over her long legs.

"I noticed that when I stepped outside a while ago." Why didn't Larry come downstairs and entertain his guests? She needed to tend to dinner.

"Weatherman predicted rain later on tonight according to the evening news," Sherman said.

Carol looked at her watch. "You'll have to excuse me a minute. I have to go look at the steaks. Larry'll be right down."

By the time she'd pulled the sirloin tips and the roasted vegetables out of the oven, she heard the bell ring and the sound of new voices in the living room.

She went in and was introduced to Clyde and Merle Houser, a couple in their early forties who seemed to be delighted to have been invited to dinner with the Gordons.

At the table she learned that Merle Houser taught English at Springview School, where Sherman taught math.

"What do people think of the new principal?" Carol asked Sherman as she passed him the meat platter.

"A lot of the staff don't like him. He's young and has never been principal before. They think he's weak on discipline and doesn't understand the type of kids that go to Springview." He buttered his roll and took a big bite.

"Why is that?" Larry asked.

"He's got this crazy idea of the whole school as one big family. We're supposed to show the kids that the school cares about them. But what happens when some smart-mouth jumps up in your face? How're you going to discipline him? Pat him on the back and say, 'That's okay, son'?" Sherman sneered.

"What's your opinion, Merle?" Larry had laid down his fork as he listened to Sherman. Now his intense gaze fastened on the English teacher.

"I don't like to speak poorly of anyone, Mr. Gordon, but I just can't trust Dr. Phillips. He's changed so many things, even the curriculum committee, which had been my responsibility for the past few years. It was a big job but I was happy to do it." The genteel quality of her voice was belied by a sharp, resentful edge.

"Why did he do a foolish thing like that?" Larry asked.

"He said he preferred a discussion of the curriculum by the whole staff." She sniffed. "As if the whole staff could ever make up its mind on something that complex."

"Bruce should've gotten that job, Larry." Sherman punctuated his remark with jabs in the air with his knife. "Your brother knows how to run a tight ship. What happened to him?"

"Bruce couldn't get out of his present contract as headmaster of a prep school upstate without losing a lot of money. But he'll be at the top of the list when it comes to appointing a permanent principal. Especially if it's clear that the interim person isn't doing a good job and lacks the support of the more experienced and valuable staff members." Larry's glance rested approvingly on Merle, who flushed with pride.

"There's already been one big fight," Sherman said attacking the large slice of devil's food cake Carol had served him. "Did you hear about it, Merle?"

"It was all over the school." Merle tasted a dainty piece of her dessert. "This is delicious cake, Mrs. Gordon."

"Who was in the fight?" Larry asked, leaving his cake untouched.

"It began with two girls in the restroom, pulling hair and kicking, then other girls joined in until it was almost a free-for-all is what I heard."

"Of course the principal suspended them," Larry said. "Do you know how many students were involved?"

Merle and Sherman exchanged uncertain glances. "I'm not sure, Larry, but there must've been five or six. Maybe more," Sherman said.

"I've not heard of any suspensions," Merle said.

"I'll get back to you on that," Sherman promised. He'd had a good evening. When the time came, he and Merle would be rewarded for keeping tabs on Phillips for Larry.

His cousin had to be discreet but his final words to them said it all. "It's very helpful for the board that we can rely on vigilant staff to keep us abreast of what's happening in the schools for which we're responsible. Our friends will be remembered."

Jenny straightened her long denim skirt, tucked in her white shirtwaist blouse and made sure the silver buckle on her belt was exactly in the middle. Then she knocked on the principal's office door.

"Come in," Scott said.

He looked up from the paper he was writing. "Morning, Jenny. Have a seat. I'll be with you in a minute." He wrote a few more lines, signed the sheet, then laid it aside.

"What can I do for you?" he asked pleasantly.

"I met with the Harvest Festival committee as you asked me to. Their plans are moving along, and I thought you'd like to know what activities the home rooms are working on."

Scott rested his chin on his steepled hands, his eyes steadily on her as Jenny continued.

"Their idea is to hold it in the gym, with each project having its own space. They're going to bob for apples, do a version of pin the tail on the donkey, carry beans on a knife, musical chairs, drop clothespins in a bottle, throw a wiffle ball into a bucket, have a sack race and at the end have a huge piñata filled with candy."

Jenny paused for Scott's comment but he seemed lost in thought.

"They want your permission to have a rap contest."

Scott dropped his hands from their steepled position and picked up his pen.

"That should be interesting," he said. "But no profanity, no suggestive or offensive words about anyone. Be sure they understand those rules. Is there anything else?"

"Several questions about money came up." Jenny almost felt impelled to hurry through the remainder of her report or come back another time. She'd never seen Scott so reserved and noncommittal. Maybe he was with other people, but never with her.

The committee's questions needed immediate answers regardless of how Scott felt or what he had on his mind. She took a deep breath, made a meaningless notation on her paper, and looked up to meet Scott's gaze.

"The students want to bake cookies, make popcorn balls,

and punch, and sell them. What about the money to buy what they need? Is it all right to sell these things and, if so, how much should they charge?"

There was silence in the office. Jenny had put the ball in Scott's court and was ready to wait as long as it took for him to return it.

Tension filled the air as Scott turned the pen over and over in his fingers. Jenny wondered if he knew what he was doing; the motion seemed to be mechanically performed by a man whose thoughts were far away.

Finally Scott said, "You and the committee take care of those things. This office will supply the money. Get it from the vice principal when you're ready."

Abruptly he stood and looked at Jenny unsmilingly. "My thanks to you and the committee for their work."

"You're welcome."

Jenny left the office with her head held high and resisted the desire to look back. Who was that man sitting in Scott's chair, and where had Scott gone?

Scott had wondered on Sunday how he'd feel the next time he had to talk to Jenny at school. Now he knew.

They both had problems and adjustments that would have to be made since they were together again as adults. Yet it was inconceivable to him that Jenny would dismiss the unique rapport they'd always had with a careless "We were children then."

As if age mattered. They were Jenny and Scott, together all of their days exploring their little corner of the world and learning what each other saw, felt, thought, feared, and understood. A wordless communication had developed between them, as well as a depth of unity they hadn't yet put into words.

When they were torn apart after Adam the natural progression of their relationship had been disrupted.

For Scott it seemed that the tide of their feeling for each other had simply gone underground. But it was still there, and when they came together, it resumed its natural flow.

He couldn't understand Jenny. If they were children then, but were now presumably mature adults, why wouldn't talking help to clear up what happened back then? Her thinking was confused and had changed just since last week.

A very attractive woman in a denim skirt and white blouse had sat across from him talking about the harvest festival committee report. But it wasn't the Jenny Mayes Cannon he knew.

His Jenny had gone away, and he didn't know how to get her back.

Chapter 11

The late October afternoon reminded Jenny of the years she'd lived in San Jose, California. Of course there'd been a three-hour time difference between San Jose on the west coast and South Carolina on the east, but increasingly she found similarities in their weather patterns.

In South Carolina and in San Jose moderate temperatures prevailed most of the year. Rain came with brief summer thunderstorms and in winter months. Christmas was likely to be in the sixties and seventies. Lawns stayed green most of the year if you were willing to put in the time and effort to nurture them.

South Carolina was more humid, she thought. Here it was already mid-October and she could still feel the humidity that had made her change into shorts and a T-shirt after she got home. She sipped from a glass of lemonade as she walked around the yard watching Nicky ride his bike from the driveway to the patio.

The earlier brightness of the blue sky was beginning to dim. In a few hours it would be dark. Jenny was seized by the need to hold onto the daylight and the warm breeze making a soft sound in the trees.

Night brought troubled dreams and distressing memories of an earlier time. She remembered when she and Scott used to sit on the grass and listen to the wind. Sometimes it spoke to her and she'd tell Scott what it said. He'd give her his full attention and never say she was silly or fanciful.

"Nice out here this time of day, isn't it?" Her dad appeared beside her dressed in his gardening outfit of worn gray corduroys and blue checkered shirt with rolled up sleeves. Albert Mayes was lean and fit with brown hair that had flecks of gray in it, a broad mouth and sharp eyes.

He put his arm around Jenny's shoulder. "I do a lot of work out here, digging up the earth, deciding what flowers or shrubs will grow best in what places. Keeping them weeded and watered and watching them grow. That's the best part."

He gestured to the tall shrubs on two sides of the yard and pointed out how in front of them he'd planted several varieties of red and white geraniums, black-eyed Susans and pansies that were like purple velvet with a ruffled fringe.

"It keeps me close to the maker of the universe and brings me peace. I'm glad to see you out here, Jenny. It's a good place for you to spend some time."

Nicky came barreling from the driveway to the patio. He stopped when he saw his grandad.

"Did you tell Mom what we did?"

He jumped off his bike and turned to Jenny. "Me and Grandad planted some flowers today, but I don't remember their names."

"They're called camellias and they're on this side of the house, where they can get full sunshine."

There were two white planters, each one holding a healthy green plant that rose at least twelve inches into the air. "They look like little trees, don't they, Mom?"

Jenny exchanged an amused glance with her dad at the way Nicky stood, hands on hips, head to one side, looking at the camellias the way he'd seen his grandad do.

"Yes, because they already have twigs with green leaves. Pretty soon you and Grandad will have to put them in the ground so they can grow tall."

Nicky's forehead wrinkled. "I don't see the red flowers you talked about, Grandad."

Jenny's dad lifted a twig. "See that little ball?"

Nicky touched a hard green ball about the size of a walnut. "You mean this?"

"Yep. It's called a bud. The bud grows and pretty soon it begins to open up, leaf by leaf, and it becomes a beautiful big red flower."

Nicky thought about it a moment, then he grinned at his grandad. "That's cool!" he said.

His grandad ruffled Nicky's hair. "It certainly is."

Jenny watched the interchange between her son and her father and was suddenly immensely grateful, for their sakes, that she'd come home. Nicky needed his grandfather on his mother's side. He had no kinfolk on his father's side.

Doug had been raised by a bachelor uncle who died before Doug graduated from college. One of the qualities Jenny had admired about Doug was his refusal to feel sorry for himself. "Uncle Chris gave me a good life. I just wish he could have met you. You're my family now," he said.

He'd proven it by spending every moment he could with her. His attentiveness made Jenny feel she had a fairy tale marriage. They'd worked, played, laughed and loved together.

When he'd died, grief left a hollowness in her that was eventually filled by her precious Nicky.

In the intensity of her suffering she sometimes thought how the people she most cared for kept disappearing from her life. First there'd been Adam, then Scott, and now Doug.

But she still had her Nicky. Maybe her dad had been right when he said Doug would want his son to be fearless and adventurous. Perhaps she should let her dad take Nicky around more.

"Dad, you know the hayride we talked about?" she said before she could talk herself out of it. "Instead of that, maybe you and Mom could bring Nicky to Springview's Harvest Festival."

She was pleased to see how her dad's eyes lit up. He understood what a change this was for her.

"You want to go to your mom's school for a lot of games and fun, sport?"

"Yesss!" Nicky whooped and started toward the house. "I'll go tell Grandma."

Her dad kissed her on the cheek. "Thanks, Jen. He's a wonderful gift to us."

She rested against him, knowing she'd done the right thing, and absorbed his comforting strength.

All day the school was abuzz with activity. Teams of students marked off their space in the gym and, with the help of the maintenance crew, arranged tables and chairs according to the project for which they'd be used. Some amateurish decorations were put up, and the huge piñata was hung with a pulley arrangement that Dave Young would handle, so short and tall kids would have a chance at hitting it. In the afternoon the food for sale was brought in and placed on tables with signs made by students identifying and pricing each item.

When Jenny was satisfied that all was ready, she thanked the students and had Sam, head of maintenance, lock the doors. She reported to Scott via phone and dashed home to change into overalls and sweatshirt, clothes that could withstand spills and sticky hands.

Students were already lined up at the door when she got back to the gym. Sam unlocked it and people signed in. Half an hour later the place resounded with laughter, groans and screams as faces got wet in the apple tubs, the clothespins wouldn't drop in the bottle and people kept missing the chair. When someone managed to be the winner, there were more noises as he or she won the cupcake.

Jenny, Dave, Lynn, and Gladys took turns handling the money box and walking around the gym to see that all was going well. Students, their families and friends filled the gym. It was vital for the event to go off without any trouble, and to that end the committee had agreed to keep an unobtrusive eye on known troublemakers as a preventive measure.

"I haven't seen any problems," Dave said as he paused in his rounds. "They're busy having a good time. I saw your Dad and Mom and I met Nicky. He was bobbing for apples," he told Jenny.

"I saw him. Is Lily here?"

"She and Devon are somewhere in the crowd."

The sack race was called, and raised great laughter and applause, especially when some of the braver teachers tried it and ended up in a heap on the floor.

Across the room, Jenny saw Scott talking with her parents, his hand on Nicky's shoulder.

Dave rang a bell and announced the rap contest. Two girls and five boys did raps about school, growing up, how to dress, and how to be cool. The applause in the gym was deafening.

"There's so much hidden talent in these kids. That's why we need the Activity Room," Lynn said.

"I totally agree," Jenny said.

Scott congratulated all the rappers, then awarded the first prize of twenty-five dollars to the girl whose theme was growing up. The second prize of fifteen dollars went to the boy who rapped about school, and five dollars went to each of the runners-up.

Students swung at the piñata as Dave pulled it up and down until finally it broke sending people scrambling for the wrapped candy.

Scott thanked the committee, the teachers and the students for their hard work. "I talked with a lot of parents tonight and I thank you for coming out. It means a lot to us and to your kids when you show your support for what we're doing here. We hope to see you again, and good night."

A group of teachers volunteered to sing the crowd out while the committee exchanged congratulations on a successful evening as they wearily gathered up their belongings and gave the money from the food sale to the vice principal.

Scott came up after seeing the last visitor out of the door. He leaned against a table. "How do you think it went off?"

"Better than I'd hoped," Dave said. "There wasn't a bit of trouble from the usual students, or anyone else that I could see."

"Maybe they're beginning to believe what you've been telling them, that this school is for them and we care about them," Lynn said.

"They really liked it that you let them have the rap contest," Gladys offered.

"Jenny?" Scott said.

"I was just remembering that I heard a group of fifth grade

girls say how good this was and how much they hoped nobody would mess things up."

"Did it sound to you like they knew someone was planning to do something?" Scott asked with concern.

"I don't know. They saw me and moved along."

"Dave?" Scott said.

"Hard to tell, but I believe in prevention. I'll ask Sam to be sure that every door and window is locked."

"You were a wonderful team," Scott said. "No one could have done more. Thanks so much and have a good weekend. You deserve it."

Dave went to speak to Sam and his crew, while Jenny, Lynn and Gladys moved toward the front. Scott unlocked the door to the teachers' parking lot and escorted Lynn and Gladys to their cars.

Jenny went into her office to get her coat and purse. When she came out Scott was going into his office. He looked tired and lonely.

Without thinking Jenny went to him. "Did you have dinner, Scott?"

He looked surprised and after a minute said, "No. I didn't."

"I didn't either, so let's go get something."

"Gladly," he said.

In the parking lot she followed him to his car. "You can bring me back here," she said.

"You have any place in mind?" he asked.

"You choose. I don't know restaurants here yet."

Scott didn't know what to think, but he was too tired to question his good fortune as the car moved smoothly into the quiet street. The night was clear with a sickle moon in the sky. He turned his favorite jazz station low and began to unwind.

"You must be tired." He glanced at Jenny who was resting against her seat, her eyes closed.

"Umm. You are, too."

"Yep, I'm whacked."

The silence was easy and tension free. Scott promised himself to stay away from any personal matters and just be with Jenny and enjoy her presence. There were three good places to get something to eat at this hour. He chose the farthest one. When they were seated he asked Jenny, "Coffee or tea?"

"Strong, hot tea. Please."

When the waiter appeared Scott gave him clear instructions for two pots of boiling water with the tea bags inside. They'd order later.

"I see you have the same problem I usually have. The water is hot, not boiling," Jenny said.

The waiter brought the tea exactly as Scott had ordered it, along with china cups and saucers, lemon slices, milk and sugar. Scott gave him a nod of approval. "Come back in five minutes and we'll be ready to look at the menu."

The tea was fragrant and bracing to Scott, who took his with a slice of lemon and a scant spoonful of sugar. Jenny put milk in hers but no sugar. After the first few sips Jenny seemed to brighten.

"When did you become a tea drinker, Scott?"

"In grad school. I drank so many gallons of coffee I got tired of it and began experimenting with tea. I'd no idea there were so many varieties. I still drink some coffee, but tea seems to refresh me in ways that coffee can't. How about you?"

"I went to London for six weeks and fell in love with tea as a vital part of my existence." Her pixie smile enchanted him. "When I got home I couldn't get through the day without my four o'clock tea. Of course, that had to be modified, but tea is still my beverage of choice."

The waiter brought the menus and they ordered cheese omelets, toasted muffins, and sliced melon.

"More tea?" the waiter asked.

"Later," Scott said.

Scott waited for Jenny to say something. Whatever it was, he'd follow her lead. She looked fetching to him in her sweatshirt and overalls, though she probably didn't think so. He tried not to look at her every minute, although he wanted to, but she'd begin to be nervous. So he glanced around the room at the other late diners.

"I noticed how you walked through the crowd tonight talking to people. Were most of them parents you'd already met?"

"I knew a few. To the others I said, 'I'm Scott Phillips, the principal.' Almost always the person would say I'm so-and-so's mother or father or some other relative or friend." He stopped while their food was served.

Jenny sampled her omelet. "This is good. I was hungry."

"One guy I talked to said he didn't have a child in school now, but he and his wife live around here. Didn't give his name. Said he'd heard rumors about a bunch of girls fighting and being suspended, so he thought he'd stop by to get a feel of the school. He said he got a positive feeling."

Jenny had stopped eating. "But, Scott, that's a lie. No girls have been suspended. Did you set him straight?" Her eyes flashed.

"Of course I did. But it's rumors like that, the ones you can't pin down and get exaggerated, that give Springview a bad reputation."

She picked up her fork again. "You're right, of course. It happens to all schools but it makes me so mad when you and most of the teachers are going beyond the call of duty to help the students and give the school a better environment."

Scott was quietly thrilled to see Jenny acting like the girl he'd known, fiercely loyal and ready to do battle for people she loved.

"I spoke with Rhonda's parents. They were friendly, and so was Amanda's grandmother. She said Amanda's mother was working. I still haven't met her and I'd sure like to," Scott said.

"She doesn't come to parents' meetings?" Jenny was surprised.

"Not since I've been here. The grandmother thanked us for what we're doing with Amanda and Steve, and said to call on her anytime if we needed to.

"There was one really bright spot in the whole evening," he said as he finished his omelet and looked around for the waiter.

"The rap contest? It was really good. Unexpectedly so, I thought," Jenny said enthusiastically. "Lynn was beside herself, because it proved her point about the talent that's in the kids."

"I agree. You never know what they'll come out with if you let them give their ideas. Are you ready for tea? Dessert?"

"Just tea, please."

"That wasn't the bright spot I had in mind," he resumed after the waiter had cleared the table. "It was having a chance to see your parents again, and visit a little, and to see Nicky. He was having such a great time. Did you get a chance to watch him?"

"I saw him trying to carry a bean on a knife and bobbing for apples." They laughed together at the memory of Nicky almost tumbling into the tub as he persistently tried to catch an apple in his mouth.

"He really goes all out," Scott said admiringly. He'd been

surprised to see that Jenny had let her parents bring Nicky without her supervising every move he made. It was a good sign, he thought.

As they sipped their last cup of tea, Scott said, "Your dad looks like he's in good health, Jenny."

"Tell me about yours, Scott," she said gently.

"He's had diabetes for years but it's getting out of control and he's had to retire. He's seventy, and the diabetes plus arthritis limits what he feels he can do."

"I didn't know that, Scott. That's not only hard for him but for your mom, too." The sympathy in her voice encouraged him to say more. This was his Jenny, the girl he could talk to about anything.

"I accepted this job because I want to put my concepts about schools into practice. The only way I can do that is to become a principal long enough to see if the ideas work. One year is too short a time. But the other reason I came home, Jenny, is because Dad and I haven't been close friends for years." He stirred his tea absentmindedly, then looked at Jenny.

"But you're his oldest son and you always got along. He was so proud of you, Scott," she said in disbelief.

"That was until I went to college. He said my mind was meant for the law and he wanted me to study it and go into partnership with him. At first I thought I would. Then I decided to go into education instead, and it caused a separation between us. I want us to be close again."

"Of course you do, and I'm certain he wants the same thing. It'll be easier now that you can see each other frequently. It'll happen, Scott. I'm sure."

He took comfort from the conviction in her voice and the certainty in her eyes.

They ended their meal in the kind of communicative

silence that had been an everyday occurrence with them. It continued during the ride back to Jenny's car. Before he saw her safely in with the door locked, he said, "Thanks, Jenny. You're a life saver."

"I enjoyed it, too, Scott. See you Monday."

He watched until her car disappeared, then drove home, expecting to sleep soundly. But he tossed and turned, his mind filled with mixed images of the festival and Jenny.

Jenny felt strange as she prepared for bed. Had anyone told her she'd end this chaotic day in a restaurant with Scott, she'd have denied it.

Stranger still was the fact that she was the one who'd invited him. It had seemed so natural, she thought as she stepped out of the shower. She'd always been able to tell when he was despondent or worried.

She pulled her gown over her head, remembering the loneliness she'd sensed. That's what had made her go to him. It had turned out okay. Nothing deep or personal except that he had told her about his dad. Maybe she and Nicky could drop in to see his parents. That shouldn't be too difficult; after all, the Phillipses had been almost like a second set of parents to her. Now that she was back home, she didn't want them to think she was avoiding them.

Before she went to sleep she had an image of her and Scott drinking tea. Just two old friends enjoying each other's company.

Maybe they could keep it like that.

Chapter 12

Scott awakened feeling sluggish and dull-witted. There'd been a foreboding tinge in his dreams that still clung to him as he tried to clear his mind and work up the energy to get out of bed. Thank goodness it was Saturday. Maybe he could take some time for himself this weekend. Go horseback riding or swimming.

The phone rang. Immediately he knew it was something to do with the apprehensiveness that had bothered his sub-conscious.

"This is Sam, Dr. Phillips. I'm at the school, and you need to get down here. There was a break-in last night, and they did a lot of damage."

"I'll be right there." The sluggishness disappeared as he called Ed Boyd, Jenny and Dave to meet him at the school as soon as possible.

Fifteen minutes later he pulled into his parking slot. Sam

was waiting for him; his broad face, usually good-natured, was now grim and angry.

"How'd they get in, Sam?" Scott's nerves were taut, his stomach had a knot in it.

"They smashed the lock on the outside door behind the stage. The door isn't used much and the lock was old." He was talking rapidly as they walked from the lot into the building. He glanced warily at the principal, knowing he wouldn't be prepared for the extent of the vandalism.

As he stepped into the central hall, Scott's jaw tightened. The walls had been sprayed with graffiti. In the classrooms, some desks had been gouged with a sharp instrument and obscenities written on the chalkboards. Posters had been torn down.

Ed, Dave and Jenny caught up with Scott and Sam midway through their survey.

"I need to call the police," Scott said. "Do any of you know who I can call who won't come with sirens blaring?"

"Captain Greer's a decent guy, but I doubt he's available this early. It's only six-thirty," Dave said. "Maybe Brad Hampton is on duty. You could ask for him."

After he made the call, Jenny met him at the door to the library. "This is the worst of all. I don't understand how people can do this. Just look at this place!"

Books were pulled from shelves and strewn all over the room. Posters lay in tatters on the floor. The six computers that had been donated to the school had all been smashed. Reading tables were overturned.

Jenny shivered and put her arms around herself. Into the silence she said, "You can almost feel the rage that made the person cause this kind of destruction."

"I just wish I could get my hands on whoever it was," Sam muttered. "He'd never do it again."

The rooms behind the library hadn't been defaced in any way. "That's odd," Ed Boyd remarked. "Maybe it was getting light or he just ran out of steam."

"Seems to me this was more than one person," Scott said. "We can't touch anything until the police come so let's go back to my office to wait. Meanwhile we have to decide how to handle the staff and students."

None had been to the end of the building that held Scott's office, and they all saw it at the same time.

WE DON'T WANT YOU HERE was painted on his door in huge black letters. Dave and Sam barely smothered their expletives. Ed was stunned, and Scott looked as if he'd taken a body blow.

"How could someone hate me that much?" he wondered aloud. "I've only been here two months."

Jenny wanted to put her arms around him. He'd done nothing to deserve this. Not only had the school he'd worked so hard for been trashed, the final insult had been proclaimed where anyone entering the building would see it.

"I'm getting rid of this right now," she said in a blaze of anger. "What do you have that I can use, Sam?"

"Jenny, Sam, we can't do anything until the police get here," Scott said quietly.

"He's here now," Dave said, and went to open the door for a tall man with close cropped hair, a firm mouth, and watchful eyes. After introductions, Sergeant Brad Hampton pulled out his notebook and surveyed the damage room by room. He showed particular interest at the stage door lock.

"This took a lot of strength," he told Sam. "No puny kid with a hammer or a wrench broke this lock."

"Seems to me whoever did it came prepared with an ax," Sam agreed.

When he was through, he gathered everyone in the conference room, which had escaped the vandalism.

"Dr. Phillips, do you have any idea who's behind this?" His notebook was open on the table, his pen in hand and his watchful eyes on Scott.

"Not at all." Scott seemed composed to Jenny as he returned the policeman's scrutiny. "The school board hired me as an interim principal after Perry Freeman died so suddenly. I began work here September first, so I've only been at Springview two months."

"Yet according to the message on your door, someone definitely does not want you here."

"Apparently. I can only surmise that my idea of the school as a family where everyone helps and supports everyone else doesn't sit well with maybe one or more of our larger students who isn't being successful."

"Needn't be a large person. Someone small could bring a helper to smash the lock," Hampton said.

Dave spoke up. "I'm head of recreation, and we do have a few strong students, but I've never heard them say anything that would indicate they held a grudge against Dr. Phillips or the school. But Jenny, what about the girls you heard last night?"

"I'm not sure if this is at all helpful," Jenny began.

"Anything, no matter how small or negligible it seems, might turn out to be helpful," Hampton said reassuringly.

After she related the conversation between the fifth-grade girls, Hampton asked if she could identify them.

Reluctant to do so, she glanced at Scott. "If you know their names you must say so, Jenny."

"But suppose they were just speaking generally? What's going to happen to them once word gets out that they talked to the police? Especially if it turns out they did hear about this vandalism and the people who were involved. How safe would they be?"

The more questions she asked the more convinced she became that this was not the way to handle such a potentially dangerous situation for three ten-year-old girls.

"I'm sorry, Sergeant Hampton. I can't do this."

"Do you know their names, Mrs. Cannon?"

"Yes, I do."

"Refusing to give the police vital information can become a serious matter, Mrs. Cannon. I want to be sure you understand that."

Jenny felt there was no one in the room except the two of them, so intense was Sergeant Hampton's regard. He was doing his job, but so was she. She knew there was a better way to gain the information from the girls without betraying the trust Scott was trying to develop between the students and the faculty. She was certain that if she talked to Tamika, Katy and Milladeen, her insight and counseling skills would lead her to the truth.

"I don't mean to be disrespectful, Sgt. Hampton." Her voice was soft, absent of the least hint of discourtesy. "Part of my job here is working with students in difficult situations. I'm sure I'll be able to get you the information you need from these girls and still not put them in danger."

"When?"

"Excuse me, Sergeant Hampton. Will you be putting the yellow crime scene tape around the school, and do you know how long it'll have to stay up?" Scott asked.

"The school grounds will have to be thoroughly examined, but the campus isn't that large. Why?"

"My idea is to let the school know about the vandalism, and to welcome the students and teachers to come help clean it up, so by Monday we'll be ready for a full day. People who came to the festival last night had a good time. I want them to have the opportunity to use that goodwill today and tomorrow. You might want to have a police presence here, and that's all right, too. If this works out, Mrs. Cannon might see the three girls before Monday."

What a strategist Scott was, Jenny thought. He didn't want the yellow tape with its negative impact around the school a minute longer than it had to be, and had given Sergeant Hampton a solidly practical reason for its early removal. At the same time, he'd welcomed the police to stay. She held her breath, hoping the strategy would work.

"I'll have to talk to the captain and get back to you on that. I have several more questions to ask." He looked at his notes. "Was there any money stolen?"

"We took in money last night and I checked it a while ago," the vice principal said. "It's all there."

"Have any items been taken that you can see?"

They all shook their heads no.

"I noticed none of the computers were taken."

"That's right," Scott said. "Smashed but not stolen."

Sergeant Hampton put his notebook down. "No money was taken, apparently none of the personal items people keep around their desks were stolen, the computers weren't stolen. This indicates that the person or persons who did this was only interested in doing damage to the inside of the building, where teaching takes place. Destruction is greatest in the library, where the books are. Chalkboards have been used to say bad things about teachers and learning."

"So you're saying this person or persons is showing his contempt for everything a school stands for," Scott said.

"Yes, and/or has a powerful grudge against Springview for some reason. I suggest that you talk about it and try to come up with some answers for me. This would be a good time for you folks to go out and get some breakfast. Except for Sam. I'll need him, so be sure and bring him back some food," he said with a touch of humor.

"How about you, Sergeant?" Dave asked.

"Just black coffee, no sugar."

Scott drove, and as he looked for a restaurant, Dave said, "I wonder how long it'll be for the news about the break-in to get out?"

"People across the street were already looking out their window at the police car," Ed said.

"As soon as the yellow tape goes up someone will call the paper and the television channels," Scott said. "It's always that way." He pulled into an IHOP parking lot. "Is this okay?"

"I love hotcakes," Dave said. They asked for a back booth and kept their conversation low. As soon as their orders were taken, the discussion began.

"Scott, how come Sam was in this morning?" Ed asked.

"He said the crew did almost everything last night, but he wanted to check that the gym was thoroughly clean and ready for Monday. He stopped by on his way out of town for a day of fishing."

"I've fished with him a time or two and we talked about where he'd planned to go," Dave added, then turned to Jenny. "I didn't realize mentioning the girls you heard last night would get you into trouble, Jenny."

Their food was served, and Jenny buttered her blueberry hotcakes before responding. She and Ed were seated opposite Scott and Dave and she addressed them both.

"Don't worry about it, Dave. You didn't say anything that wasn't true. Scott, I apologize for not doing what you told me to do about telling Sergeant Hampton their names."

He was her boss, after all, and he could take it that she disobeyed his instruction, not only in front of the police, but also in front of the vice principal, plus Dave and Sam. Not a pretty picture.

She wondered even now if she should have waited until they were alone to apologize as she saw Dave and Ed turn slightly away from her and act as if she and Scott weren't in the same booth. But she couldn't wait any longer to get the bitter taste of disloyalty out of her mouth. And since Dave and Ed had heard the whole thing, they needed to see how Scott handled it.

She was too nervous to eat as she waited for his comment, so she pushed her food around her plate and took a sip of water.

Scott cut a piece of ham but didn't put it on his fork.

"If I should ask you or any other staff member to do a specific job—such as write a report on something of that nature—and you categorically refused, I'd consider that a serious administrative matter."

He cut another piece of ham and laid it beside the first one. Then he put his fork down and looked at Jenny soberly.

"Naming the girls, however, turned out to be a matter of conscience which you explained very well. I'm not sure what consideration the police give to one's conscience, and I'd hate to see you tagged for contempt of court or as an accessory after the fact."

Jenny closed her eyes and swallowed hard. What a disaster it would be if she ended up in court and what effect would it have on her grant application? She couldn't back down now. She had to protect the girls.

When she looked at Scott, his eyes gleamed with warmth, and his mouth quirked with a little smile.

"My best advice to you is to hope the police allow us to

put Springview back together this weekend, and that you use your creativity to figure out some unobtrusive way to get your girls there so you can talk to them."

"I will, I promise," Jenny said and discovered that her appetite had returned.

During the rest of the meal they drew up plans for getting the graffiti off, then encouraging the students to decorate the walls with fast-drying paint.

"Lynn Bartlett could be in charge of that," Jenny suggested.

The maintenance crew and other willing people could be assigned to work on the desks and the chalkboards.

"What about the door to your office?" Ed asked. "We could cover it with sheets of paper for now."

"No," Scott said emphatically. "I want people to see it. We're not hiding anything except Jenny's girls. I'm hoping that the more people see what ignorance can do, the more willing they'll be to help us combat it. After all, it's their school. We'll figure out later what to do with the door when we talk to Sam."

"Gladys Fellows is going to be heartbroken when she sees her library," Jenny said.

"That's where most of the student help can be used. Will you please organize that with her, Jenny?"

"I'll talk to her as soon as we get back to school to prepare her for what she's going to see."

The yellow tape encircled the campus by the time they returned. A police officer let them through, and they delivered the coffee to Sergeant Hampton and breakfast to Sam. They were introduced to Captain Greer, a compact man of military bearing, who was in the library.

He closeted himself with Scott, then announced he saw no reason to keep the tape up after his men were through scouring the building and the grounds. "If we're lucky, we might find a spray paint can that can provide us with a good set of prints. The books in the library were definitely handled by the vandals, but also by many students. It's most likely that gloves were used anyway. The instrument used to smash the computers hasn't been found, and was probably brought here for that purpose, and to break the lock on the door that got him or them inside. Give us another two hours or so and you can start cleaning up," he said. "I'm sure I needn't tell you that if you find anything that is unusual or out of place, you let me know at once."

Jenny was feeling relieved that he hadn't said anything to her, when he called her name and took her aside.

"Sergeant Hampton told me about the girls you overheard at the festival last night."

"Yes, sir."

"I'd like to hear it from you."

Jenny related the sparse details then waited.

"You know these girls?"

"I do."

"Explain to me why you won't identify them?"

Jenny repeated the reasons she'd given earlier to the sergeant.

"You understand the consequences of your action, Mrs. Cannon?"

She'd thought Sergeant Hampton a weighty man, but Captain Greer was much more intimidating. Somehow, she felt the full force of the law from him. She had to take the best care that she could of the girls. That was her calling and let the chips fall where they may.

"We'll look forward to hearing from you very soon, Mrs. Cannon," he said, and left her with a brief nod.

With a sigh of relief she called home to explain about the

break-in, then was pressed into service to answer the phone at the secretary's desk. Scott took the calls from the newspaper and the television channels as well as the parents who insisted on speaking to the principal.

By the time the yellow tape was removed by the police, there was a crowd of people wanting to enter the building. The news had jumped from student to student and teacher to teacher and Jenny, taking names as they entered, found that probably one-third of the entire school population had shown up.

Dismay, outrage, shock and anger filled the building at first, as they wandered up and down the hall and looked at the classrooms. Although warned by Jenny, Gladys Fellows couldn't control her tears when she saw the devastation in the library. Jenny hugged and comforted her as best she could then walked with her around the space, notebook in hand, organizing the most efficient way to restore order.

Students, wide-eyed at first, became vocal at what had been done to their school.

Scott left his phone and began to talk to them and answer their questions. The first one was always, "Who did this?"

His answer was, "We don't know, but the police are working on it. We need a lot of help putting things back together. What would you like to do?"

By mid-afternoon a part of the wall had been cleaned and a group of students were happily decorating it, under Lynn Bartlett's careful eye, with their own signed creations. Every classroom had people working, while the library had almost more helpers than could be managed.

As she went back and forth on her errands Jenny thought there was almost a festive air in the crowd as they worked together in an unusual camaraderie. She hadn't seen the three girls yet, but she was confident they would show up.

The Eyewitness News team came in, their cameras photographing the wall painting, the library, and several classrooms.

The commentator zeroed in on a boy with droopy pants and braided hair. "Why'd you give up your Saturday to come here?"

The boy stopped painting a picture of a football player. "Because this is my school and I want it to look nice."

Jenny was called away, but she saw other students being interviewed, and made a mental note to be sure to watch the channel when she got home.

At Scott's request she'd ordered pizza, snacks, and soft drinks which came as the television crew left. As she guided the delivery to the cafeteria she saw the three girls she'd been looking for working in the library.

"Tamika, can you, Katy and Milladeen come help me get this food set up, please?"

"Sure, Mrs. Cannon," Tamika, a short girl wearing jeans and sweater, said.

Milladeen, slim, and with hair extensions down her back, said, "This is awful, isn't it, Mrs. Cannon?"

Katy, the tallest of the three, also in jeans and a white top, walked beside Jenny. "I never thought this would happen to our school. Did you, Mrs. Cannon?"

Since Katy was the one Jenny had heard express the hope that no one would mess things up, her comment was encouraging. Jenny had looked up the girls' school records and found them to be good students with excellent attendance whose parents always attended the required conferences. They did have older brothers and sisters, and Jenny knew full well that school records did not reveal the whole picture.

"What I want to know is who did it," Tamika said.

"Maybe someone who feels like he was mistreated when

he was here. You know how some kids think everyone's against them even when they aren't." Jenny threw this out.

"My uncle's like that," Milladeen said. "He's a pain to get along with." She tore open a huge bag of chips and put one in her mouth before emptying the rest into a bowl.

"I've only been here a short while, so I don't know who might feel like that about Springview," Jenny said. She placed a stack of paper plates beside the pizza boxes and hoped the girls would follow her thinking. She didn't want to ask them direct questions if it could be avoided.

"When my brother was here a few years ago, Springview had kind of a tough reputation, but the guys that fought and got suspended are all in high school now, I think." Tamika laid out paper napkins and cups.

"Yeah, there was the guy that was always in trouble," Milladeen said. "Had a funny name. Jojo. That was it."

"My sister was in his class. I think he left town," Katy said.

"So there's no Jojos around that you know of." Jenny began to open pizza boxes while glancing casually at the girls. There were no secretive looks; their expressions remained the same—innocent and youthful—as they busied themselves at their tasks.

"This is a great disappointment to Dr. Phillips and the rest of us. We were all so pleased at the way the Harvest Festival went last night. Everyone was having so much fun," Jenny said.

"That's just what I thought!" Katy exclaimed. "I told Tamika and Millie I hoped nobody would mess things up, because the school is better since Dr. Phillips came."

Jenny wished she could hug Katy. Her intuition had been correct. The child's remark had carried no sinister undertone. In fact, it had been the opposite—a sincere hope that all would stay well at her school.

She needed to pursue one more point with Katy, who had begun opening the boxes of cookies.

"What'd you mean by messing things up?"

"Last year we kept having things happen, like fights in the schoolyard, kids talking back to teachers, and then our grades weren't good. But Dr. Phillips talked to all of us when he came. He said we should be like a family and help each other. Most of us liked that, because he treats us that way. The only thing bad that's happened before this break-in was the fight between Rhonda and Amanda, and they didn't even get suspended. It was a little mess, but not much." She looked at Jenny to see if Jenny understood.

"I see what you mean, Katy. Dr. Phillips would be so pleased to know that you really listened to him. Is it all right with you if I tell him what you said?"

Katy looked shy. "I guess so. All three of us feel that way." Tamika and Milladeen nodded.

All the food was ready. "Thanks for helping, girls. Now if each of you could go round and tell everyone to come eat, I'd appreciate it."

She went in search of Scott and found him being interviewed by a newspaper reporter. She was invited in and answered a few questions, then Scott passed the reporter on to Ed Boyd.

As soon as they were alone, Scott let his guard down and Jenny saw the tiredness in the slump of his shoulder and the lines around his mouth and eyes.

"Will this day ever end?" he asked, leaning back in his chair and closing his eyes.

"It will. You need some food and it's ready in the cafeteria." She also relaxed in her chair.

"Okay. We'll go in a moment."

Still with his eyes closed, he said, "You talked to your girls, didn't you?"

"How did you know?"

"I know you, and I know it turned out to be a casual remark, just as you thought it might be."

"Because?"

"Because your intuition, especially where kids are concerned, is usually right."

"I'm so relieved, Scott. I'm not anxious to be on the wrong side of the law but I had to protect those girls. You should have seen their innocent faces."

"I did, Jenny. When you were ten."

Chapter 13

Dave breezed into the conference room carrying the Sunday paper, a box of donuts and several cups of coffee in a cardboard carton.

"We made the paper twice," he announced.

Scott, Jenny, Ed, and Sam were breakfasting on ham and egg biscuits and coffee Jenny had picked up on her way to the eight o'clock meeting they'd decided on Saturday night. The wall had to be finished and the rest of the books shelved.

"Twice? I only talked to the reporter once," Scott said.

Dave handed him the paper. "Check his story on page one and see if it's accurate."

"Page one? Must not have been much happening yesterday," Ed remarked.

Scott scanned the article quickly. "He did a good job, especially when he quoted the students. That's the important message." He sounded pleased as he returned the paper to Dave.

Dave said, "I'll read what's on the editorial page."

"I can't believe we made the editorial page," Jenny was impressed.

"Wait'll you hear it," Dave said as he found the article.

Springview School, trying under its interim principal Dr. Scott Phillips to overcome its previous reputation of fighting, frequent suspensions and low grades, was vandalized Friday night by person or persons unknown. Unfortunately, this is not unusual. What is unusual is that students and teachers are working together to repaint the walls, clean up classrooms, and put the library back together. The school's six computers were smashed. Dr. Phillips and the school are to be commended for their teamwork and strong commitment to Springview.

Jenny applauded. Ed, Sam, and Dave joined in. Scott flushed.

"You all know that no one person deserves credit. Like the paper said, it's teamwork."

"Everyone saw the television news last night?" There was general assent. "When they ended the segment showing you, Scott, standing by that door, undaunted, praising the people who showed up because the school meant something to them, I was so proud to be working here. We might be a good team, but that's because you're a good team leader." This from Ed.

Still flushed, Scott gave a mock bow. "I thank you one and all. Now on to business. First, you need to know that Jenny talked to the three girls yesterday. They knew nothing about the vandalism and Jenny has passed that on to the police. For today's schedule, we'll do as much as we can until noon, then you all need to go home and relax, get some rest so you'll be ready for Monday. The kids who were working on the wall said they'd be back this morning. Anyone else who shows up can shelve books. And Sam, you'll need how many for the classrooms?"

"I could do with six, but ten'll be better."

Sam needn't have worried. Jenny thought it was the story on television that brought people out who hadn't been here on Saturday. There was almost too many, but between the team members, every pair of hands was put to work.

They began winding down the activity at eleven-thirty. A roster had been kept, but even so, at noon, the team walked through the building making certain everyone had gone and it was secure.

Jenny was in her office when she heard Nicky calling her name. Startled, she rushed into the hall to see Nicky and her dad with Devon and Lily.

"Nicky and I wanted to see the walls your students painted," her dad said.

"You'll like the pictures," Jenny said, hugging Nicky. She'd missed him yesterday and was looking forward to being with him this afternoon. The sun was shining and she longed to be out in the fresh air after being cooped up.

Her dad took Lily by one hand and Nicky by the other. "Look at this football player. He looks real, doesn't he?" They moved slowly down the hall.

Jenny knew there was something in the air. Hypersensitive as she was where Nicky was concerned, it was more than a coincidence for her dad to bring Nicky to the school at the same time Devon and Lily came.

Devon's eyes sparkled with excitement. "I've got a great plan, Jenny!"

"I knew something was going on," Jenny said.

"We're going to have a picnic. All of you have worked so

...ard and so long this weekend, and haven't had time to ...elax. What you need is to get out in the open and forget the ;chool until tomorrow. I've packed some food in the trunk)f the car."

She hesitated. "I wanted Nicky with us for your sake and or Lily's, so I called your dad and asked him to meet me here. You're not angry, are you, Jenny? Lily and I could've picked iim up, but I know how careful you are about him."

A picnic! What a glorious idea. But of course she couldn't ;o. She needed to do a little shopping and her laundry. Devon neant for all of them to go, which included Scott, and that night be awkward.

She wasn't at all sure where they stood with each other ifter the events of the weekend, which had forced them to work together closely for the sake of the school. That had urned out to be effortless and instinctive, like two well-made pieces of a single unit created to work together smoothly. Time after time, with only a word or a glance, they'd know what the other needed or was thinking about.

"Mom! Lily said they're going on a picnic and they want is to go. Can we, please?"

Devon looked reproachfully at her daughter. "It just slipped)ut, Mom, because Nicky's so much fun."

"There's plenty of food, Mr. Mayes, if you'd like to join is, too," Devon said.

"Thanks, but I'm going to work in the yard a little. It's nice)f you to do this for Jenny and the others. They've had a hard ime, and a picnic'll help them be ready for tomorrow."

Jenny felt that to back out now would make her look ill-empered and discourteous, so in the end she and Nicky ollowed Dave, Devon and Lily in Scott's car. Sam went fishing ind Ed said he had a business deal and took a raincheck.

"Good luck," Dave said and winked at Ed as he left.

"Don't tell me he's seeing someone." Devon grinned a Dave. Ed's bachelorhood was a sorrow to Devon, who wante her friends to be as happily married as she was.

"I'm pretty sure he is, but I don't know the lady so don' bother to ask," he said and grinned back.

"Were you roped into this, too?" Scott asked Jenny as they followed Dave's car onto a country road.

"Definitely. I'd planned to do some shopping." She trie to fix her lips in a pout, but the more the car flew along wit sunshine pouring over her and birdsong echoing from th trees, the harder it was to feel put upon.

"There's a bright side to everything, Jenny. Look at the mone you'll save. The picnic won't cost you a cent. Right, Nicky?"

From the back seat, where Nicky had been listening t every word, came a firm, "Right, and a picnic's more fun tha shopping."

"See. You're outvoted. You may as well enjoy yourself."

Scott smiled at her, looking more carefree than she'd see him in days. Her spirits lifted and, for a brief moment, wit Scott and Nicky smiling at her on this bright afternoon, Jenny felt that all was right with the world.

"Look, Mom. Look at the horses."

Nicky pointed at a field that held a number of horses. Som were grazing, several stared over the fence, and on the far side a few seemed to be running for the joy of it, stretching thei elegant legs and arching their necks.

Scott slowed the car and they all three looked in silence a the beautiful sight.

In the front seat Scott lightly touched Jenny's hand, and in the back seat Nicky sighed in sheer delight.

Dave made a left turn, and shortly after another left, onto

road that climbed a hill. He brought the car to a stop and gestured for Scott to pull up beside him.

"This is picture-perfect, Dave. How'd you find it?" Jenny stood under a large tree which still had orange and red leaves on it. A green meadow stretched out in front of it, and in the far distance she could see farms. Lily and Nicky were already whooping as they chased each other on the hill.

"I did my practice teaching about twenty miles from here. When I got frustrated I'd get in my car and just drive. One day I saw this place and fixed its location in my mind. Devon and I have been back here several times."

"I can see why. It's having an effect on me already," Scott said and yawned.

"We have to eat first, before you get too relaxed," Devon said good-naturedly. "Take hold of the other end of Dave's blanket and spread it out over there." She pointed to a level spot.

"Yes, ma'am, Sergeant, ma'am." The men saluted while Jenny laughed and began to take the food out of the trunk.

Scott had been keeping an eye on Nicky, who was chasing Lily. When the children got a little distance away he walked down the hill toward them before Jenny got worried or nervous.

"Time to come and eat," he said. "Let's see how many steps you have to take to get to the food." When Nicky reached the highest number he knew, Scott pitched in.

"I did a hundred nine steps to get here," Nicky told Jenny proudly. He plopped down next to her. Scott sat on his other side. Large paper plates were filled with barbecue, coleslaw, baked beans and rolls. Lemonade or iced tea was poured from gallon jars.

"This is so good, Devon." Jenny savored the seasoning of the meat. "Dave, you were so lucky to get a girl who could cook. How did you meet?"

"She used to come to the football games at the Universit of South Carolina and go crazy over me," Dave said with straight face.

"You wish," Devon retorted. "The truth is, he used to com to the library where I worked and hang around so much Mis Swanson had to ask him to leave."

"Did you or did you not watch me play football? Jus answer yes or no." Dave winked at Lily who smiled.

"Yes, but…"

Dave interrupted her. "I rest my case."

Devon ignored him. "I didn't even know there was a Dav Young on campus until my junior year. I wasn't interested i football. Then one day he came to the library and needed hel in research for a paper in education. He invited me to a game and I went." She passed the barbecue around again.

Dave took another rib. "You like this meat, sport?" h asked Nicky who was chewing on a small piece of rib an getting the sauce all over his face. He nodded yes.

"The truth, Jenny, is I had no idea if Devon could cook o not. I just thought she was the most interesting girl I'd met. The she invited me home to meet her family and she cooked dinner."

"So she threw you a pass you couldn't possibly fumble," Scott teased.

"Here I am, still eating her good cooking and loving it." His bantering words were belied by his tender glance, whic made Devon blush.

"That reminds me, Scott," Dave said, "you know who els was on the USC team before I left? Bruce Gordon, Larry' younger brother."

"Was he as good as Larry?" He shook his head as Jenny offered him the coleslaw.

"He was okay, but not as fierce as Larry. Jenny, I bet you

idn't know about Scott's football career because it was after our family moved to California."

"I remember the two of you and Richard playing at ootball," Jenny said.

"We got pretty good in high school didn't we, buddy?" Dave looked at Scott.

"I guess we did. That seems so long ago," Scott said reflectively. He reached for his cup then looked at Jenny. "I nade quarterback and Dave was a tailback, and together we ad a pretty good time, especially when we played the team cross town. Their high school was in the affluent section, so hey had a lot of stuff Brentwood High didn't have. But most f the time they couldn't beat us."

"Larry Gordon was their quarterback and he couldn't stand s, especially Scott. Twice Scott made the touchdown that ok the division championship away from Larry."

"Did you also play football in college and have girls go razy over you?" Jenny asked mischievously.

"I played, but I don't know about the rest." Scott threw his ead back and drained his cup. He didn't want to think of hose college years, when Jenny Mayes should have been the irl waiting for him after the game instead of the others who ostly wanted to be seen with a popular football player.

"Larry Gordon. Why is that name familiar?" Jenny asked.

"He's the Lawrence T. Gordon who serves on the school oard," Dave replied.

A chill swept over her. She made an involuntary gesture oward Nicky, putting her hand on his back. He was safe. She eeded also to touch Scott, and with the thought his hand overed hers on Nicky's back and they looked at each other. ust Jenny and Scott with no years between them.

"Dessert now, or later?" Devon asked.

"Later," Dave decided. "A picnic's not a picnic without a ball game." He jumped up, went to the car and brought out bats and balls. He looked at Jenny and Devon who were putting food away.

"Jenny, you look like you can move pretty fast. I pick you for my team."

"I can move fast, too," Nicky said. "Can I be on your team?"

"You sure can. Here, catch the ball." He lobbed the soft ball slow and easy, so it fell into Nicky's outstretched hands.

"Way to go, Nicky," Scott said exchanging a smile with Jenny over her son's head.

"You're on my team, Lily," Scott said. "And I guess you and I will have to help your mom run fast for our team."

"Watch what you say," Devon threatened, "or you'll not get your dessert."

They decided the goal would be four short home runs. With laughter, cheers, a few falls and assists, Dave's team won.

The second time around Scott's team won, by which time Devon decreed they'd worked off enough calories to have dessert.

The children opted for cookies instead of the rhubarb pie, then were distracted by the games Devon brought out and placed on a smaller blanket for them.

"I see you're an old hand at this," Jenny murmured.

"Kids are tired by this time," Devon answered. "We may be, too, but this quiet end of the picnic is sometimes the best part of the day."

How true, Jenny thought. Dave and Devon were sharing their pie and talking softly. It occurred to her that Dave had seen very little of his wife in the past few days. How generous of them to make this afternoon possible for her, Scott and Nicky when they could have kept it for themselves. Then she

ecalled the atmosphere of love and unity she'd felt in their
home, and decided that sharing was an integral part of it.

She felt Scott's gaze and turned to him.

"This is nice, isn't it?" He was so close she could feel his
breath on her cheek.

"Yes, it is. Are you relaxed now?"

"More than I've been in a long time. Dave and Devon are
true friends."

"I was thinking of them also."

"Nicky and Lily are getting along as if they were the same
age." Jenny thought she detected a note of pride in Scott's ob-
servation.

He put his arms around his knees and looked at her. "So
what did you do for sports in school?"

"I ran track."

"Did you really?"

"And I played tennis."

"In high school or college?"

"Both."

"Were you good?"

"I won a few awards, but I did it because I liked it. The sen-
sation of moving smoothly and feeling the earth under your
feet. You must know how it is, because you run in the park."

"It isn't the same as running on a track. In the park you
have to watch out for people and animals, but it's better than
nothing and it's convenient."

"True."

"Are you still running?"

"Not since Nicky was born. I'm terribly out of shape, but
I look forward to the time when I can get back to it."

"You don't look the least bit out of shape to me," he
murmured.

Her only reply was a slow smile.

They were interrupted by Nicky, who wandered over and leaned against Jenny.

"Ready to go home?" she asked.

"If we can see the horses on the way back," Nicky said, rubbing his eyes.

Jenny stood at her window contemplating the starry night. So much had happened since she'd awakened that morning. Yet she was reluctant to climb into her bed.

She felt at ease with Dave, Devon, and Scott, almost as if she were a normal young woman leading a normal life. Not one filled with guilt and transgression that she couldn't dispel no matter how she tried.

The afternoon had been pleasant, pleasurable, and peaceful.

Would it be so terrible if she met each day as it came, seeing if it could also be normal? Especially with Scott?

Chapter 14

Leaves were falling, carpeting the ground in colors from palest yellow to brightest red. A mild November wind blew them around, reminding Scott of how, when he was Nicky's age, he'd loved to play in piles of leaves.

His early morning drives to work were peaceful and enjoyable. Traffic was sparse and he liked to mosey along lost in his thoughts, in no rush to get to Springview. That's why he left his apartment early.

He noticed the Jacksons were getting their house painted, and the hardware store had big red and white signs announcing a clearance sale.

At a stoplight, he saw a new billboard about the circus coming to Columbia, the capital, showing a colorful picture of elephants, clowns and girls standing on horses. Nicky would sure like that, and he wondered if Jenny had ever taken him to the circus.

She seemed to be easing up on the boy. Yesterday, she

hadn't been over-protective, and he'd played like any boy his age. Running, falling, yelling and having a wonderful time with Lily and everyone else.

As for his precious Jenny, he couldn't keep up with her mood changes. She'd gone from remoteness to asking him out to eat on Friday night. Then at the picnic yesterday, she'd been the Jenny Mayes he used to know. Despite her earlier refusal to talk about their years apart, he'd felt that since Dave, Devon and he had spoken of their high school and college years, maybe she would also. He'd kept his questions specific and she'd answered each one without hesitation.

On the way home, with Jenny beside him and a sleepy Nicky in the backseat, he'd been envious of Dave whose car held his wife and his child.

If only that could happen for him.

Scott began the day with a schoolwide meeting. He described precisely what had happened on Saturday and Sunday. Because it was their school he wanted them to know from the principal all about the vandalism. He thanked everyone who had helped and asked were there any questions.

"Who did it?"

"We don't know."

"Are the police trying to find out?"

"Yes. However, if anyone here has an idea of who might be responsible, you can help us by telling anyone in the office or any teacher.

"Do you think we'll get a name from anyone?" he asked Ed as they walked back to their offices.

"An anonymous note would be a good thing." Ed didn't seem optimistic.

"If we could be sure it wasn't used just to get someone in trouble."

"That's the chance you take," Ed said as he turned into his office.

Later in the morning, Scott had a call from Joe Alston's secretary. "Dr. Phillips, the school board wishes to know if you could be present at a special meeting tonight. This is short notice, but Mr. Alston said they won't keep you long. Their regular meeting begins at seven, but they'd work you in before that at a closed-door session. Could you be here at six-fifteen?" She gave him the address and thanked him.

Scott was surprised at first, then decided that the board wanted a firsthand account of the break-in. That should be no problem. To be on the safe side, he jotted down events and times in a notebook and left work a little early so he'd have time to dash home and change, as this would be his first formal meeting with the entire board. As he put on a blue shirt and chose a red silk tie, he glanced at the names of the board members listed on the brochure from his desk.

Joe Alston and Lawrence T. Gordon he knew. The others were Mary Lee Fisher, Cliff Laird, Walt Mills, Kay Morgan and John Ring.

The board met in the town hall complex, where Joe Alston greeted him and ushered him into a small conference room with a rectangular table and ten chairs.

As introductions were made, Scott and Larry shook hands briefly.

"It's been a long time, Larry," Scott said pleasantly.

"It has indeed." Although Larry's voice was cordial, his eyes were cold. Scott was given the seat at the end of the table. He immediately sensed that this meeting might turn out to be something more than a casual question and answer session.

He'd had some dealings with school boards in Connecticut but never in the role of principal. Tonight he was here as principal of Springview and no matter what the board said or did, he would defend and protect his school in a worthy and dignified manner.

"Dr. Phillips," Joe Alston began, "we heard about the vandalism at Springview on television and in the paper, but we felt we needed to hear about it from you." He gave Scott an encouraging glance.

Scott began with the harvest festival as the reason Sam had stopped by the school the next morning and had discovered the break-in. He described the entire series of events that followed.

Cliff Laird, a bald man with a trim gray mustache asked, "Do you have a security person at Springview?"

"No, sir, we do not."

"Why not?"

"There wasn't one in the budget when I arrived. Our head of maintenance, Sam Pickens, the vice principal, Ed Boyd, and I all have a full set of keys. We know all the locks and between us we keep an eye on everything."

"Do you have any enemies, Dr. Phillips?" Lawrence Gordon asked.

"None that I know of."

"The message on your office door was very specific."

"Yes, it was."

"I wonder why you felt it was necessary for that to be shown on television, Dr. Phillips." Scott heard the disparaging undertone in Larry's voice. "Wasn't that rather brazen?"

The gloves were off. This was the same Larry he'd known in high school. Even though he was now a banker and vice chairman of the board, he hadn't lost his mean spirit. He'd just covered it over with a shallow veneer of success.

"I don't think it was brazen at all." Scott deliberately turned his attention to the other six board members. He might as well make his speech now, letting them know where he stood. "If we want students to understand that the school exists for them to learn and succeed, the adults who run it have to be trustworthy. Be open and honest with them. They know right away if you're not sincere. I had nothing to hide. At Springview they know I want only the best for them. If someone doesn't like me and what I'm doing, that's their business but I've done nothing wrong so it's best to let everyone see the door."

Reverend Walt Mills, minister of a large black church, said, "I was troubled to hear of a fight involving a number of girls. Could you clear that up for us?"

Now how in the world did that piece of misinformation get to the board? So much had happened since Jenny had counseled Rhonda and Amanda, he had to think fast to recall the details.

"I'm afraid you were misinformed, Reverend Mills. Two girls had a minor scuffle in the restroom because one girl called the other girl's brother dumb. There was no one else in the restroom. We broke it up immediately. No one else was involved."

"Were the girls suspended?" Reverend Mills asked.

"No, sir. They were given demerits and counseled and there's been no more trouble."

"Have there been any other fights?" John Ring asked.

"None. We try to provide an atmosphere of friendliness and helping each other so students won't feel the need to fight. There've been several close calls on the playground, but so far a teacher has been near to remind them of the rules against fighting and to encourage talking instead."

"Very good," Reverend Mills said approvingly. Kay Morgan also seemed pleased.

Other questions followed concerning why students were permitted to paint the walls Saturday, were the services of the educational consultant being used to full potential, and was it appropriate to have rap at the festival.

Scott became convinced that, as Dave had warned, there were indeed people at Springview who not only were against him and his ideas, but were steadily feeding information and rumors to a person or persons on the board.

As the time drew to a close, Larry Gordon said, "Dr. Phillips, you must understand that in view of Springview being an at-risk school, and in view of your interim status while we search for a permanent principal, it is our responsibility to pay very close attention to all that happens at the school on your watch." His eyes didn't blink as he laid down the challenge.

Scott held very still, determined not to visibly react to Larry's naked threat, but he noticed that the other members seemed embarrassed, flicking a curious glance at him and at Larry. Scott saw Joe Alston take a breath, but he didn't need Joe to defend him.

He looked Larry straight in the eye. "I would expect the board to do no less, Mr. Gordon. The well-being of the school community as a whole is certainly above the interest or rationale of any one individual."

"Very well said, Dr. Phillips," Joe Alston said approvingly. He rose to his feet while looking at the wall clock. "We truly appreciate your giving us these valuable insights on your work at Springview. It seems to me you've made a good beginning in a difficult situation. Please let us know when the culprit who vandalized the school is found."

There was a smattering of applause as the meeting broke up. Scott didn't linger. He didn't want to make personal friends on the board. At the end of the school year he had to win their votes to become permanent principal based on the credibility of his work. Had the school, as Larry rightly said, improved on his watch?

He couldn't help the fact that Joe Alston saw him positively, and that Larry Gordon saw him negatively, based on their knowledge of his past.

He had to admit it was worrisome to know that someone on the board had a pipeline to someone on campus, and that one or the other was willing to distort events—as witness the fight between the girls. As far as he had heard, the fight hadn't even been talked about that much at school because it had been handled quickly and decisively, in a way that neither girl wanted to brag about it.

He couldn't waste energy on it. Springview was a public institution and therefore open to the community it served. He'd just have to stay on the alert and not risk making foolish mistakes.

The next morning he called Ed and Jenny into his office and told them what had happened at the board.

"You both need to know that everything we do is under serious and continuous scrutiny by the board. At least some of them would like me to make a blunder big enough to take me out of contention for the principalship."

Ed had been in academic administration a long time and knew its pitfalls, Scott thought. Also he had an unflappable personality, unlike the other person he was talking to, Jenny Cannon. He could tell she was already about to explode.

"Then those people aren't concerned about the students at all," she exclaimed, hand waving in the air and eyes flashing.

"People on school boards don't always make the students their first priority," he said. "You've been in education long enough to know that unhappy truth, I'm sure." He met her fiery glance with a composed attitude meant to calm her down.

"You can't get rid of politics and people seeking to gain

and exercise power," Ed told Jenny in his quiet voice. "Confidentially, that was one reason I was glad to find this opening, so I could leave the district I'd been in for ten years. The power struggles were unbearable. I even took a cut in pay, but it was worth it."

"But the same thing is happening here, isn't it?" Jenny protested.

"Not like where I was. From what Scott says, it appears to be one or two people, but the chairman seems to think Scott can do the job, since he recruited him. So do I. This is only the end of the first grading period, so we have the rest of the year to show the board how we can turn the school around."

Scott listened to Ed, who was generally a man of few words. Although they worked well together, Ed rarely spoke of his personal life and Scott hadn't known how he'd felt about his former position.

"Thanks for the vote of confidence, Ed." Busily polishing his rimless glasses, Ed glanced up and nodded.

Scott could see how Ed's wise comments had helped Jenny to calm down. She was sitting back in her chair and the fire had gone from her eyes.

"Jenny, if you can continue doing things like defusing the fight situation and the testimony of the girls yesterday, we'll stay in good shape."

"The fight still got blown all out of proportion, and apparently they were ready to believe the worst," she grumbled.

"We can't help that. All we can do is keep our emotions in check and carry out our program." He looked at her steadily and sent her a silent message, words he couldn't voice with Ed in the room.

Stay with me on this, Jenny. Your grant and my permanent

position are at stake here, as well as the students. We need to help each other stay steady on the course.

Jenny drew in a deep breath. "I agree with that," she said. As she left the office, she flashed a smile at Scott and Ed. "Next year this door will be decorated with a sign that says, 'Welcome, Dr. Phillips, our new principal!'"

A car she hadn't expected to see was in the driveway when Jenny arrived home. The sporty black coupe had a back vanity plate that said HYPER. Jenny broke into a smile. H for Helena, Y for Yvonne, and PER for Perry.

She hadn't seen her oldest sister since last year, and they hugged each other tightly at the door.

"You didn't tell us you were coming." Jenny said.

"It's a spur of the moment trip, but Mom said she has a bed for me, since you, for some strange reason, are sleeping in the attic." Helen smiled.

"Not an attic. It's the dormer room, and I like it," Jenny retaliated. "Let me look at you, girl." She held Helena at arm's length, taking in the five feet, ten inch flawless figure that had first caught a photographer's eye while Helena was in college. The modeling she did then became a career after college. She was thirty-five but her caramel skin had no wrinkles, and her thick dark hair clung to her well-shaped head like a cap of satin.

"Glamorous as ever, but aren't you a little thin even for a model?" Jenny didn't mention the sadness in her sister's eyes, nor the brittleness she sensed when they touched.

"That's exactly what I told her. I'm sure she isn't eating enough, but maybe while she's here we can persuade her to eat a little more."

Jenny was proud of their mother for not using the dreaded words, fatten her up! But Mom was right.

"Don't you two worry. I'm fine," Helena declared.

"How long can you stay?" Jenny asked.

"About four days. I was between jobs and bored, and Woody's on a case in San Francisco. Thought this would be a great time to just get in the car and point it toward South Carolina. I left yesterday, stayed overnight in Richmond, and got here an hour or so ago. It was an easy trip."

"Have you seen Nicky?" Kenny asked.

"He ran out to greet me and bring me into the house. He's absolutely adorable, Jenny. He isn't in school yet?"

"He goes to kindergarten."

"Where is he now, Mom?" Jenny asked.

"With your dad at the market, but they'll be back soon."

"I brought him some stuff, Jenny. I hope you don't mind," Helena said.

"What kind of stuff?"

The only nephew and grandson thus far in the Mayes family, Nicky had received so many toys over the years that Jenny felt she had to tactfully call a halt to this over-consumerism. Every year she had passed on to a children's agency the items she found excessive or inappropriate for her son.

"You can look at them first and take out whatever you don't like. It's really a joy for me to be able to select things for my only nephew. This time I went for some learning toys."

"Let's look at them now, before he gets back."

In her upstairs room, Helena opened one of the two bags she'd brought. Out came four books graded for six-year-old children, a large picture dictionary, a small baseball mitt, a remote-controlled truck, a New York Giants cap and jersey, and a plastic laptop computer designed to teach phonics, numbers, and other learning activities.

"How'd I do this time?" Helena sounded anxious.

"You're getting better." Jenny picked out two books and the truck. "These are good choices, but he already has them, so some other lucky children will profit from your generosity, Sis. Thanks. He'll love everything else."

Helena had picked up the small jersey, and was stroking it almost as if Nicky was already wearing it. Jenny heard the downstairs door slam and the sound of Nicky's steps on the stairs, but not before glimpsing the longing on her sister's face.

Later that night, she recalled that expression. Helena's gifts had been a great hit with Nicky, especially the laptop which he and his aunt had played with after dinner. Helena had gladly promised to spend time with him and the laptop tomorrow when he came home from kindergarten.

She and Jenny put Nicky to bed, then settled themselves in Helena's room. Jenny's initial sense of Helena's sadness and fragility had increased throughout the evening. Now that they were alone she didn't waste time.

"What's hurting you, honey?" she asked. "Don't say you're all right, because I know better. That's why you came home." They were sitting side by side on the bed, and she put her arm around Helena.

Helena was looking down at her hands, turning them over as if they were unfamiliar to her. Her fingers were long, slim, and, as always, beautifully manicured.

Jenny had been envious of how Helena's hands looked so perfect. She, too, had begun her career with such hands, but then came Nicky. Then she had neither the time nor the need to sustain that image. For years she'd done her nails herself, keeping them trimmed, neat, and unpolished, so that she could do for and with Nicky whatever came up. Still, she found herself admiring Helen's hands while she waited for an answer to her question.

"How many years have I been married?" Now Helena was twisting her hands.

"Eight years," Jenny said. What an odd question.

"I'm beginning my thirty-fifth year, and I had just turned twenty-eight when I married Woodrow. Before that I was involved in establishing a modeling career."

Jenny listened, trying to understand what Helena was getting at as she reviewed these facts, known to both of them. There was no emotion in her sister's voice. Only the twisting of the hands conveyed her agitation.

"The first few years after we were married, Woody was intensely busy setting up his law practice, because he'd had a late start. Remember?"

She glanced at Jenny as if for corroboration that this was accurate.

"I remember that the times we got together I saw very little of him because he was working long, late hours," Jenny agreed.

"I didn't fully realize at that time how much I wanted a family. I guess our two careers had so filled our lives that when the thought came, I always figured there'd be time next year."

The despair Jenny saw in Helena's eyes gripped her heart.

"I can't tell you how much I want my own Adam, or my own Nicky, or a darling little girl. A child out of my own womb. I'm barren, Jen!"

"Are you sure?" Jenny was dismayed. She'd assumed Helena and Woody weren't interested in having a family. The years had gone by without the appearance of an offspring, and they never talked about it.

Now all she could do was put her arms around Helena. "I'm so sorry, honey," she murmured and held her until she felt a lessening of tension.

"You know all those methods doctors tell you to try, like

keeping an ovulation chart? We've tried them all, but nothing has worked."

"How does Woody feel about this?"

"He blames himself, because he wonders if it's his fault."

"What do you mean?" Jenny asked.

Helena went over to her suitcase and lifted out a night-shirt. It was decorated with tiny hearts that read My Funny Valentine.

She held the pink garment lightly. "Woody thinks that because, after trying everything else, we decided to try in vitro fertilization. We had such hope, because we knew several couples who'd gone that route and finally had a child."

She stopped speaking and swallowed several times, as if her mouth had gone dry.

She held the nightshirt close to her breast. "Last week we got the result. It didn't take."

Jenny, watching with horrified sympathy, thought it was as if a sudden thunderstorm had hit her sister. One minute she was speaking quietly, and in the next she was overtaken by a violent downpour of wrenching sobs that left her shaking. Jenny jumped up and went to her.

"Come here, honey," she said and gently led Helena to the bed, laid her down and cradled her in her arms. Occasionally she stroked her back, wishing she had wonderful words of wisdom that could soothe her weeping sister.

Long minutes went by before the sobs gradually died away.

"It's a good thing I had this nightshirt." Helena threw the sodden garment on the floor. "I'll have to get another one to wear to bed." Her half smile was shaky, her face blotched, and her eyes swollen.

"You had a lot of grief stored up," Jenny sad. "You had to come home to let it out."

"I knew you'd understand, Jen. I have a friend or two, but they're not family."

She kissed Jenny on the cheek. "See you tomorrow, and thanks."

Chapter 15

There may be truth in the poet's declaration that no man is an island, Jenny mused on her way to work, but it was equally true that each person has some hidden inlets and defended channels no one else has access to. Like Helena, whose confession last night had taken her by surprise.

When Jenny, Patty and Helena had been growing up here in Brentwood, it had been Patty who was closest to Jenny. The four-year age gap between Jenny and Helena had been deepened by the difference in their interests. Everything about the world of fashion had fascinated Helena from childhood on, and the only reason she'd gone to college was because her parents had insisted on it.

Jenny's interest in fashion was tied to necessity and she'd gone to college because she loved it. It was Patty who seemed to understand how Jenny felt about Scott, and who gently teased them both at times. Helena, busy with her own friends, seemed to ignore it or had occasionally criticized it.

All three sisters had grown closer as they moved into adulthood, but Helena had never before disclosed such an intimate matter to Jenny. Infertility was beyond the scope of Jenny's experience, but she could imagine what it might have felt like had she been married for seven or eight years and not able to conceive.

Some women, and some men, too, wanted only children who came from their bodies, which seemed unfortunate. There were so many children of all ages and backgrounds who desperately needed to be included in loving families. Had Helena and Woody considered this yet?

She reached Springview, parked, and went into her office. But before she got caught up in what awaited on her desk, she recalled that at no time had Helena mentioned prayer as something she'd turned to in her dilemma. Was she also lacking in faith?

Part of her job description as an educational consultant was to identify research-based programs to be used as prevention for some of the behavioral problems displayed by the students. In Chicago she'd found serious issues involving physical violence, bullying, drugs, and alcohol abuse, with some sexual overtones.

Thank goodness the students at Springview were younger, and although many of them came from homes where financial stability was a day-to-day effort, the environment was light years away from what she'd had to deal with in Chicago. The schools here were smaller and there was a better socioeconomic mix.

From her list of possible activities, she chose a field trip, and talked with Luis Gomez, a new social studies teacher.

Luis was stocky and agile. Dave had remarked that the

Play the Lucky Hearts Game

and get...
2 FREE BOOKS
and a FREE MYSTERY GIFT...

yes! YOURS to KEEP!

I have scratched off the silver card. Please send me my **2 FREE BOOKS** and **FREE mystery GIFT**. I understand that I am under no obligation to purchase any books as explained on the back of this card.

Scratch Here!
then look below to see what your cards get you... 2 Free Books & a Free Mystery Gift!

168 XDL EFYC

FIRST NAME

LAST NAME

ADDRESS

APT.#

CITY

STATE

ZIP CODE

(A-LH-06)

Twenty-one gets you **2 FREE BOOKS** and a **FREE MYSTERY GIFT!**

Twenty gets you **2 FREE BOOKS!**

Nineteen gets you **1 FREE BOOK!**

TRY AGAIN!

The Reader Service — Here's how it works:

word was out about Mr. Gomez. "He's new, but you don't mess with him." It seemed that not only was he the eldest of eight children whom he'd helped raise, but he also had been in the service.

She invited him to sit and asked, "What do you think of field trips?"

"They're useful if they have a point and are well organized. Are we going to have one?" His dark eyes sparkled with interest.

"If we can agree on one to show Dr. Phillips and he approves it. The theme is 'Downtown as History.' There are four historic sites a few blocks from here, within walking distance. Students should grow up knowing the history of their town and they'll absorb it better if they see it and can ask questions about it. This, combined with a classroom exercise, should make an impression."

"I like that, and I have another idea to go with it," Luis said.

By the end of the class period, they had a detailed plan which Jenny took to show Scott.

"Luis has nine boys and ten girls in this social studies class. The buildings around the town square are only four blocks away. He'll have the boys, I'll have the girls. We propose to ask the woman who wrote the town history if she could meet us there on Friday, and walk around the square with us, describing what happened and answering questions. Back in the classroom Luis will give the students an oral quiz and have a discussion based on the importance of knowing one's local history." She knew this was a good scheme that would enhance the learning for their students.

"This is fifth or sixth grade?" Scott asked.

"We thought we'd try it out on fifth grade first."

"Very wise. The town hall is just across the street. Why don't you show them that as well?"

"That would be even better." Her smile at his suggestion was spontaneous. "Anything else Luis and I might have forgotten?"

"Only what we talked about regarding our public view that might cause us trouble with the board. Do you need an extra teacher to help police the students?"

"Luis didn't think so, and he's the one who'll have the boys." Jenny closed her notebook. "This is the first time I've seen you today. How are you?"

"Better for seeing you, Jenny. Terrible cliché, but true. All is well with you and Nicky?" The warmth in his eyes created an answering gleam in her.

"We all had a surprise yesterday. Helena drove down from New York and will stay a few days."

"I haven't seen her in years. How is she?" Scott asked.

Jenny knew she didn't have the right to tell Scott how Helena really was at this point in her life, so she gave him a sketchy update instead.

When she was finished, Scott said, "I do remember now seeing a picture of her as a model. She was very good-looking."

"She still is." Scott was looking at her as if trying to decide to say what he was thinking. "What is it, Scott?"

He didn't evade her question. "I was just remembering the feeling I had that Helena never liked me."

Jenny was shocked. "What gave you that idea?"

"She was never friendly, like Patty or your parents. Maybe it was my imagination. Anyway, it's not important." He brushed the air. "How's Patty?"

"She's married to Sterling Anderson, a contractor, and they have two girls, eight and six. They live in Lexington."

His face relaxed into a smile. "I'd like to see Patty with her daughters. Have they been down yet to play with Nicky?"

"That's supposed to happen soon."

They were interrupted by the final bell for the day, and as Jenny made her way through the crowded halls to her office, she could only think of Scott's impression of Helena's dislike. Such a thing had never occurred to her.

Several hours later, Nicky and Helena were telling anyone who wished to listen of the wonderful afternoon they'd spent together, where they'd explored everything that was in the park.

"When Aunt Helena and I got back we were 'austed, Mom." Nicky flopped back on the couch.

"Tell your mom what it was that exhausted us the most, Nicky." Helena plopped down beside him and ruffled his hair.

Whatever it was, Helena had profited from it, Jenny thought. She wasn't the same tension-filled, shaky woman who'd arrived yesterday. Her cheeks had a healthy flush, her hair had lost some of its sleekness, her eyes were bright and clear as she looked at Nicky. They grinned at each other mischievously.

"We went on the swings and then on the merry-go-round." Jenny could see that Nicky was holding himself back as he looked at her.

She played along. "I don't see how that made both of you so tired."

"We did it over and over and over and then we got 'austed!" He turned to his aunt. "Can we do it again tomorrow?"

"We'll find some other kind of fun for tomorrow," she promised.

The neighbors across the street had dropped by after dinner, so it wasn't until Jenny was in her bedroom laying out clothes for the next day that she and Helena had a chance to be alone.

"How're you feeling, Helena?" She held up a pair of black pants, changed her mind, and exchanged them for a pair in charcoal wool.

"Much better than I did yesterday. I slept late, had a nice breakfast with mom and spent the afternoon with Nicky." She examined the white-on-white tailored blouse Jenny was holding next to the pants. "Not that one. Don't you have anything that's rose?"

"Come look," Jenny invited, and took a seat to let Helena complete the outfit. It was easier and it always looked better than her choices.

"Doesn't this look smart?" Helena had put a pale rose sweater with the pants, a scarf with gray and rose tint, and a pair of brushed silver earrings. "Wear black leather pumps to set it off. Okay?"

"Thanks. I'll enjoy wearing it."

Helena perched on the corner of the bed. "Mom said you're working with Scott Phillips. What's it like being with him everyday?" she asked curiously.

Jenny took the question at face value, as if Scott hadn't said he felt Helena disliked him. "It was strange at first. Actually I was going to walk away from the job, but changed my mind."

"I'm surprised you didn't walk away," Helena kept her eyes on Jenny.

"Really? Why do you say that?" Maybe Scott was right.

Helena shrugged. "He's not my favorite person."

Puzzled, Jenny said, "Why?"

"You know why." Helena voice was crisp.

"You mean because of Adam?"

"What else?" She had gathered the end of the coverlet on the bed into her hand and was making tiny pleats in it.

"But you know he had nothing to do with Adam's drowning." Jenny heard her words as if they had been spoken through a fog.

"What I know is he didn't save Adam." She looked at the quilt, not at Jenny.

"It was too late by the time he got to the pond, Helena," she exclaimed.

"Why are you defending him?" Helena stared at Jenny.

"Because it was my fault. Mom told me to go find Adam, and I didn't go when she first told me to. If you have to blame someone, blame me." She took a long unsteady breath but held Helena's gaze.

"I can't blame you. You're my sister." Helena sighed and resumed making her pleats.

Jenny didn't know what to say. The whole conversation was so unlike Helena, especially her combative undertone. Had she been holding blame against Scott all these years when subconsciously she knew it was Jenny's fault? Jenny flinched away from this idea even though it might have substance. But Helena had never indicated that she felt this way.

Jenny stared into space, trying to calm herself and make some kind of sense of where she stood with her sister. What she knew for certain was that Helena, reserved and undemonstrative, had experienced an upheaval in her life that had driven her home. It was up to Jenny to be a part of the comfort Helena was seeking, not a part of the problem.

Helena said quietly, "I talked to Woody today."

"Oh? How is he?"

"Pretty much like I am, trying to get past this. Spending a lot of time on the golf course. That's his therapy."

"I see."

"When he asked how I was, I said I felt better today, especially after spending time with Nicky. He's a godsend, Jenny." Unshed tears made her eyes shiny.

"For me, also," Jenny said.

"Woody wants us to go away together as soon as we both get back."

"That sounds like a great idea, Sis."

"That's what I told him."

"Have you thought of going to a spiritual retreat of some sort? You might find it healing and helpful."

"That might work," Helena said thoughtfully. "I haven't been down that path for so many years it just never occurred to me. I'll tell Woody tomorrow."

No matter what Jenny tried, sleep eluded her, so she found herself once more staring out her dormer window at a night sky, which this time was cloudy.

Her conversation with Helena kept her thoughts shooting off in all directions. For instance, why had she jumped to Scott's defense when Helena said exactly what Jenny had held as truth all this time? That somehow he was blameworthy, and therefore the bond between them had been destroyed.

Yet despite some setbacks, the evidence of the same bond seemed to be reestablishing itself almost instinctively. As when she had invited him to a meal after the festival because she saw him looking tired and alone.

Did that mean she no longer associated the drowning with him? But if not, why did she continue to have the frightening nightmares? Perhaps they would subside as time went on.

Could this be where faith dared to begin to hope—given the fact that she could release Scott from guilt?

The longer she stared at the night, the more fanciful her musings became. Faith could be thought of as a prism whose light colors the focus and the characteristics each person holds up to it. Hers was guilt, a guilt so long-standing that it had obscured the light.

Helena's capacity for faith had become negatively affected

by her inability to fulfill her function as a woman and bear a child. Was the loss of Adam a part of that equation?

To Jenny, it seemed more that in Helena's severe emotional distress she had confused losing Adam with losing a potential son or daughter of her own.

Weary of these conundrums and suppressing a yawn, Jenny returned to her bed.

Whatever had caused her distraught sister's outburst, Jenny would be sure to let her know she was loved and all was well between them.

Chapter 16

Jenny lined the girls up, three abreast, for the four-block walk
to the square where Mrs. Tessie Martin was to meet them. The
tenth girl, Milladeen Aiken, walked with her. Behind them
came Luis Gomez who had his nine boys also three abreast.

Jenny was at the front of the column, Luis at the end. They
attracted a few smiles as they walked briskly, warned ahead
of time that no straggling would be allowed. The Downtown
as History field trip was on its way.

Mrs. Martin, a matronly woman with a firm voice and a presentation she kept lively with anecdotes, captured the students'
attention. This was what Jenny had hoped for. Most had their
notebooks out as they heard about the oldest pharmacy in the
country that still had old-fashioned exhibits of how some pills
were made and also had a rumored ghost of the first owner.

A clothing store, a rehabilitated theater and a restaurant that
had been in the same family for generations filled out the list.

When asked how many students had been in these places, half of the hands went up.

The last place was the town hall across the busy street. The students were talking animatedly about Mrs. Martin's stories as they filed into the building. Jenny and the girls went first, staying close behind each other to give room to people who were there on business.

Suddenly, Jenny heard a crash and muffled noises. Everyone turned to see what had happened, including the people in the wide hallway.

"Don't move," she told the girls as she hurried to the back of the line, where several boys were getting to their feet.

"What happened?" A glance at the boys' faces assured her this was not the result of a fight. In fact, the boys looked sheepish as Mr. Gomez got them quickly back in line.

"Anyone hurt?" Jenny asked.

"No. The last boy in line tripped over his shoelaces and pushed the boy next to him who pushed the third one. They all went down. Just an accident."

"Let's move on then. I hope no one in here took a picture."

Mrs. Martin's story of when this building became town hall and all that went into it was brief. Jenny was thankful, because the fifth graders had been distracted by the boys falling, but they gave the speaker a good round of applause.

Jenny hadn't been back in her office fifteen minutes when there was a tap on her door and Scott came in.

"Apparently your field trip was a success," he said solemnly.

"Please have a seat," Jenny said wondering how he knew unless he'd already talked to Luis. "Yes, it went very well except for a little mishap at the end."

"I've had three calls from town hall, including one from the mayor himself. I hardly think mishap is the right word."

Jenny's heart sank. "What were the calls about? All that happened was a boy tripped on his shoelace and there was a domino effect because the kids were walking in a close line. The boy and two others fell. They got up and we went on. That's all there was to it."

"Not according to the mayor. What he heard was there was a scuffle between the boys, which made three of them fall. He thought it was too bad they couldn't act better in the town hall!"

"But that's not true!" Jenny was on her feet.

"The second call was from someone who wanted to know if we intended to sue the town hall, and the third one was from a reporter who happened to be there and wanted information to put in the newspaper." His lips were set in a grim line.

Jenny's eyes were wide and filled with indignation. "All of that—"

"Sit down, Jenny."

It was the restraint in his voice and the weariness in his eyes that Jenny responded to. She sat down and waited.

"Tell me what happened from the time you left here."

Ordinarily, when Jenny was telling anything to Scott, it was easy and comfortable. This time she felt he was examining every small detail of her report. His eyes never left hers. Surely he didn't think she was misrepresenting the event to keep herself or Luis in the clear?

If he was foolish enough to think she'd lost her integrity he'd just have to think that. She clasped her hands on her desk when she was finished and held his glance. She didn't know what to expect.

"This is exactly what you and Ed and I talked about after the school board meeting. Everybody who works in town hall or who was there will spread the story, and most of them will get it wrong. Sooner, rather than later, the board will hear all about it."

She was the one Scott had been concerned about, because of her emotional volatility. She'd assured him she would be careful and yet, several days later, this tiny mishap had occurred under her supervision in the most public place in town.

When she could stand the silence no longer, she asked, "What did you tell the mayor?"

"That I'd get back to him as soon as I'd received my staff report."

"Since I'm the one who was there, I'll be happy to go back and tell him precisely what happened," she said.

"Which would give him the opportunity to say the principal was hiding behind his staff." Scott stood up. "Thanks, anyway." He closed the door soundlessly behind him.

Jenny pounded her desk softly to relieve her frustration. She wanted to laugh and cry at the same time: laugh at the silliness of the incident and cry at the pain it was causing Scott. Heaven knows what the long range effect might be— all because some fifth-grade boy hadn't tied the extra-long laces in his shoes that were part of a fashion statement.

Now she had to laugh at herself because there was no point in trying to make sense of the ins and outs of life.

This was only the beginning of November. She had fashioned other ideas and activities to help students who needed it become interested in learning and to be able to practice what they learned. One that she was excited about was called "It's My Turn."

After Scott told her what the fallout was of the field trip, she didn't know if she would be permitted to use the new concept. She didn't even know if Scott would still keep her on as his educational consultant. The agency could send him someone else.

She shivered at the image of what that would look like on her grant application. She couldn't say she hadn't been warned by Scott. Her grant and his selection by the board to be principal might both be at stake.

Supposing she resigned. Wouldn't that be the honorable action to take? It would relieve Scott of the possibility of any more episodes that would reflect badly on him and his school. It would also relieve him of having to let her go.

She'd never walked away from a difficult situation in her work life before, and she squirmed at the thought. However, she'd never had Scott Phillips as her boss before, and she would do anything she could to keep him from harm's way.

Could she replace this position with another somewhere in South Carolina so she could keep Nicky close to his grandparents? She might have to postpone the grant application for a year, but she could do that if need be.

North Carolina was a possibility as well.

There was a lot to think about over the weekend. Helena would be leaving early tomorrow morning so she'd spend this evening with her.

But Saturday she'd begin researching some alternatives and thinking through the doctoral program.

What she didn't want to think about was leaving Scott.

Chapter 17

Saturday was turning out to be one of those days that happened to Scott now and then. He guessed everybody had them. They start out okay, and then one thing happens, and another, and the next thing you know the day has disintegrated.

Scott had slept an hour later than usual. That part was good. After a leisurely breakfast he decided to give his apartment a good cleaning. For him that meant running the vacuum, gathering all of the papers and trash to be disposed of, and cleaning the bathroom.

The vacuum refused to work for no reason that he could see, the bleach he was using in the bathroom splashed on his jeans, and the trash bin outside was filled to overflowing, which meant he'd either have to take his three bags back upstairs or put them in the trunk of his car where the garbage would smell up the trunk! So he did what he hated seeing others do. He added to the overfill, even though he knew the trucks wouldn't come on the weekend to empty the bin.

He picked up his clean laundry. No problem there. He dropped off his cleaning, presented the ticket for the items he'd left last week, and waited patiently for the lady to find it. Minutes passed. "Are you sure you didn't already pick it up?" she asked, a worried look on her face.

"How could I? I just gave you the ticket for it."

"It doesn't seem to be here," she said, looking at the ticket.

"Please look again," Scott said, trying to be civil.

The upshot was that the manager was called, who helped the clerk look until his pants were found, under R instead of P.

Maybe I'd better go back to bed, he thought.

Instead he took a stack of reports from his briefcase which he really hadn't intended to work on, but maybe a bit of familiar routine would make him feel better. He was an hour into the stack when the phone rang.

"Hey, buddy. This is Harry. A bunch of us are gonna play pool and get some food. Wanta join us?"

Keep working or hang out on a Saturday night with some guys? He should go. Might make him feel better. They'd have a lot of laughs.

"Thanks, Harry. I'm stuck with a stack of reports. Let me know next time." He should've gone. He'd enjoyed the previous night out with Harry and his friends because it turned out he'd known two of them from high school.

It just didn't suit him tonight, so he might as well keep laboring on the reports. He put on a jazz CD and tried to put everything out of his mind while he worked. When he pushed the completed reports back in his briefcase, he was surprised to see that it was already eight o'clock.

No wonder he was hungry.

He wasn't about to look in the refrigerator. Not the way his day had gone. He got in the car, went to the nearest fast food place, and out of sheer frustration got a huge hamburger, fries, and a chocolate milkshake.

There was a nip in the air tonight, but the sky was clear. He was in no hurry to get back to his lonely unvacuumed apartment. What had happened to the busy social life he'd always had? A Saturday night like this rarely had happened, and if so only by his choice. Now it was the norm. He could've called Tiffany, but she was likely out with Watson, and anyway, he had no appetite for the Tiffanys of this world.

His only hunger was for the Jenny Mayes Cannon he knew. If he could just hear her voice. He turned the Lexus home, went in and dialed her number. It was late and he promised himself he'd only let it ring once, and if she didn't answer...

"Hello."

"Jenny, this is Scott. Is it too late to call?"

"It's only a few minutes after nine. What's wrong? Where are you?" Her voice was filled with anxiety.

"I'm home and nothing's wrong. What made you ask that?"

"You've never called me here so I was afraid something had happened." Scott still sensed her uncertainy and he set out to reassure her.

"No, honey, it's just been one of those days when nothing goes right. Will it bore you if I tell you about it?"

"I'm listening."

Scott told her in detail about the vacuum, the spilled bleach, the overfilled trash, and the almost-lost cleaning, making it as amusing as possible. He was rewarded by Jenny's sympathetic comments and occasional chuckle.

By the time he was through, all of the frustrations of the

day had vanished. He relaxed into his chair, long legs stretched out, the phone pressed to his ear and his eyes closed.

"Is Helena still here?"

"No, she left this morning."

"I wanted to call you yesterday evening, but I figured she was still here. Did you read in the paper about that up-and-coming activist, Lee Baldwin, from Mississippi coming here?"

"Yes, but I didn't remember it was last night."

"I went with Dave and Devon. He's supporting the democrat who's running for the vacant congressional seat. It was a packed house, Jenny. He's very articulate, and was particularly effective because he knew the candidate and all about the local and state politics."

"Sorry I missed him. Did you see anyone from Springview in the audience?"

"Yes, but there was also someone I didn't expect to see."

"I'll take a wild guess. Lawrence T. Gordon."

"The man himself."

"I don't believe it. What was he doing there?"

"It's smart to know the enemy, and Larry isn't dumb."

"Did he see you, Scott?"

"Looked me in the eye and nodded. One more mark against me, I suspect." He hadn't acknowledged that before, but saying it to Jenny, he knew it to be true. Larry had never minded mixing fair means with foul to achieve his goal.

"Are you serious, Scott?"

"You know I don't lie to you, Jenny."

"He scares me, Scott, a person like that is dangerous because you don't know what he's liable to do," Jenny said, her voice a little tremulous. "He has no principles, only goals, and I'm afraid of what he might do to get you out of that job. Even though you'll be the best candidate, I don't want anything to happen to you."

Scott held the phone tighter. If only he could be with Jenny at this moment. She cared about him. Was fearful on his behalf. She didn't want anything to happen to him. He needed to tell her how her caring made him feel, but he knew he couldn't. She'd retreat again.

"Thank you for saying that, honey, but I don't want you to worry. Let me tell you how I see the situation. Knowing what you're up against is half the battle. The other half is doing the best you can regardless of any other circumstance. I'll admit the town hall fiasco yesterday threw me off a little, and if I upset you, I apologize. It was so unexpected, and a prime example of making a mountain out of a molehill. It won't happen again. You probably didn't feel too good about it, did you?" He waited with some trepidation for her answer because he knew he'd come on strong to her.

"You're right, I didn't," she said.

"Forgive me?"

"Yes. I'll try to be more circumspect in the future."

"You must be Jenny Mayes Cannon, an educational consultant who cares passionately for the students she's here to help. I'll keep on being the interim principal who does the same and hopes to make a significant difference using methods he believes in. If they decide at the end of the year that they don't want my methods and me, I'll simply take them somewhere else. At least I'll have had a year to test them out and see what works and what doesn't."

"We won't be scared off?"

"Nothing will scare us off."

"I want to jump up and down and yell hooray!" Jenny laughed excitedly.

"I'm feeling good myself," Scott confessed. "There's just one thing, Jenny."

"What is it?"

"Don't walk out on me. Sometimes I sense the need in you to cut loose. Please don't." He tried to keep his voice calm but emotion surged in his throat.

She didn't reply at once. Had she already decided to leave? He clutched the phone and waited.

"I won't break up the team, Scott."

Jenny had put on a bright face even though she'd only had four hours of sleep, her mind twisting and turning with the possibilities of securing a new position quickly and making living arrangements for Nicky here if her parents would keep him. That thought alone tied her in knots.

Helena was leaving after an early breakfast.

"Will you stay in Richmond tonight?" Jenny asked.

"No. I think I'll push on through."

"That's a lot of miles," Dad said worriedly. "Will you be okay by yourself?

She gave him her brilliant smile. "I've done it before, and I want to be home when Woody gets there."

"You'll be very careful, won't you, dear?" Mom added.

"I will, and I promise to call as soon as I get in."

Jenny was impressed. That was a rare concession from Helena.

Just before she left, Helena ran upstairs to drop a light kiss on Nicky. She'd insisted he shouldn't be awakened for her early departure. She turned to Jenny who had gone with her and hugged her tightly.

"You don't know how much you've helped me, Jen. When I woke up this morning I was certain for the first time that I was on the right path. I know Woody and I will make the right decision."

As they all stood later waving goodbye, Jenny puzzled over her sister's words. She'd only listened while Helena spoke of her fertility problems. She had thought of adoption as the natural solution but hadn't mentioned it. They'd had the little difference of opinion about Scott and the drowning, but surely Helena wasn't referring to that.

Whatever it was, she appreciated that Helena left with a positive attitude about her marriage and a family.

Her lack of sleep had left her listless, and as she dragged around doing her laundry and cleaning her room, she felt the beginning of a headache, which grew in severity so that her previous idea of spending hours in the library had to be put aside.

Fortunately, her dad invited Nicky to go with him on several errands. Nicky was fascinated that grandad intended to teach him how to pick out tires for the car, then get the car washed and then have lunch somewhere.

Her mom went shopping, and the blessed quiet of the house was irresistible. Jenny went to bed and slept. It wasn't until after dinner that she thought of using her laptop to begin the research for another job.

She looked for half an hour and found nothing interesting. Maybe she'd do better tomorrow. Her heart wasn't in it today. She put the computer away and played with Nicky until his bedtime.

What an odd day it had been, she thought, as she picked up a book and nestled in her most comfortable chair. She'd found it in the family room and asked permission to use it in her dormer. The upholstery was a blend of blue and green which she'd accented with two small emerald pillows.

She was wrapped in a warm robe, listening to the soft music from the radio and reading her book, when her phone rang. She picked it up immediately and was surprised to hear Scott's voice.

Was something wrong? Apparently not. She relaxed and smiled as he recounted the frustrating events of his day. He went into great detail but she didn't care, it was lovely to just sit and chat with him.

Last night he, Dave, and Devon had gone to hear Lee Baldwin. She couldn't help feeling a little envious. She should have been there with them. The four of them got along so well. Maybe she'd drop a hint that—no. Don't do that. She was supposed to be putting some distance between herself and Scott.

Scott ran into someone there he didn't expect to see, and she knew it had been Larry Gordon, the same man whose name had given her a chill when Scott and Dave had mentioned him at the picnic.

"He scares me, Scott," she'd said, because her intuition told her this man would do anything to keep Scott from getting the job.

He began to explain how he saw the situation, and in doing so brought up the field trip and the calls from town hall which had thrown him off. He apologized for upsetting her and asked how she'd felt about it.

Not good, she told him, and he asked her to forgive him; it wouldn't happen again.

Jenny couldn't believe what she was hearing. Had she been well, she might already have applied for a new job via the Internet, because she'd been so sure that resigning was the best thing to do.

Scott went on to reiterate that they must stay who they were and pursue their visions for Springview. If the board gave the job to someone else, at least he'd have the experience to see how his ideas worked out.

She felt excited and empowered to work even harder for

her project's success. But he'd made a request that'd thrown her for a loop.

"Don't walk out on me. Sometimes I sense the need in you to cut loose. Please don't."

She could hear the emotion he was trying to suppress and it made her feel weak inside.

That's why he'd called her tonight. The connection between them had passed the message that she was getting ready to leave. His involuntary response had been to pick up the phone and pin her down.

He was waiting for her reply, but she was overwhelmed by the sudden realization of another force at play rearranging her life. In response to it she had no alternative except to assure Scott she wouldn't break up the team.

She laid the phone down but she didn't pick up the book. In moments like this her only warmth was knowing Scott was near. Their connection, so unlike any other, sustained her.

She only wished it could be closer.

Chapter 18

Jenny ran lightly down the stairs. Her mother was in the hall pretending to be dusting the table near the door where the mail collected.

"Are you sure you feel well enough to go to work? I'm certain you could take a sick day. You never have." A line of worry wrinkled her forehead.

"I had two days of rest, which is a lot more than I usually get, Mom. Believe me, I feel fine. See you later." She dropped a kiss on her mother's cheek and went out the door.

She was glad to be wearing her cinnamon brown pantsuit because the temperature had definitely dropped during the night. She liked the brown leather half boots she'd found. They were comfortable as well as smart.

Would Scott think they were smart? She zipped along the street, her spirit high as she tried to recall if Scott had ever paid her a compliment since they'd been at Springview. She thought he might have. Yet how could she expect him to unless he did the same with the other female staff?

But of course she wasn't "other female staff." She was the female he'd called Saturday night and talked nonsense with about his day, then seriously about his strategy for managing Springview the remainder of the year. She'd been truly surprised when he talked about the board passing him over for the permanent position.

To face the fact that no matter how much he accomplished, the board might not choose him was not only realistic but courageous. It would release some pressure from all of them and make the job more enjoyable. She admired him for his clear vision, his confidence and integrity. It was not in him to shortchange the school community just because he might not be at the helm next year. She was fortunate to have such a man as her supervising principal.

She parked the car in her slot next to Ed and walked into the hall. It looked shiny, almost as if it was new to her. She moved slowly along the portion where the students had painted their artwork and appreciated their clever representations of what was meaningful to them.

Had she noticed before the striking detail in this woman's face, as if she was about to speak? Or this person running? It was almost a stick figure, yet you could feel the energy in the arms and legs. Up in a corner was a doll house, slightly aslant. In each piece of art there was something to be commended, even though the students were untutored.

The only reason Jenny had been sent to Springview was to assist in developing methods that would stimulate and enhance their desire to learn and their success in doing so. She had to find a way to use this wall to show them what they had achieved and how those same elements could be used in learning.

When she got to her office, even it looked unfamiliar. Then it occurred to her that mentally she had detached herself from Springview when she left the school Friday. She hadn't meant to come back to stay, and that's why this morning she felt like she was returning unexpectedly to a dearly-loved place.

The knock on her door a few minutes later admitted Scott.

"You're here," he said with a wide smile. "Good morning."

She smiled back. "Of course I'm here, and good morning to you."

"I just needed to reassure myself. That's a great outfit you're wearing."

"I'm glad you like it," she said.

He nodded once and was gone.

Scott had needed to assure himself that she was here and had liked what she was wearing. Contented and pleased, Jenny settled down to make notes on the student artwork.

Talking with Lynn Bartlett about it later that morning, they planned ways to incorporate it into the art segment of her activity room program.

"Depending on their interest and progress, I can see us putting on an exhibit for the public in the third or fourth grading period." Lynn was excited and confident this could happen.

Looking at her animated face, Jenny wished there were more teachers like Lynn. She knew that Lynn would work overtime, and with the sensitivity to reach the shy student who had the talent but had never received the recognition or encouragement of that talent.

Dave Young came to her table at lunchtime. "We missed you Friday night," he said, unwrapping a large whole wheat sandwich filled with ham, cheese, lettuce and tomato.

"Helena was here, and I forgot that was the night Baldwin

vas speaking. Scott said you and Devon went. What'd you
hink of him?" Jenny's half a tuna sandwich looked puny beside
)ave's. She pushed her bag of corn chips across to him. "Can
ou use these?" She'd be lucky if she could eat her yogurt.

"Thanks. I thought he had the mark of a savvy politician
nd can go far if he keeps himself straight. Did Scott tell you
ve saw Gordon there?"

"Yes. Do you think he could be a serious threat to Scott?"
)ave had known Gordon as long as Scott had, and she trusted
is opinion.

"The word is that Larry intends to manipulate matters so
hat his brother Bruce gets his job." He picked up the second
alf of his sandwich.

This was news to Jenny. "That's the guy who was at uni-
ersity with you?"

"That's him."

"Why didn't this interim job go to him?"

"He's working at a prep school and didn't want to pay the
enalty of leaving at short notice."

"Unlike Scott, who had to pay a lot to break his contract,
ut did it because he wanted this chance above anything else,"
enny said.

"There's no comparison between Bruce and Scott. Believe
ne, I know them both," Dave asserted. He finished his
andwich and fixed Jenny with a sober glance. "Merit has little
o do with it when you're dealing with a Larry Gordon and
ny influence he might have over other board members.
lemember that, Jenny, and so will I."

Jenny pondered these words as she walked back from lunch
o her office. On the way she met Sergeant Hampton who
sked if she could spare him a few minutes. Was he going to
uestion her again about the girls' testimony?

"We're still investigating the break-in, Mrs. Cannon, and I wonder if you have heard anything about it from any students?" He sat across from her, his steady glance on her. She was glad she had nothing to hide from that intense regard.

"I've heard nothing, Sergeant Hampton. I wish I could help you find the person because I think we'd all feel safer."

"It may have been a former student, someone who was known to be a troublemaker but who may have dropped out of sight since leaving here. Does that suggest anyone you might have heard of?"

Something stirred in Jenny's mind. She tried to bring it into focus. Had one of her fifth-grade girls mentioned an older guy with a funny name?

"Jojo," she said.

Sergeant Hampton said, "What about him?"

"Someone mentioned him as a person who was always in trouble, especially in high school, but they think he's left town. That's all I heard. Does that help?"

"Everything helps. Thanks, Mrs. Cannon. Was there a last name?"

"No, there wasn't."

After he left, Jenny wondered if having a single name could help the police, but if the student had been in trouble, the name might be known to them.

She dialed Scott's office to report Sergeant Hampton's inquiry, but there was no answer, so she left the message. As soon as she hung up, her phone rang.

"Jenny, this is Gladys. Can you come get Amanda? She's here in the library crying."

"I'll be right there."

She found Amanda at a corner table, her head down and her shoulders shaking. A girl was trying to comfort her without success. She seemed relieved when Jenny appeared and sat down beside Amanda.

"Amanda, dry your eyes and come to my office where we can talk." Even as she made the suggestion, Jenny saw it wasn't workable. Amanda was too deeply upset and she would attract attention walking all the way to Jenny's office. After a hurried whisper with Gladys, she was able to help Amanda from the main room into a small workroom with a table and chairs. She got a box of tissues from Gladys and put them in front of Amanda, who was still sobbing.

"Take your time, Amanda," she said gently. "Get it all out and when you're through, we'll talk about what's troubling you so I can help."

This seemed to bring on a fresh downpour. "No one can help," Amanda wailed, holding another wad of tissues to her eyes.

"What happened, Amanda? Did someone hurt you?" Jenny asked.

The girl shook her head no.

"Did something happen in your classroom that upset you?" Again a negative shake of the head, but Jenny was encouraged as she eliminated possibilities through her questions.

"Tell me what happened at home that is making you cry." This was delicate territory, but it had to be something serious, and Jenny had to know what it was if she was going to help the girl.

Although she wasn't yet ten, Amanda was tall for a fourth grader, had no trouble with her lessons when she applied herself, had a creative talent and a gregarious personality. Jenny's experience told her that unless Amanda learned self-discipline, her high spirits would often get her in trouble. She could well imagine that there would be problems at home sometimes.

The sobs had stopped and as she dried her eyes, Jenny saw Amanda's face for the first time. He eyes were swollen and red. She looked at Jenny with a despair that sat oddly on such a young face.

"I can't go home and I don't know what to do."

"Why can't you go home, Amanda?" Jenny asked.

"Because my mom will never forgive me."

"Forgive you for what?

"I took some money and I told her I hadn't seen it."

"How much was it?"

"A five dollar bill."

"Why did you take it?"

Her features crinkled up as if she was going to cry again. "I don't know why I do things I know are wrong. Last night I wanted to stay up to see a show and Mom said I couldn't. My homework was done and I didn't see why she said no. So I was kinda mad at her, and this morning, when I saw the money lying on the table, I took it. She asked my brother and I if we'd seen it. We both said no. She gets so mad when we lie to her so I don't know why I did it. I know she won't forgive me this time."

"You've done this before, Amanda?"

"You mean take money?"

"That's what I mean."

"Just once before, but that was way last year." She gave the time as if that made a difference.

"What kind of punishment will your mom give you?"

"You mean if I go home?"

"Yes."

"Ground me for a week or two, I guess, but I don't know, because it wasn't just taking the money, it was lying about it." Her voice wavered as she realized herself the enormity of her action.

"What will your dad say?"

"He walked out on us when I was four. He lives with his girl-friend, and my brother and I don't see much of him. I don't think he cares about what happens to us." She shrugged her shoulders.

"Are you afraid your mom will beat you?"

"She never does that. She'll get that look that says she's disappointed in me. Then she'll remind me of the Ten Commandments."

"What'd you spend the money on?"

"I didn't spend it." She took a bill from her pocket and smoothed it on the table. "Here it is."

Jenny now understood that this was mostly an act of defiance and rebelliousness, but it had consequences which would only grow as Amanda matured if she could not halt them now or at least give her some controls to use.

"Amanda, I want you to sit quietly, think about this situation with your eyes closed. When you're through, think of what you'd really like to happen."

She watched Amanda fidget at first, then she settled down, covered her face with her hands and thought.

Amanda opened her eyes. "I'd like to go home, talk with my mom, and have her forgive me."

"Okay. Let's practice, so what you really want will be what really happens. I'll be your mom, so you start talking."

Jenny didn't know if Amanda would buy into this, nor did she know what Amanda's mom was like, but it was worth a try.

"I don't know what to say," Amanda lamented.

"That's because you're only thinking of yourself and how you feel. Are you talking to your mom just to make yourself feel good, Amanda?"

"Well, a little bit," she said sheepishly, "but mostly I want my mom to talk with me and then feel better about me."

"Keep your mom in mind and start again. Usually when you get home, where is your mom and what is she doing?"

"She's in the kitchen getting ready to cook."

"Okay. Pretend I'm at this table peeling potatoes when you come in."

"Hi, Mom. Can we talk?"

"Hi, Amanda. Sure. Have a seat."

"Mom, here's that money." She laid the bill on the table. "I'm sorry I took it and lied about it. Will you forgive me? Please?" Her voice wavered again. Jenny had no doubt of Amanda's sincerity. What she wanted from this young girl who had so much potential was for her to have a deeper understanding of what she'd done, so this could become a significant milestone in her life. Therefore, as Amanda's mom, she would not be persuaded easily.

"I'm glad to have the money back. I owed it to Mrs. Burke next door. It's easy for me to say I forgive you, but how do I know you won't do something like it again, Amanda?"

Amanda looked at Jenny in surprise. Caught up in the strong emotion of the moment, she hadn't analyzed the future.

"How do I know I won't do it again, Mrs. Cannon?" she asked.

"Didn't I see your grandmother at the harvest festival?"

"She came because my mom had to work."

"She seemed to be a very wise person. What would she tell you?"

"She always says that she can forgive me, but can I forgive myself? Because until I do, and then ask God's forgiveness, it's all just words. I have to feel—I forget the word—its re-something."

"Remorse."

"That's it. Can you explain it to me?"

"You do something wrong. It makes you feel guilty because you know it's wrong. It's hard to put out of your mind because you understand how wrong you were. It makes you feel so terribly bad that you decide not to ever do it again. You ask God to forgive you, ask the person to forgive you, and you forgive yourself because you know you won't do it again."

As she spoke she watched Amanda's face to see if she was making a very complex matter clear.

"That's why I was crying, because I felt so guilty."

"Amanda, I think if you explain this to your mom like we've talked about it, she'll understand and give you another chance."

The young girl's face brightened with hope. "I'll try it, Mrs. Cannon. Thanks."

She picked up her bookbag and left the room. Jenny followed more slowly and, after thanking Gladys, went back to her office.

If I can explain guilt, remorse and forgiveness so a nine-year-old can understand it and act on it, why can't I?

What is it in me that won't let me be forgiven?

Chapter 19

No one likes hospitals except the people who have to wor in them, Scott mused as he climbed the steps of the Brentwoc Community Hospital, and he was no exception. His dad ha been brought here an hour ago with complications of diabete according to what his mom had told him over the phone.

"What kind of complications?" he'd asked, alarmed at th news.

"I don't know yet. That's why he's in the hospital."

The reception area of the hospital had been expanded an refurbished since the last time he'd seen it. No more straigh back chairs lining the green walls. Now there were groups comfortable chairs in pastel colors, the walls were crear colored, and more windows added sunlight to the room.

A candy stripe lady with a clipboard greeted him. "Ma I help you?"

"I'm here to see Ward Phillips," Scott said.

"He's in 3G. Just take the elevator to your left and get off at the third floor," she said, and took a step away from Scott to greet the next person.

The elevator was crowded, and, as it stopped on the second floor for people to get out and others to crowd in, it occurred to Scott that this was his first time seeing one of his parents in a hospital.

He wasn't sure how he'd feel, and his steps slowed as he got off at the third floor and turned right down the corridor toward 3G. The door was closed. What did that mean? Was the doctor in there?

Scott knocked on the door and opened it. Whatever was happening, it was his father in the room and Scott had a right to be there. The first person he saw was his mother, who hurried to him.

"I'm so glad to see you," she said. His strong, courageous mother leaned against him, and he involuntarily put his arm around her to give her support. She looked almost frail, which told him more about his dad's condition than anything.

He hardly recognized the man hooked up to tubes who was lying in the hospital bed, a cover pulled up to his chin. His face was drawn and pale. He looked old, weak and tired. Totally unlike the man Scott knew as vigorous-minded and dominant, even when he wasn't feeling well.

Scott had to get past the lump in his throat before he could say "Dad?" He didn't know if his father was conscious, he was lying so still and seemed to be hardly breathing. But there was a flutter of the eyelids which heartened Scott.

He found his dad's hand under the coverlet and held it for a moment. It was warm, and although there was no responsive pressure, the life in it gave Scott hope.

"Tell me what happened," Scott said as he went to sit beside his mother.

"I was in the kitchen preparing lunch when I heard this noise in the living room. I ran in and found your dad on the floor unconscious. The ambulance was there in three minutes and brought him here."

"What's the diagnosis?"

"It's a diabetic coma. His blood glucose level dropped very low and that's what brought it on."

"Has it happened before?"

"No. He's started sweating and trembling a time or two, which is a symptom, but medication and food always kept it from going any farther." She kept looking at the bed and Scott sensed that she was blaming herself for what had happened.

He covered her hands with his. They were cold, and as he rubbed some warmth into them he tried to reassure her that she wasn't at fault.

"Knowing Dad and how stubborn he can be, it's likely he missed a medication at the time he was supposed to take it or was doing something he shouldn't have been doing."

"I told him not to reorganize his law library in the study, but he's been wanting to do it for some months and he started on it last night. He was so pleased he began again right after breakfast."

"That's what brought it on. Did you tell the doctor?"

"Yes, and he agreed."

"So what's next?"

"He's going to keep him here for a few days for more tests and to get him completely stabilized before he permits him to go home."

"Sounds like a good idea, Mom. Don't you think so?" He wanted her to have a chance to regain her strength before having to deal with his dad, who wasn't the easiest patient in the world. He hoped this setback might catch the attention of Ward Phillips and make him more amenable to following the demands that diabetes incurred.

"I do think so. I don't want us to lose him because of his own stubborn ways." Her voice wavered.

"He may be stubborn about some things, but he's strong-willed and intelligent about what matters, like his family, so don't worry, Mom. He'll be home in a few days. What you need is to get some rest. Okay?"

"I feel better just talking to you. Thanks for coming right away. I'll go home pretty soon."

"Good. I'll see you again after work."

Back in his office Scott found it difficult to concentrate on his in-basket. The image of his dad, weak and silent, dependent on tubes, stayed in the forefront of his consciousness. After he'd frittered away an hour, he called Jenny's office.

"This is Jenny Cannon."

Thank God she answered. "This is Scott. Are you busy?"

"Not that busy. You want to see me?"

"Yes. I'll be right there."

At his first knock, instead of saying "Come in," she opened the door for him, then closed it immediately. She gave him one searching look, then put her arms around him.

This was what he needed. Scott pulled her close and found in their nearness the comfort and solace he craved.

After a long wordless moment, they separated, and she gestured him to the chair in front of her desk. She pulled another chair beside his and asked, "What's wrong, Scott?"

He told her in detail, beginning with the call from his mother and ending with the fact that his whole image of his father had changed from one of health to vulnerability. "I'm finding it difficult to deal with that," he confessed.

"But he's going to be all right, and he'll be strong again." She took his hand in hers.

"My head tells me that's what'll probably happen." He looked at their clasped hands. Hers was smooth and soft, yet had a firmness to it. He squeezed it gently and received an instant squeeze in return. "I held Dad's hand like this. It had some warmth but no strength."

"You know that will come back."

"He's had the diabetes for years, plus arthritis, so I don't know why this hits me so strongly."

"This is the first time you've seen what the diseases can do to him. How old did you tell me he is now?"

"Seventy his last birthday." Seventy had just been a number before, representing the decade after sixty and the one before eighty. Eighty had seemed to be when people began to age, not seventy.

"It's only a number," Jenny said, echoing his thought. "Sometimes it comes with a health crisis, sometimes not. Your dad has no heart problems, has he?"

"Not that we're aware of."

"After this, his doctor, your mom and hopefully your dad will all pay strict attention to the regimen he has to follow."

Scott relaxed in his chair as they talked a while longer. He held Jenny's hand and couldn't take his eyes away from her expressive face when she continued to set his mind at ease.

He didn't want to leave Jenny, yet he knew he must go back to work. This atmosphere of security she created, was it the same for all her students as it was for him? Is this how she'd persuaded Amanda to go home and talk with her mother? His objective intelligence told him that obviously some of the same elements had to be present.

Subjectively he wanted her interaction with him to be

special, intimate, unique to their relationship. Maybe it was juvenile to feel this way, he thought, pressing her palm to his cheek, yet he asked, "Why did you open the door and put your arms around me?"

"Because I knew something had happened to upset you deeply."

"How did you know?"

"By what was in your voice and the emotion I sensed."

"You were right. I had to come to you because I couldn't get any work done. I couldn't settle. I needed you, Jenny."

His fervid glance brought heat to her face as he pressured his lips to the palm of her hand. "People like us belong together, Jenny," he whispered.

Before he was tempted to go farther in breaking his vow about his behavior toward Jenny at school, he quickly got up and left her office. But the image of his father had been replaced with an image of his darling Jenny, eyes wide and face luminous at his declaration.

He hoped she would keep the moment and the declaration as deep in her heart as it was in his.

Saturday delivered Ward Phillips home in an ambulance with a stern warning from his doctor about what he could and could not do, eat and not eat.

"But my son Richard is flying in to see me today. I don't want to be wrapped in pajamas and a robe. I want to have my clothes on," he grumbled.

"You may get dressed as long as you stay in your chair most of the time," the doctor said.

"Eight hours?" Ward asked.

"Fine, if your wife watches you closely. And that's that. End of discussion."

Now in early evening, as the dusk deepened, Scott sat on one side of his dad's chair while Richard sat on the other. Their mom was putting the finishing touches to dinner and the enticing aroma of roast beef filled the air.

Richard, three years younger than Scott, looked so much like their father that it was a joke in the family. Their personalities, however, were worlds apart. Dad was serious, goal oriented, responsible and successful in his chosen career.

Richard was happy-go-lucky, yet always fell on his feet. He never professed a goal, and once out of college was attracted to the flash and dash of New York City, where he fell into an underling's job in Wall Street. Now at thirty-one he was a moderately successful investment broker, still unsure of what he wanted to do as a career.

Maybe it was because of their difference, Scott thought, as he saw Dad smile at one of his brother's stories that Dad admired Richard so much. Maybe it was because Dad knew early on that Richard would never be a lawyer, and so he hadn't been disappointed in him as he had been in Scott for a different career choice.

Dinner was eaten on tray tables around Dad's chair and it seemed to Scott he enjoyed being the center of attention as he ate what he described as pap while the rest enjoyed roast beef. But Richard kept them entertained with his adventures until it was clear the five hours were up, as Dad's energy flagged.

When he was settled in bed and Richard had assured him he could tell his two sons exactly where he wanted each of his books placed in his library the next day, the bedroom was cleared, and in the kitchen Mom served banana cream pie and coffee.

"The doctor said he would have a full recovery in due time

as long as the regimen is followed, so we don't have to worry."
Scott saw the clear relief in her face and was thankful.

"Will you need any help?" Richard asked, all laughter gone.

"None that I can see. Your dad was really scared, so I think
he'll do what he's supposed to do. Of course, he'll grumble,
but that's his privilege."

"Absolutely, we wouldn't want him to change that much."
Richard's grin was back.

"I'll see you later, Mom. I'm going with Scott, so leave the
door unlocked."

"There're plenty of keys for my children. Here's yours,"
she said and hugged her sons as they left.

In the car Richard said, "I'm relieved about Dad. Mom, too.
I think he's going to be okay. Funny how you never think
about your parents getting old, and then wham! It hits you in
the face. Know what I mean?"

"I said almost the same thing to Jenny the day he went to
the hospital and I saw a sick old man instead of Dad."

Richard turned his whole body toward Scott in surprise.
"Jenny. D'ya mean little Jenny Mayes?"

Scott smiled. "Not so little anymore. She's Jenny Mayes
Cannon now."

"She came back to Brentwood also?" He chuckled. "That's
not so surprising. She always did follow you around. What
does her husband think of that?"

Scott parked the Lexus. "I'll tell you when we get upstairs."

"I thought some of my stories were good," Richard said
when Scott had told him how Jenny had come to Springview,
"but yours beats mine for coincidence." Shoes off, legs
propped up on the couch as he sat across from Scott's easy
chair, he looked searchingly at his brother.

"So Jenny Mayes went ahead and got married. You didn't,

but I remember you were thinking about it with that girl Emma, in Connecticut. What stopped you?"

"She wasn't interested in having a family, and that put a stop to it for me."

Scott could see Richard turning that over in his mind and forming his next question, which would be about Jenny and Scott. How much should he tell his brother about the true situation? Richard could be trusted, he had no doubt of that. Perhaps if he opened his heart to Richard, it would help him understand himself better.

"What's the relationship between you and Jenny now?"

"It's hard to describe, because it goes back and forth. At first she decided not to stay because of our past history. You know we hadn't seen each other or been in any contact at all since the day of Adam's funeral, eighteen years ago."

"I didn't know that. I always assumed that you'd been in touch because you were so close."

"She wouldn't see me or talk to me after Adam, then she went to San Jose a few days later, and that was that. We both had some adjusting to do when we found we'd be working together."

"How was it for you?"

"I kept getting Jenny Cannon mixed up with my Jenny, Jenny Mayes. I found out accidentally that she and Cannon had had a son, Nicky, who is six years old. She hadn't even told me, and when I faced her with it, she made a feeble answer that it hadn't come up. I was hurt and angry, then I discovered she's almost obsessive about protecting him."

"You like him?"

"Yeah. He's a good kid, friendly. He and I get along really well."

"She lets you see each other, that's a step forward, isn't it?"

"I never go to the house. I see him in connection with school affairs and things. When I make one step forward, she takes two back. Then she'll do an unexpected thing, like make me go to a late meal with her because she sensed how tired and lonely I felt that evening. Yet when I try to talk to her about old bonds, she denies it in words, says that was kid stuff."

"Is she good at her job in the school?"

"She's brilliant. She's great with the students, knows how to defuse situations, comes up with new ideas for hiking kids' interest in learning."

"Do you know how she feels about you, Scott?"

"She's let her guard down lately and seems to feel more comfortable with me. When I came from seeing Dad in the hospital I went to her office. She knew without my saying a word that I was in bad shape, and put her arms about me until I felt better."

"Wow! That's impressive," Richard's eyes were wide. "No matter what she says or doesn't say, her feelings for you are deep."

Scott's face saddened. "If so, I don't know if she'll ever acknowledge it, Richard."

"You don't mean because of Adam? Like you said, he was buried eighteen years ago."

"He won't stay dead."

Richard just stared at him in astonishment.

"She thinks I could have saved him. I think maybe I could have if I'd been able to find him sooner. I want to talk about it with her and get the whole guilt issue resolved, but she shies away like a frightened colt, which makes me think she feels guilty, too. We were both supposed to look for the boys earlier, but got to teasing each other about Tiffany, who was hanging around."

Scott leaned back in his chair and closed his eyes. "Adam is always between us, Rich," he said wearily.

After a thoughtful silence, Richard asked, "Want my opinion?"

"I wouldn't have told you all of this if I didn't." Scott opened his eyes to look at his brother.

"It's a shame for you two to waste your lives like this when you should be building a good marriage together. I'm not a psychologist, but I do know that in the investment business there comes a time when the client will say yes or no. All your senses have to be alert for that moment, and you must seize it when it comes. That's what you have to do with Jenny. She sounds confused to me, and subconsciously she may be waiting for you to force the issue. Had you thought of that?"

"Not in those terms but I see what you mean," Scott said. "Enough about me. What's with your current love life?"

Richard grinned. "Funny you asked, because I did want to get your take on this girl I've been dating steadily for the past eight months. Name's Cynthia, and we work in the same building. She grew up in a small town in Illinois, went to university in Chicago, moved to New York to see what it was all about. I met her family the Fourth of July holiday. Reminds me of my own family."

"What is it you like about Cynthia compared to other girls you've known?"

Basically we want the same things out of life, we laugh at a lot of jokes together. We fit in ways that's not happened before."

"Have you thought if she'll stick when you decide not to be a New York investment broker anymore?"

"You're so cocky smart," Richard said with a chuckle. "How'd you know what I was thinking?" He tossed a small cushion at Scott.

"Known you long and known you well, bro. What's your next venture?"

"I'm thinking of taking some of my investments and buying a business of some kind. Don't know what kind or where yet, but I've a yen for living in my own house and raising a family. Who knows, I might even end up around here."

"Will Cynthia go for that?"

"Haven't asked her yet, but from the comments I've been throwing out, I think she's as ready to leave the Big Apple as I am."

"Thanksgiving's coming up. Bring her home for the weekend and see how that works out."

"Hey! Great idea. Thanks."

"Just returning the favor."

Chapter 20

Scott's weekend had been intense, especially Saturday. On Sunday he and Richard had taken a run before breakfast, then spent most of the day with their parents. Reorganizing their dad's library had turned out to be unexpectedly interesting, as many of the books had reminded him of a particular case.

He'd state the facts, appoint Scott as the prosecutor and Richard as the defense, then listen as they argued the case. As judge, he'd give the decision. He also changed the positions, making Richard prosecutor and Scott the defender. The exercise challenged Scott in a way he hadn't been challenged in years, and he thought it was the same for his brother. They wanted to show Dad the kind of sons he'd raised. The element of brotherly competition added zest, as did Mom's pert comments from time to time.

When Scott and Richard stood at his bedside to say goodnight, Dad had said, "Thanks, boys. This has been one of the best days of my life."

The glow of his dad's approbation stayed with Scott, and seemed to make his work at Springview lighter. Even the problem Ed and Dave brought him when they came into his office on Tuesday didn't loom as large as it might have.

"I thought we'd gotten rid of bullying, but it's back," Ed said. "Dave just told me of an instance, so I brought him to you so we can nip it in the bud."

"The worst offenders are usually sixth graders," Dave said "They're bigger, stronger, and can intimidate smaller kids by their size. So each year they graduate, it means we've got a chance to discourage the kids who were in the fifth grade last year from becoming bullies. On the playground we all try to keep a very close watch for it but it take place inside as well. The ones with a taste for it get slick and sly so they won't get caught."

"Can you give me a recent example, Dave?" Scott asked.

"Yesterday I'm in the hall at lunchtime, so it's filled with kids. Two boys are holding a big conversation. There's a boy in front of them, and instead of going around him, they pretend they're so busy with their talk they don't see him until the last minute. They separate, so he's in the middle, and they bump him hard, then walk on as if nothing happened. He fell, but the boys walked on as if nothing had happened."

"It couldn't have been an accident?"

"Not with these boys."

"How can you tell with certainty?"

"I watch kids on the playground. I see kids who are picking on someone and I begin to keep an eye on them. They tend to select targets, either a kid who they know isn't going to fight back, or a kid they don't like because he's smarter, or other kids like him, or he has money. They've got all kinds of ways to harass and intimidate without getting caught, like pinching hard, knocking his books down, taking his lunch, making him give them money, spilling drinks on him and making fun of him on the bus knowing other kids aren't going to come to his rescue."

"I saw some of that on my last job," Scott said reflectively. "Dealing with it effectively is not easy. When we suspended the students, the parents, especially the fathers, raised a big stink. Said their sons played a little rough but that's what would teach them to grow up as men. Or you got a father or a mother who bullied their son and the son passed it on to someone weaker."

"The way the school's been going since you got here has helped, but there'll always be the few whose need to exert their power over someone else is stronger than doing the right thing," Dave said. "Those are the ones we've got to do something about."

"You have names?" Scott asked.

"Names and descriptions."

"Who do you see as the main target?"

"A fifth grader named Billy Cross."

"Why have they picked on him?"

"He's smart, quiet, teachers and students like him. Has pocket change most days, which they take." Dave paused. "I almost think the main reason they pick on him is because no matter what they do he goes on as if they hadn't done it."

"I don't want to know who the bullies are. I'll watch Billy and see what happens so I'll have firsthand knowledge as evidence in addition to what you've seen," Scott decided. He hated bullying. It was like an insidious poison in a school if it got a hold on the student body, because it was based on the psychology of fear. Like any poison, it took strong medicine to treat it. He hoped he'd be able to find that medicine in time and apply it.

His next task was planning the special staff meeting scheduled for the coming Friday morning when the school was closed for the teachers' workday. Jenny and Ed joined him in the conference room with their materials laid out on the tables.

"This is the attendance graph you wanted." Ed handed Scott the easel-sized paper. "It does show that attendance is steadily improving."

Scott grinned like a schoolboy. "We'll start off with that, because it means we all must be doing something right."

"This one shows attitude, which is much more difficult to measure," Jenny said holding up her graph. "But according to the criteria we agreed on, this also is improving."

Scott held up the third graph. "This one for grades is what the district is interested in. I want to talk about it last, because if attendance and attitude are in the positive mode, the grades should reflect it. They do. Not as much as they will as the year goes on, but they are definitely up."

They hadn't been certain what the graphs would show, as each had worked independently, but the good news was irresistible. They laughed and exchanged high fives.

With confidence, they planned the remainder of the agenda, including several new projects involving not only staff but also parents and students.

When the meeting was over, Jenny gathered her materials and lingered after Ed had gone. She'd seen Scott only briefly the day before, with no time for conversation.

"How's Mr. Phillips?" she asked.

"Better. I haven't had a chance to tell you that Richard

came from New York on Saturday morning and stayed until Sunday night. Picked up all our spirits."

"I can believe that." Jenny's face lit up. "Is he still full of laughs?"

"He is. He was surprised to know you were here, and wanted to know all about you. You'll get a chance to see him Thanksgiving."

"I'll look forward to that. Is he married yet?"

"That's one reason he's coming. He's bringing a girl home to see what she thinks of Brentwood and his family."

"How romantic. Someone he's known a long time?"

"Eight months. Not nearly as long as I've known you, Jenny."

Force the issue, Rich had told him. He stroked her hand and smiled into her eyes.

She blushed and got hurriedly to her feet. "I'm glad your father is better, Scott. Please give him my regards," she said as she left the room.

Looks like Rich was right, Scott thought with pleasure.

On Thursday Superintendent Ryan Glover was escorted into Scott's office by his awed receptionist.

"Superintendent Glover to see you, Dr. Phillips," she announced.

"Sorry to burst in without an appointment, Dr. Phillips. I'm Ryan Glover, and, since I haven't had a chance to meet you yet, I thought I'd just drop by."

Glover topped him by an inch, had some gray in his hair, and deep blue eyes in his narrow white face. He seemed genial as they shook hands and Scott welcomed him to Springview.

The lines of command between a district superintendent and a lowly interim principal were many and Scott knew this man, no matter how genial he was, had not happened to "drop by."

"May I show you the school?" Scott asked.

"Be glad to see it. I heard about the students' artwork after the break-in. That was a good idea you had."

"You may have some budding artists here," he said at the end of the painting.

"We think so, and one of our best teachers is working with them."

He examined the library and the repaired door behind the stage. Scott invited him to visit a classroom or two, but Glover declined.

When they returned to the office, Glover asked, "Where is the door that had a message on it for you?"

"It's the one you came through."

Glover turned around to look at it. "Is it new?"

"No, it isn't. Maintenance cleaned it up and put it back on its hinges."

"The mayor told me there was a fight in city hall but I suspect that wasn't the whole story."

"Indeed it wasn't." Scott gave Glover the accurate details. "While I'm about it, allow me to also give you the actual details about a fight between two girls in the restroom." Glover listened impassively and Scott couldn't tell what thoughts were going on behind his steady glance.

"I understand you worked in Hartford before coming here. Did you like it?"

"Yes, but I like Springview better. I went to school here myself. Also I have ideas about this school that I want to put into practice as principal. I'm starting them this year as interim, and hoping they'll be successful enough that the school will be better for them."

"It's been an instructive visit, Dr. Phillips. I'm sure we'll see each other again," Glover said as he got to his feet.

"Thank you for coming, sir."

Scott sat in his chair looking out of the window and reviewing the past hour. He pondered its meaning and possible implications.

Early the next morning, he met Jenny in the Brentwood Room, where they made sure coffee, tea, juice, platters of fruit and pastries were set out for the meeting. Then he took her aside into a small room off the stage.

"Superintendent Ryan Glover paid me a visit yesterday, unannounced," he said.

"You mean the district superintendent?" Surprise was followed by alarm. She laid her hand on his arm. "What did he want?"

"The same thing the school board wanted when they called me in. I give him credit for coming himself. He said he wanted to see the student artwork. First he said he hadn't met me and so he just dropped by." He waited to see if her response to that would be the same as his.

Her expressive face twisted in disbelief. "Baloney! What was your take on his reason?"

"He'd heard the same pack of half-truths the board heard and was checking it, and me, out."

"Did you like him, Scott?"

He'd asked himself that question. "I liked that he came here, that he was sufficiently impressed by some of the artwork to ask what we were doing for those students. I liked that he said the mayor told him about the fight in the city hall but he suspected there was more to it. He asked about the office door and about the Hartford job."

"As a person did you like him?"

"Not a matter of liking or not liking, he was too impersonal. He didn't set out to charm me or I him and that's okay."

"Do you trust him?"

"That's the real question. At this point I think he has an open mind about the school and its interim principal."

"That's good enough. Let's hope he keeps it."

Chapter 21

Walking around the backyard, Jenny thought the superb
weather was the quintessential definition of autumn. The sky
was a bright blue, but not the lush blue brought on by
summer's heat. It had an edginess that blended in with the air
which tasted like the finest apple cider and sleeked her skin
with its invigorating touch.

It was a Saturday and she was free from the classroom.
What more could one ask! She felt the need to work in the
garden, a mindless task, satisfying in the result of weeds pulled
from around the beds of fall flowers her dad had set out earlier.
In addition to gathering and carting away the inevitable debris
of leaves and branches that piled up here and there.

Her mind turned to yesterday, when Scott had been at his
eloquent best at the staff meeting, as he described the meaning
of the graphs. When he set goals for the next nine weeks, she
felt the wave of support he inspired as the room echoed with

applause. She'd been so proud of him, and to her surprise, found herself wishing she could tell him so in front of everybody.

Actually she'd been sort of floaty about Scott ever since he had come to her office with the story of his dad; he'd told her later that they belonged together. Maybe it was because she'd instinctively opened herself to his pain so she could lessen it for him by sharing it. When he kissed her palm it coursed through her like electricity, and when he said, "People like us belong together," he was simply stating a fact known to her in the deepest reaches of her being.

Known, but heretofore unacknowledged.

That knowledge had surfaced again, when Scott, telling her of Richard's visit, had mentioned the girl coming with Richard for Thanksgiving. She'd innocently asked had his brother known the girl long and Scott had said eight months. "Not nearly as long as I've known you, Jenny." She knew she'd blushed and had left him quickly.

His implicit message had been clear to her in her new frame of mind. Richard, after only eight months, was bringing his girl home to meet his family, whereas Scott had known Jenny all of her life, so what were they waiting for?

Was it dad's illness that had caused the change in Scott? Mortality, the inevitable corollary of birth, was always present, but coming close to the possibility of it in a loved one, as Scott had, changes how one looks at one's own life.

There was a forcefulness now in his relationship to her that hadn't been present before. She was aware of it whenever they were together and it made her tingly and, well, floaty. She was over thirty and could only describe her feelings like a teenager. But that was okay. She was enjoying it for now.

In her work around the yard she'd come to the camellias. True to what her dad had explained to Nicky, several of the hard green balls had changed. From their inner core, they had slowly begun to loosen, and she could see the tips of the myriad red leaves pushing against the green walls. Now that the process had started, the bud would open more each day until the whole beautiful camellia blossom was unfurled. Nothing could prevent the blossoming except a violent storm. Jenny hoped that wouldn't happen.

In the afternoon she took Nicky to the park for an hour, then shopping, where she indulged Nicky by letting him get a jacket and cap set he didn't need, but wanted. For herself, she bought an outfit she passed three times before giving in to the urge to buy it. It was the fresh pink color that she couldn't resist. The scoop neck cashmere sweater had cap sleeves, and the circle skirt flared from her waist to a sequin-accented hem. A sterling silver necklace with rose quartz drops and matching drop earrings couldn't be left behind.

When she got home, she looked at it again before hanging it in her closet. She hadn't a clue as to when or where she'd wear it but it didn't matter. It spoke to how she was feeling now.

While they were eating dinner Patty called to say she and Sterling and the girls would be coming tomorrow to spend the day. Jenny knew that her mother's primary reaction would be joy and her second would be "We don't have enough food. We'll go to the store after dinner."

Jenny's main concern was Patty. Had she been able to dismiss her suspicions about Sterling's reasons for working late with his clients? Was their marriage now back on the right track?

She had just finished icing the double chocolate cake the next morning when Nicky ran in. "They're here, Mom," he said, and dashed out again.

By the time Jenny washed her hands and joined her parents outside, Nicky had Alicia and Katy in tow, ready to show them his bike and other treasures.

Patty hugged her tightly. "I'm so glad to see you," she said. "I've things to tell you later." Her smile, and the way that Sterling's eyes followed his wife's every move, reassured Jenny that Patty and Sterling had reached an understanding.

The pre-dinner hours flew by with impromptu visits to the garden, first by Dad and Sterling while Patty helped Jenny and Mom in the kitchen, then the adults sat on the porch and watched Nicky and the girls rip and run at their game.

Dinner began at one and stretched for nearly two hours as Sterling described some of the more unique construction requests he'd received. They were still talking about the man who wanted a burial spot on his property for the first car he'd ever owned, when the phone rang.

"Scott's bringing Elly and Ward over to see us," her mother announced when she returned to the table. "Ward had a little setback with his diabetes, and I'm delighted that he's feeling well enough to come over," she explained to Patty and Sterling. "Scott said he's so glad he's going to see you, Patty. Let's clear the table for now and have dessert when they get here."

All Jenny could think of as she went from table to kitchen was that Scott was coming here with his parents. He hadn't been here since she'd arrived, nor had she seen his parents, although she should have.

She ran up to her room as soon as the table was cleared. She was still in the jeans she'd put on this morning. Would her folks think anything if she changed to something less casual? She didn't care, she was going to do it anyway.

She put on a woolen skirt with tiny black and white checks, topped it with a look-at-me flaming red sweater, and a demure silver necklace and drop earrings. She desperately wanted to put on her three-inch black heels, but thought that'd be too much. After redoing her makeup and hair, she went downstairs in her black low-heeled sandals decorated with a silver ornament.

Fortunately Scott and his parents were arriving as she came into the hall, so her attire went unnoticed at the moment, although Patty gave her a wink.

There was a confusion of greetings as Scott's parents spoke with Jenny and Patty, whom they hadn't seen for years, and Sterling, and the three children. Scott had to renew his ties with Patty and meet her family.

Through it all, Jenny was intensely aware of Scott in his pleated black slacks and collarless white shirt. Their eyes had searched and found each other immediately in the hubbub at the door. For a long wonderful moment they communicated, then joined the family group.

In the living room, Scott managed to take the chair between Patty and Jenny. "Did you like living in San Jose, Patty?" Scott asked.

"It was fine after I made friends there. Everything about it was different from living here, wasn't it, Jen? We used to talk about it in our room at night. Remember?" She looked at Jenny.

"California seemed to be light years ahead of Brentwood," Jenny agreed. "The kids at school thought we were country and quaint, and I guess we were, but we decided to show them we weren't behind when it came to grades. We were on the honor roll every time." Her eyes sparkled at Scott as they continued talking about growing up in San Jose.

It suddenly occurred to Jenny that she was doing what Scott had tried to get her to do several times—talk about her life after Brentwood. She'd refused, but now it was so natural. Was it because Patty had begun the memories, or was it because her attitude had changed? She saw no reason to hold that part of her life back from Scott.

The sounds around her subsided as she followed that thought. Had she come to the place where she was ready to deal with Adam? To let go of her guilt and believe God would forgive her? If she was, when and how had it happened? What was the next step?

"Earth to Jenny," she heard Patty say. Patty and Scott were staring at her.

"Sorry," she said. "I guess I was daydreaming."

"I'm going to help Mom with the dessert. Why don't you and Scott go outside and gather up the kids."

"I've kept my eye on them through the window," Scott said as they went outside. "They're okay."

"Hey, Dr. Phillips." Nicky ran beside Katy as she rode his bike up to the porch. As Alicia joined them he said, "This is my mom's boss, and I've been to his school where the kids painted pictures on the wall."

"Time to come in and wash your hands for ice cream and cake," Jenny said.

Nicky attached himself to Scott. "I'm glad you came to our house. Aren't you glad he came, Mom?"

Alicia held Jenny's right hand, Katy her left. They were swinging them high and talking to Nicky, who hadn't waited for an answer to his question.

"Are you glad?" Scott murmured, his eyes holding hers.

"You know I am," she said.

At the table Jenny seated Nicky beside her and served him his cake and ice cream. She felt Scott's presence as he took the chair beside her, and almost wished he hadn't. He made her breathless. She ate small bits of cake and drank sips of coffee to make them go down. When he held her hand under the table she had to keep her eyes on her plate until he released it. She was afraid her trembling would show.

After they left the table, she got Nicky and the girls settled with his laptop and several other toys, then helped Patty clear the table. When they were alone in the kitchen, Patty said, "Take Scott outside and show him the garden before his dad decides it's time to leave. Go." She gave her a little push and a smile.

"Patty said I have to show you the garden before you leave," she told Scott when he came into the kitchen with some coffee cups.

"Bless you," Scott told Patty as he handed her the cups and followed Jenny through the back door.

They stopped by mutual consent near a shadowed corner where there were no windows.

"Don't you ever wear that outfit to work, Jenny." His eyes blazed with a fire that made her tremble.

"Why not?" she asked.

"Because I won't be able to keep my hands off of you," he growled and pulled her into his arms.

She wrapped her arms around him and thought her heart would burst with joy. Then, with one hand, he held her head gently so they could see each other.

"I want you to look at me when I kiss you for the first time, my Jenny. I want you to know it's me."

The words alone lit a spark in her, and when his warm supple lips touched her, with an infinite tenderness that spoke of a promise of passion and desire, she kissed him with a response that held nothing back.

He groaned and tightened his embrace. Each kiss was like a drink of water to her. "I didn't know how thirsty I've been," she said.

"I knew." Scott kissed her again. "My soul's been parched for years waiting for this."

"Scott." Patty called from the back door. "Your dad wants to go."

"I hate to let you go." He crushed her to him and kissed her fiercely.

"I'm missing you already." She kissed him back and kept her arm around him until they came to the back door.

"You go on in, Scott," Patty said. "Jenny, everyone'll know if you go in looking like that. Come with me for a minute."

In the bathroom Jenny washed her face in cold water, combed her hair, and washed her face again, but the inner glow was still there. "At least your mouth doesn't look as swollen," Patty teased and Jenny blushed.

They went back into the living room together to tell the Phillipses goodbye, and Jenny found herself able to look at Scott and mention she'd see him at work the next day.

"You coming to see us again?" Nicky asked, swinging on Scott's hand.

"Yes," Scott said.

"Good," Nicky said firmly, and went back to play with Katy and Alicia.

"Honey, we're going to have to think about leaving pretty soon," Sterling said to Patty after the door had closed.

"I need half an hour with Jen first. Okay?"

"Fine. Take as long as you like. I just don't want to get on the road too late."

"Where you going, Mom?" Katy asked.

"Up to Aunt Jenny's room."

"Can I come?"

"Not this time. We're going to talk while you play with Nicky."

"They're so different," she told Jenny as they went up the steps. "Alicia stopped wanting to tag after me by the time she was four."

"They do change," Jenny said. "Nicky has, just since we've been back in Brentwood. He's much more independent and he's more rough and tumble than he ever was. I guess that comes from having friends at school like Tod, and Dad saying I need to let him be more like Doug. I still worry about him, though. He's all I have."

"How can you say that, Jen?" Patty arranged herself on the bed and leaned against the cushion after nudging off her shoes.

Jenny said in the chair. "What?"

"That Nicky's all you have? If that's true, what is it I've been watching all afternoon between you and Scott? The electricity between you was so hot I couldn't stand it, and I figured you were ready to explode. That's why I sent you outside. Scott isn't playing with you, and I don't think you're playing either."

Jenny felt herself turn two shades redder. "Do you think anyone else noticed?"

"Sterling did, but I don't know about the parents. When did all of this happen? When I was here you didn't say anything about it."

"You know our past. We found out that the bond we had was still there, but I didn't want to do anything about it. Still, it came up between us every now and then. When he first heard his dad was ill, he came to my office, and it was as if I knew exactly how he felt, so I tried to help him feel better. It really worked, and he said that people who felt like we did belonged together."

"That was it?"

"I guess so, because ever since then I've been feeling like this about him."

"Have you talked about it?"

"No."

"Not even when I sent you outside?"

"We didn't exactly talk," she murmured, blushing again.

"Oh, Jenny, was that the first time in all these years that you kissed each other?" Patty said softly.

Jenny nodded her head.

Patty looked at her sister with great affection. After a silence she asked, "What happens now?"

"I don't know."

"Maybe you don't, but I can tell you for certain, Jenny Mayes Cannon. You not only have Nicky, you also have Scott, and you need to remember that. Don't get tied up in something and neglect him, or forget that he's in your corner, no matter what."

"Does he know he has such a staunch friend?" Jenny asked.

"I was always his friend. He knows that."

"What happened between you and Sterling after your lunch with me in the park?"

"I did what you suggested, trusted in the marriage we'd built and that he was telling me the truth. I apologized to him, said I'd been a little jealous because we no longer had our time together. He said maybe he'd been too intent on making money and didn't take time to realize how it was affecting our home life. He came back to our bed, and we began to talk to each other like we used to when we were first married. It's been getting better, and the girls have picked up on it, too. That's why I wanted us to come home for a day, so you could see how you helped us."

"He seemed very happy today. I saw how he watched you all of the time."

"Actually he told me the other day that he was surprised

and a little pleased that I was jealous, and he wants to take me away for a second honeymoon. The girls are going to stay with his folks over Thanksgiving while we're away. He won't tell me where we're going."

"That's terrific, Patty."

After everyone had left Jenny went up to her room. She relived her moment in the garden with Scott and a bubble of joy rose within her.

She'd just turned out the light and gone to bed when her phone rang.

"It's Scott. I'm sorry to call so late, but Harry came over and he just left. You in bed?"

"Yes, but not asleep. I was thinking of you."

"I'm not going to keep you, Jenny. I just needed to hear your voice, and I needed to say thank you, with all my heart. We made a big step today."

"Yes, we did. Finally."

"The other thing I need to say is there's no going back, Jenny dear. Do you understand?"

"Yes. No going back from here. I don't want to. Do you?"

"Never. Goodnight, dearest Jenny."

"Goodnight, dearest Scott."

Chapter 22

The change of Lynn Bartlett's room from one of several homerooms had been effected as a pilot project, one Jenny intended to use in her application for the doctoral grant.

Now students came once a week for several hours to learn about and practice arts, crafts, music and role play. These were not only an end in themselves, but developed as learning tools.

Already the Activity Room, as it was called, had become a favorite of the students. Lynn Bartlett knew how to capture their interest and keep it through the particular segment they were studying.

As she had foreseen, the students discovered that the creative imagination they used so casually could now be harnessed and developed in ways they hadn't dreamed of.

"I always wondered how those guys made comic strip figures look so real," a fourth-grade boy who loved to doodle said. His doodling had turned to drawing figures, which he was making into his own comic book. His close buddy was helping with the story line.

Role play was one of the more popular segments, and Jenny never ceased to be amazed when a student used puppets, dolls, or dress-up clothes to play the role of someone else. The insight and empathy they displayed seemed remarkable to her. More and more she understood why Lynn had been persistent in offering these ideas to the students.

Another significant segment had to do with listening skills, in which Lynn first played several tapes and had the class say back what they heard. When she played them the second time, they wrote what they heard. The third time she read what was on the tapes, students were amazed at what they missed, misinterpreted, or simply didn't hear. Then she trained them in listening skills. Later the students made up their own lessons and presented them.

The positive feedback from their teachers was one of the quickest outcomes of the Activity Room segments.

Jenny was talking with Lynn on Tuesday after class when she got a call.

"Mrs. Cannon, this is Brentwood Community Hospital and I have a call for you."

Jenny turned pale, put out a blind hand to Lynn who sat her in a chair.

"Mrs. Cannon, this is Mary Wise from Nicky's school. He fell from a tree and he's unconscious, but the doctor said he'll soon come around. Could you come?"

"I'll be right there." She told Lynn what had happened. "Tell Scott. I have to go to Nicky."

She never knew how she got from Lynn's room to the hospital, where the nurse immediately took her to the emergency room. Nicky, white-faced and still, looked small in the long bed. There was a long scratch on his left forehead and his arm was in an awkward position.

"Are you—?"

"I'm his mother," Jenny interrupted. "Where are you taking him?" The person was getting ready to move the bd.

"We have to x-ray his arm. You can wait for him here."

"No. I'm going with him, and you can't stop me," Jenny said.

"We need you to fill out his paperwork, Mrs. Cannon," the nurse said.

"I'll do it when I come back," Jenny said holding onto the bed.

The orderly looked at the nurse who raised her brows and nodded for him to proceed.

Jenny held Nicky's hand during the forty-five minutes it took before the orderly wheeled the bed back to the emergency room.

"Why isn't he opening his eyes?" Jenny demanded of the nurse who brought her the clipboard of papers to fill out.

"Doctor will be here in a few minutes to answer your questions, Mrs. Cannon," the nurse said.

Jenny filled out the papers automatically and handed them back. Her mind seemed to be filled with clouds of confusion. All she could think was another sign had been made that she was not forgiven. She had let herself begin to be happy with Scott, and see what had happened. She wouldn't do it again, she vowed. Just let Nicky be well.

She became aware that Dad and Mom had come in and were sitting beside her. She answered their questions dully, all of her attention on her son's still body.

A short, stout cheerful man wearing a white coat came in. "I'm Doctor McGinnis," he said. Looking at Jenny holding Nicky's hand, he said, "You're the mother?"

"I'm Jenny Cannon, yes. My parents, Mr. and Mrs. Mayes."

"Your boy's going to be all right. When they brought him in he was in pain from the fall and scared. I gave him a little sedative to make him comfortable. He has a gash, as you can see, that might require a stitch or two, and he'll have to get his arm set. We'll keep him here tonight, and if all goes well, you can take him home tomorrow."

"He's never been away from me for a night in his life," Jenny said.

The doctor looked surprised, glanced at her parents, then said, "You may stay with him in his room tonight if you wish."

He bent over Nicky, lifted his eyelid, looked at his chart, and satisfied himself by checking his pulse and listening to his heart. "He's a healthy boy," he said approvingly.

After the doctor moved on to another patient, the nurse said, "We'll put him in a room as soon as we have one ready. It'll take a while. Why don't you make yourself comfortable in the reception area? There's also a cafeteria, if you're hungry or thirsty."

"I'll stay here," Jenny said.

She went with him when they put a cast on his arm and wondered what he'd think when he woke up with this new addition. He'd probably find it a novelty at first, until it began to itch.

When they got back to the emergency room, the first person she saw was Scott sitting with Mom and Dad. He got up at once.

"I came as soon as I could." He stood next to her beside the bed. "How is he?"

"They're keeping him tonight to see how he does. I'll be able to take him home tomorrow."

"You must have been so frightened, Jenny. You look like you're in shock." He reached out to turn her face to his. She moved back so sharply his hand dropped, and he looked at her with surprise and hurt.

He needed to leave before she succumbed to finding in him the solace that only he could give her. That wasn't permitted, and he had to shield herself again with the armor of denial and distance. She had to begin now or she wouldn't be able to do it.

"You don't have to stay, Scott. Thanks for coming."

She didn't look at him, but she felt his shock at her dismissal. She waited but he didn't move.

"I don't know what's going on here, Jenny, but I'm not moving unless you can look me in the eyes and tell me to leave." He had lowered his voice so no one else could hear it, but she knew he meant exactly what he said.

She tried not to think at all as she looked at him. "You may leave now, Scott. Thanks for coming."

"There's nothing I can do for you?"

"Nothing."

"You don't want me to sit with you until Nicky wakes up?"

"No."

"You don't need me in any way, Jenny?"

Why was he prolonging this agony and making her lie over and over? She needed him in so many ways; how could she tell him no? She had to swallow before she could say a firm "no."

She would not let herself feel the pain she saw in his eyes before he made them blank, turned on his heel and walked away. She watched him stop to speak to her mom and dad. Dad got up and went out with him.

Mom came over to the bed. "I thought Scott was going to stay. That's what he said when he came."

"There was no need to. The three of us are here."

Dad came back just in time to be in on Nicky's moving to a room in the pediatric ward, where the colors were bright pastels and the walls bore playful animals.

Nicky's eyes opened when the orderly carefully moved him from the emergency room into his new bed. He was still groggy from the sedative in his system.

"Nicky," Jenny said, and his eyes focused on her.

"Mom? What happened?"

"I want you to tell me what happened, Nicky." Her voice was firm as she held his hand. Could he remember everything?

"Take your time and see how much you can tell Grandma, Grandad, and me."

Obediently, Nicky opened his eyes and thought. Jenny knew the instant he remembered. He opened his eyes. "I did a wrong thing, Mom. You want me to tell you anyway?"

"Tell us, and then we'll see about the wrong thing."

Nicky seemed a little relieved.

"There's a tree near the boys' restroom. It's not one of the biggest ones, but it's big enough to climb. They tell us never to climb it." He stopped and looked at Jenny to see how she was taking it.

"Go on," she said.

"Tod and I bet each other we could do it. I went up and got to the first limb. When I reached for the next one, I fell."

"Who was there?"

"Only Tod. I just laid there and cried because it hurt bad. He ran and got someone. Then they called an ambulance and I got to ride in it."

"Did you know you broke your arm?"

He looked at the small cast on his left arm. "I knew it hurt and looked funny. How long do I have to wear it?"

"Dr. McGinnis will tell you tomorrow."

Grandad said, "How're you feeling right now, sport?"

"I think I'm hungry. Are we all going to eat here?" He had no experience with hospitals and was fascinated when

Grandad produced dinners from downstairs for the three of them, while a nurse brought Nicky's in on a tray and arranged it over his bed on a little table that swung out.

Dinner was followed by a little television, until Jenny saw Nicky trying to keep his eyes open. He said goodnight to Grandma and Grandad.

"You going too, Mom?" He clutched at her.

"I told you I'm staying with you," Jenny said, holding his hand.

"All night?"

"I'll be the first face you see when you wake up in the morning," she said.

"I can drop you off a few items for the night," Dad aid.

"Don't bother, it's only a few hours, and I'll be all right."

Jenny made herself comfortable in a nest of blankets the nurse had brought for her to put in the lounge chair. She answered calls of concern from Dave and Devon, Lynn Bartlett, Gladys Fellows and Clare Minor. She watched two news shows, then an adventure movie, and finally around midnight, a rerun of *Goodbye, Mr. Chips*. The story of an eccentric schoolmaster who lived a rich life in the sheltered world of an English boys' school had been a favorite of hers since college days.

She shouldn't have seen it. It brought her too close to the one person she was trying not to think of, Scott.

It had been so lovely to be able to think of him, to recall how he looked at her with tenderness and admiration. To feel again, instead of having to be remote and emotionally isolated. The feelings that had come alive for Scott were so different than the ones she'd had for Doug, even though they'd been married.

She thought she knew why. She and Scott had chosen each

other from the beginning of their lives. Not with mature understanding, but nevertheless a choice had been made. What had attracted her to Doug was that he reminded her of Scott. Her brief life with him had been interesting and pleasant. Then it was over, leaving Nicky as its treasured legacy.

When circumstances had made it possible for her to meet Scott again, the richness of their early years was still there. All they had to do as adults was to acknowledge it and move forward into the sweet abundance of the reminder of their lives that was waiting for them.

Scott had understood this almost at once. She hadn't. She had been held back by the ghostly Adam and the living Nicky.

She had failed to protect Adam, and was stained by that guilt. The few times she had thought that perhaps the possibility of forgiveness was due her and she'd hoped for the rebirth of her faith, she'd been slapped back. When her marriage had gone so well and she'd found she was pregnant, it had seemed to her this was surely a sign of divine forgiveness. She'd been radiantly happy. Then a few months later Doug had been killed outright in a skiing accident. She'd learned a lesson and vowed to focus herself on her son and his protection.

Nicky had flourished, she worked hard at her career and asked for nothing more. Then out of the blue she'd been placed in Brentwood with Scott. She'd tried hard to resist any relationship with him except on a professional basis. Despite herself, her spirit opened up to him and she acknowledged they were the two halves of a whole.

They had shared the first kiss in their whole lives. It had been like drinking pure water for the first time. That had been on Sunday. This was Tuesday. She knew Nicky's fall was a warning, for the fall could have been so much worse. He could have been permanently damaged, even killed. She understood a warning when she received it.

You are not forgiven, was its meaning. That happiness is not for you!

Jenny slumped into her blankets and let her despairing soul cry out.

"Why isn't happiness for me? I know I did wrong, but God knows how remorseful I've been all these years. I'd bring Adam back if I could, but I can't.

"How can I give up Scott when I've just found him? Already I've hurt him so much. I can't keep doing that day after day. I'll have to leave Springview, but I don't want to."

Every thought increased her grief, and the tears kept coming until she was in a state of exhaustion.

She had tried to say prayers before but they hadn't helped. Still her last thought before drifting off to sleep was a plea.

"Help me, please, dear God."

Chapter 23

Elly Phillips didn't know when she'd been so excitedly happy. First had been the call on Tuesday from Richard.

"Mom, I'm bringing a friend with me for Thanksgiving. Okay?"

"Of course it's okay. Who is it?"

"A girl named Cynthia Tucker. We're driving down, arriving tomorrow night."

"You'll stay here, I hope. You know we've plenty of room."

"Thanks, Mom. Tell Dad we'll see him."

Richard had never brought a girl home. Never. She could hardly wait to tell Ward. He didn't get excited like she did, but she saw the gleam in his eyes and the softening around his mouth.

"Cynthia Tucker. Hasn't mentioned her before, has he?"

"Not to me. But it must mean he's serious about her, don't you think?"

"Calm down, Elly. I don't want you to get your hopes up and then be disappointed. I will say that he must be considering the possibility that this young lady might fit into his future."

"That's good enough for me. They're staying here, so I have a lot to do."

"I don't want you working yourself to death, Elly. You keep this house clean enough for the First Lady to visit."

"Thank you, Ward." She dropped a kiss on his cheek. Such compliments from her husband had been scarce lately, and her heart lightened. He had been showing such improvement and the visit with the Mayes had been like a shot in the arm. This was going to be a great Thanksgiving. She could tell.

The next call had been from Mikey. She hadn't seen her youngest son since a fast visit in July. He was making up for lost time at twenty-four, going to college in Durham, North Carolina, and working part-time at a rehabilitation center, the same one that had saved his sanity, he often said.

"Mom, I'm coming home for Thanksgiving. Who'll be here in addition to you and Dad?"

"Scott, of course. Your brother Richard's coming and he's bringing a young lady named Cynthia Tucker with him!"

"That should be interesting! Tell Scott I'll bunk with him."

The last call had been a little later, and was from her daughter, Alnetta.

"Mom, I know I spoke with you last week and said I didn't know about Thanksgiving, but we are coming just for the day, and I'll bring a pecan pie. Okay?"

"Better make it two pies, Net. Your three brothers will be here, plus Richard's bringing a friend named Cynthia Tucker." She waited for the explosion she knew was coming.

"What? Rich is actually bringing a girl after all this time? What did he say about her?"

"That's all he said. They're driving, be here tomorrow night."

"You want me to come tomorrow and help you?"

Elly hesitated. Alnetta was pregnant with her first child, and, although the help would be welcome, she didn't know about her being on her feet.

"Why don't you talk it over with Roy? You can call me back."

By the time Alnetta and Roy arrived next morning from Jamison, one hundred miles east of Brentwood, Elly had changed the linen in the three bedrooms, made the bathroom glisten, and written multiple lists concerning food, tables, and house chores.

Ward opened his arms to embrace his daughter. He wished she hadn't waited until thirty-five to get pregnant, but she seemed to be healthy. "You feeling all right?" he asked. At five feet, five inches she carried the weight well.

"I'm fine, Daddy. You're the one we worry about. But you're looking better each time I see you."

"Don't overdo yourself. You and Elly put Roy to work." He smiled.

"I already have my list," Roy retorted.

"Actually, so do I," Ward said. "I've got silver to polish."

Scott came over in late afternoon to join the working party. The big house was filled with the fragrance of pies and cookies and hot rolls. A huge pot of beef stew was simmering on the back burner, and several kinds of salads were resting in the refrigerator.

"I'm not sure what people will want to eat tonight," Elly said.

"How about cornflakes and milk," Scott teased.

"There's all kinds of cereal and gallons of milk," Elly replied.

The moment they were all waiting for came about eight p.m. when Richard opened the door, bringing with him a petite young woman with velvety-smooth dark skin, skillfully braided hair, gold hoops in her ears and no makeup on her chiseled features. Her long eyes sparkled with interest as she looked around the room.

Richard took her directly to his parents. "Mom and Dad, this is Cynthia Tucker," he said simply.

"I'm so happy you could come," Elly said and hugged her.

"Welcome," Ward said, looking at her warmly and shaking her hand.

"I'm very glad to be here," Cynthia said with a wide smile.

Richard beamed, and with his arm on Cynthia's shoulder said, "Everybody else, don't rush the girl. Take your time. We're tired and hungry, and I think I smell beef stew."

"Pay him no mind," Cynthia said. "I come from a large family myself, so let's not be shy with each other."

Scott was the first to reach her. "I'm Scott, and welcome to the family. I hope you'll like us." He kissed her on both cheeks then stepped away for Alnetta.

Dinner was a noisy affair, during which they learned that Cynthia edited publications for an educational agency whose office was in the same building as Richard's, that she was the eldest of three, and her home was Alton, Illinois.

Mikey didn't arrive until ten-thirty when everyone was beginning to yawn. It had been a long and busy day.

"Sorry to be so late." He kissed Elly and hugged his dad. "Had a last minute emergency at the clinic."

Over a heated-up bowl of stew, he visited briefly with everyone. Before leaving with Scott, he said, "There's nothing like coming home to family. God Bless."

Elly's heart was full as she said her nightly prayers. All her children were doing well, except for Scott. He had participated in all of the laughter and warmth that flowed through the house but she had seen the sadness in his eyes. "Take away his sorrow and give him ease," she prayed, and hoped she would find him in better spirits the next day.

"What time do we have to be at the house?" Mikey asked. He scratched his unshaven chin and sipped the hot coffee Scott had given him.

"Dinner's at three, I think, but they'll be expecting us long before that." Scott hadn't been able to stay in bed until Mikey woke up. He'd run a little, then showered and dressed. He was on his second cup of coffee.

"I went to bed and died I was so tired." He looked at Scott. "You still run every morning?"

"No, just weekends. Want some breakfast?" At five feet ten, Mikey was wiry, but even so, to Scott he looked like he needed some calories.

"Yeah, I'm starving."

"Good. Get your shower, I'll make breakfast and tell Mom that we'll be there when we get through."

Scott cleared the table of papers, books, and mail, found his checkered place mats, and transferred the small potted plant from the windowsill to the table. He added plates, silverware, juice glasses, and napkins. Satisfied with his hospitality efforts, he grilled sausage, toasted bagels, and was about to crack eggs when he remembered that Mikey liked his hardboiled.

"Hey, you clean up good," Scott said ten minutes later when Mikey appeared. He had a broad forehead, well-defined eyebrows over deepset brown eyes that were clear as daylight, a generous nose, and full lips. He wore his hair in a ponytail tied with a narrow leather band. With his jeans he wore a navy blue sweater and a thin silver chain.

Mikey said, "I'm impressed," looking at the table. "Do you entertain often?"

"You're the first guest to eat at this table, so mind your manners."

After the food was served and Scott sat down, Mikey said, "You like being home, Scott?"

"This school job is great because I'm getting a chance to try out my ideas, and of course it's good to be close to Mom and Dad. But we can talk about that later. What I want is to catch up with you on what you've been doing."

Mikey carefully cracked open one of his eggs. "Thanks for these, by the way. Didn't know you remembered. How do I look to you?"

"You look good. You look healthy and content. I think that's the other word I'm looking for," Scott said.

"That's your answer. The work I'm doing is making me that way. I'm twenty-four, the rehab clinic helped me find out who and what I am, I'm in school preparing myself for a career to help other people who were lost like me, and I'm putting in some hours at the clinic getting practical experience."

"When will you graduate?"

"Next year. I may stay on for a graduate degree. Depends on how it all goes." He finished one egg and started on the other.

He was being very deliberate, and Scott, buttering his bagel and putting jam on one half, knew there was more to come.

"Let me tell you how you look to me, Scott." He put his egg down and turned his whole attention to Scott.

Scott braced himself. In Mikey a combination of sensitivity and compassion drew people to him and gave him an insight that Scott realized was now being shaped and disciplined for the difficult career he'd chosen.

"You look physically healthy, and when you talk about your job you are in control and confident. But there's a shadow on your spirit and pain in your eyes that doesn't go away, Scott."

Scott took a big bite of bagel and pushed it past the lump in his throat. How did his little brother see all of that so quickly?

"It's Jenny, isn't it." Mikey made it more of a statement than a question. He began eating his eggs, giving Scott time to respond.

Mikey already knew about Jenny coming to Brentwood for the job and bringing Nicky with her. Scott began with their dad's illness, which made him seek out Jenny, to the family visit to the Mayes home, and ending with Nicky's fall and Jenny's deliberate rejection of him.

He found that telling Mikey about it made him relive the pain all over again. He clenched and unclenched his fist under the table. When he glanced across the table at Mikey all he saw was affection and nonjudgmental acceptance.

"I think Jenny is very frightened," Mikey said after a long moment.

"Frightened? I don't understand." That had never occurred to Scott. "What is she frightened of?"

"I'm not sure," Mikey said thoughtfully, "but given the fact that you care about each other, fear is the only emotion strong enough to make her have that reaction."

He ate his egg, while Scott pondered the notion of fear rather than something personal that had made Jenny push him away.

"What about Nicky? Is he home from the hospital yet?"

"He's okay. Mr. Mayes called to tell me he's home and doing fine."

They were interrupted by a loud knock. "Richard," they told each other as Scott went to open the door.

"See, I told you they were just lazing around," Richard said, ushering Cynthia in.

"Good morning to you, too, and welcome to my humble abode, Cynthia." Scott offered food and coffee, which they refused, having eaten at the house earlier. Scott, looking at a radiant Cynthia, wondered why it had taken Rich so long to decide she was the right one for him. There was a glow about her whenever she looked at him, which he returned. Scott knew the true reason Rich had brought Cynthia over. He wanted his brothers' approval of his choice. Scott had no problem giving his right away.

"I don't know how my crazy brother had the good fortune to meet you, dear Cynthia, but I'm very glad he did, and I hope he hangs on and you'll be kind." Not very elegant but positive.

He raised his glass to her and was pleased to see her blush.

"Meeting you, Cynthia, and bringing you here is probably the most intelligent thing our brother has done in his whole life. Here's to you." Mikey raised his glass to Cynthia, who gave him and Scott a luminous smile.

Rich, beaming with pride, put his arm about Cynthia. "Now that I've been insulted by my brothers, let's all go and show Cynthia around the neighborhood. Especially Springview, where we all went to school and where big bro is now the principal."

After the sightseeing they went home, and everyone got involved in a leisurely fashion with the dinner preparation.

Scott thought his mom had outdone herself with the variety of delicious foods that accompanied the huge golden brown turkey his dad carved with swift efficiency.

As plates were filled and conversation flowed, he wondered what was taking place at the Mayes house. Had Patty and Helena come home, and were they all at the table now? What was Jenny feeling?

Alnetta punched him in the rib. "Eat your dinner while it's hot." They stayed at the table for hours, eating, laughing, telling jokes, and filling Cynthia in on many family anecdotes, especially ones involving Rich. Scott was certain that she would be present next year as Rich's wife. He wouldn't be surprised if the engagement was announced soon. There was an aura about them that was special.

Cleaning up was another family activity, then they played games and listened to music. It was during this time that Scott missed Jenny the most. Had things been right between them, he could have persuaded her to spend this time after the dinner with him. She'd said she was anxious to see Rich and to meet Cynthia. He tried to put her out of his mind. Then Cynthia and Rich would exchange a glance or a touch and the need for Jenny would pierce him again.

At one such moment, Mikey appeared beside him. "Let's go outside to get some air," he said quietly. They sat on the porch and looked at the stars. There was no conversation, but in Mikey's empathetic calm, Scott gradually grew composed.

Alnetta and Roy left after dessert, and the evening began to wind down. Scott took Mikey back to the apartment, where they spent some time talking about their work.

"I'm trying to work with youngsters in ways that will keep them from becoming your clients," Scott said.

"I know, and maybe I can give you some pointers from the young ones I deal with."

When he went to bed later, Scott realized he hadn't thought about Jenny these last few hours.

Chapter 24

Friday morning was crisp and cool. Scott enjoyed his early run, and was surprised to find Mikey up and dressed when he returned to the apartment.

"I intended to join you this morning but I was too late," Mikey explained.

"I was earlier than usual. Didn't sleep too well, so got on up and out. Always makes me feel better."

"How about I make us some hotcakes?" Mikey asked.

"Great. Make yourself at home."

Their conversation this morning was mostly about the family. "Dad seems to be pretty good," Mikey said.

"There's no doubt that he's getting better all the time and Mom isn't as worried." Scott set the table and made fresh coffee while Mikey cooked.

"Feels to me like he's understood what he must do to

have any quality of life and, being an intelligent man, has decided not to fight the medication." Mikey ladled batter onto the griddle.

"Have you been to see Net and Roy?" Scott put butter and syrup on.

"Not yet. Maybe you and I can work on a trip there some weekend."

"Yeah, especially when the baby gets here. Those look pretty good." The cakes coming from the griddle were a uniform brown and fluffy.

At the table they traded ideas of what Rich would decide to do next, as both were convinced he was tired of New York. Mikey thought he might marry Cynthia and go someplace like Alaska, just because it would give him a new challenge. Scott thought he'd marry Cynthia, like yesterday, and start an investment business in an unlikely place, like Brentwood, and become a big success.

When breakfast was over, Mikey said, "I'm ready to answer the first thing you asked me yesterday morning, Scott. I have to go to the pond to do it, so get your jacket and let's go."

Scott had avoided the pond since returning to Brentwood, and he didn't want to go now, but he knew he had to for Mikey. He parked the car on the street where their old house was. It had been painted and looked cared for.

The path through the woods was still there, used, no doubt, by the kids now living in the neighborhood. He was uneasy as he approached the tree from which he and the other boys had swung across the pond as a sign of their status as "big boys."

Opposite the tree, Mikey stopped. The pond looked smaller to Scott now, but he saw that it could still be a danger to small children.

"I told you years ago how I felt because Adam died and I

was still alive. Do you remember that, Scott?" Mikey, hands in pockets, spoke softly, his eyes on the sluggish water.

"Very well. You were having trouble at school, and at home because of how you felt."

"A boy whose father was one of the firemen on duty when Adam drowned told other kids that I let my friend drown even though I was older."

"Yes. You told me, and I told you you were not responsible."

"You always tried to help me, Scott, but nothing anyone said made it better, and that's how I went from bad to worse. I thought drugs would help, but when their influence was gone, I felt worse, not better. Sometimes I had terrifying visions of Adam."

Scott couldn't speak, but he put his hand on his brother's arm.

"One day after a particularly bad session I had a moment of clear thinking. A voice told me that if I wanted to be free of the pain and guilt, I had to let it go. I dragged myself over to this rehab clinic to a guy who had told me that he would help me when I was ready. That was the beginning of my healing."

He turned to Scott. "I had to let it go. No one else could do it for me. Do you understand?"

"I hear you, Mikey."

"You have to decide to let it go. So does Jenny."

"I'm not sure I understand how to get to the point of letting go," Scott said.

"Listen, Scott, if I'd had the discipline you've had to resolve your guilt, I'd never have gone as far down the drain as I did."

"But I haven't resolved it, not like you. You had faith in yourself to overcome it. That's what I admire," Scott said.

"We're all different and we don't go about it the same way. Can't you see that your whole life has been devoted to working with young kids, protecting them from harm in the way you teach them responsibility, caring and helping each other instead of only thinking of self? You have paid over and over for the burden you took on here at this pond."

Mikey's vision enveloped Scott. He stood aside from himself and for a moment saw the Scott Mikey described. If only this were the true Scott!

"I haven't been here since that day, Scott. I could never make myself come. Being here with you was something I had to do. I had to face it as my final step. Thanks for coming with me."

He held out his hand. Scott took it, then embraced Mikey, trusting the gesture would convey all that was in his heart.

After lunch at the house Mikey left for Durham. Rich and Cynthia said they'd be back for dinner, which left Scott free until then.

He filled his car with gas and set off to find the road back to the hill where Dave had taken them for the picnic. He took his time, and when he saw the field with horses, he knew he was nearly there. He parked the Lexus where he'd parked it before.

The air was just cool enough to make him appreciate the jacket he wore. He stood under the tree and wished he had Jenny with him as before. No, that wasn't quite true. The reason he'd come to this hill was to be alone and with no waiting schoolwork to distract him. This was a rare opportunity to have the undisturbed time to get some perspective on the present and the future for Jenny and him.

He sat on a cushion of leaves and leaned back against the tree trunk. The meadow stretching out still had some patches of green. He could see thin columns of smoke rising from a few farmhouses beyond the hill.

Was there a connection between all that Mikey had said at the pond and his earlier suggestion that Jenny had backed away from him after Nicky fell because she was afraid?

What could she be afraid of? Did she see him as some kind of threat? He certainly wasn't a threat to her precious Nicky. All he wanted for the boy was to one day have him as his son. Yet instinct told him Nicky was at the core of Jenny's strange behavior.

Scott recalled how on Sunday he'd been thrilled to find Jenny reacting to the same emotional tension that had him stretched thin as a wire. All the guards she'd put up against him had disappeared. When she came so willingly into his arms he was transported beyond his dreams to a new reality.

They'd agreed there was no going back for them. "I don't want to," Jenny had said.

Yet that's what she'd done only two days later at the hospital after Nicky fell.

"I don't need you." She'd looked him in the eye and he felt the prick of the knife in his gut.

Could she possibly have seen Nicky's injury as some sort of sign? Not that it made sense to him, but he knew Jenny tended to be obsessive about her son, although he thought she'd relaxed some lately.

Or maybe in her mind she'd linked Nicky, now six, with Adam who was drowned at six.

If she was lost in that dark wilderness of fear, she'd cut him off just when she needed him most. If that's where Nicky's fall plus her guilt plus confusion had thrust her, the worst thing was for her to be alone, without his understanding support. Yet what was left?

He couldn't be with her. He couldn't talk to her. But in the connection between them he sensed that she was in distress.

There was only one source that could take away Jenny's anxiety and give her peace and a clear understanding.

He wasn't much good at formal prayer, so he just bowed

his head reverently and opened his heart and mind and let God
see the depth of his concern for Jenny.

Scott sat there a long time. It seemed to him that the air
became hushed and fragrant and it had a peculiar light.

Refreshed spiritually, and physically calm, he got in his car
and drove home.

Chapter 25

It had begun Wednesday afternoon when Jenny was dressing Nicky after Dr. McGinnis had said he could go home.

"Mom, I thought Dr. Phillips liked us," Nicky said.

"Of course he does. Why'd you say that?" She looked up at him from where she was pulling a sock on his left foot.

"He didn't come see me when I fell."

"Yes, he did, honey." Jenny was horrified that she'd neglected to tell her son that his friend had come right away. Scott's presence had meant only one thing to her, that she had to send him away. She hadn't thought at all that he and Nicky liked each other and that Nicky might expect him to come. How selfish she had been. She'd make it up to Nicky some way.

"When did he come?" Nicky asked.

"When you were asleep."

"Can we see him today?"

"I don't think so, honey. They're busy at his house with

family coming in for tomorrow. Remember what tomorrow is?" Maybe she could get him onto another subject.

"Thanksgiving. Who's coming to our house?"

Before she answered that question the wheelchair arrived that was to take him from his room to the car. His interest captured by that new adventure, Nicky forgot about Thanksgiving and not seeing his friend.

Jenny was relieved to see that once he got home Nicky was his usual lively self, especially when Tod came over. Jenny and Tod's mother were less than enthusiastic about the tree climbing, but Nicky had gained hero status in Tod's eyes. He begged to be the first one to write his name on the cast.

Jenny's first thought had been to ban Nicky from seeing Tod, but had soon realized that wouldn't work since they attended school together. She'd have to wait for the right moment to get him to understand the seriousness of what his unthinking action could have produced.

Nicky's energy began to flag by dinner time. When he was putting on his pajamas, he said, "Can I talk to Dr. Phillips, Mom?"

Jenny thought Nicky had put Scott out of his mind. If she called his number and he answered, what could she say?

"You want me to call him for you, Nicky?"

"I want to talk to him myself."

"That's fine."

They went up to Jenny's room and she dialed Scott's number. She let it ring four times. "There's no answer, honey."

Nicky looked so disappointed, she said, "We'll try again tomorrow."

Patty and Sterling called later that evening with best wishes for a good Thanksgiving from their bed-and-breakfast hideaway in Connecticut.

Jenny picked up the phone the next morning when Helena called. "I'm glad you answered, Jen, because I want you to know Woody and I are working things out. We're in the Bahamas for Thanksgiving week. Tell everyone hello."

"No one's coming to our house for Thanksgiving?" Nicky asked.

"My two cousins are coming. They'll be here pretty soon and I was hoping you could help me get some flowers to put in the house," Grandad told Nicky, whose face brightened. "Sure, I can help you with that."

Cousins Lucinda and Leona Mayes arrived from Charlotte with several boxes of homemade cookies.

"We heard Nicky was here and we thought he'd like these," Cousin Leona said.

"There's chocolate chip, oatmeal and plain sugar cookies," Cousin Lucinda explained. "You don't want to eat too many at one time."

The sisters were first cousins to Dad, and Jenny remembered that all through her childhood they had brought cookies when they came. Now they were retired from the classrooms they had taught in for thirty-five years and were enjoying traveling. Their conversation was never dull.

"We did something last month that I bet you'd like," Cousin Lucinda told Nicky, her little eyes sparkling in her round face with its plump cheeks.

Nicky, fascinated by their stories, asked, "What was it?"

"We went up in a hot air balloon!"

Nicky's eyes stretched wide. "Were you scared?"

"A tiny bit at first but it was something we'd always wanted to do. It was very exciting, Nicky. When you get bigger, you and your mother should try it," Cousin Leona declared. She closed her generous mouth decisively and nodded her head in positive emphasis.

After the turkey and dressing and all the other foods Mom had prepared with her help were eaten, Jenny cleared the table and brought in the dessert. The cousins liked rhubarb pie above all else, and that's what Mom had made. The pastry was flaky and tender, the fruit just tart enough.

"You've outdone yourself, Elly," they said.

"I'm glad you like it. There's one for you to take home."

The cousins never spent the night. Immediately after dinner, they began to gather up their wraps and the pie.

"Enjoyed our visit, as always. Jenny, you and Nicky here to stay now?"

"I'm not sure yet," Jenny said.

"We'd love to have you home again. Don't make up your mind in a hurry." Cousin Lucinda gave her a searching glance with this advice, and shook Nicky's hand, which gave her another boost in his estimation, and signed his cast.

"Nicky, you be more careful. Don't you fall again," Cousin Leona said, no smile this time as she signed his cast. "You can't worry your mother like that." Another shake of the hand and they were gone.

"It was good to see them again, Dad. They're a breath of fresh air."

"They are. Sometimes I find myself envying them," he said wistfully.

"That probably goes both ways," Jenny said, putting her arm around her dad.

That night at Nicky's bedtime, she didn't wait for him to ask her to call Scott, but took him up to her room and dialed the number. Again it rang without an answer.

"I promise we're going to keep trying until we get him,

honey," she told her son, who surprised her with the obvious disappointment he showed each day at not making the connection with his friend.

Devon called Friday. "Can you and Nicky come over? I haven't seen you in a while and Lily misses Nicky."

Jenny didn't know what to say. Had Dave and Devon heard about what had happened at the hospital? If she was going to have to leave Brentwood, was it wise to deepen the relationship with the Youngs?

"Jenny? Is today not a good time for you?" Devon asked as Jenny hesitated.

"Today is okay. I was just wondering what would be a good time to come."

"Any time after one."

Devon was welcoming and showed no sign of anything except to see how Nicky was coming along. Jenny relaxed and let herself enjoy being with Devon and Lily, as Nicky told them about his fall and his hospital stay and offered his cast for them to sign. Lily took him off to play some games in the far end of the family room.

"Have you had to go through this with Lily?" Jenny asked.

"She's had some scrapes, but not a fall, and no casts. Did he hurt his leg?"

"There are some bruises on his left leg, but his jeans protected his skin. Thank goodness it didn't happen in warm weather when he would have been wearing shorts."

"I came up with three brothers and, believe me, you get used to sprains and broken limbs, especially when they get big enough to play sports."

"You're warning me to take this in my stride. You're probably right. We see it at school all of the time." Devon's attitude, concerned yet casual, reflected that of her parents. She had to concede that they were right, especially since Nicky had only the fading bruises on his leg, the scratch on his forehead, and the cast, which he already was learning to ignore, as physical signs of this fall.

The conversation turned to Thanksgiving, family, and anything else that came to mind between the two women, who were becoming friends.

This was what stayed with Jenny when the visit was over. Devon was a woman with whom she could become close friends, one of the few she'd met in the past few years. She hungered for such a relationship, especially since Patty didn't live in Brentwood. She didn't want to give that up, but she'd have to if she put Scott out of her life.

That specter which she had suppressed to get through the holiday now came rushing back full force. The same anguish and confusion she'd gone through that night at the hospital overtook her.

Seeking relief she went into the backyard, and, on her knees, began pulling weeds wherever she could find them. She didn't want to leave Scott or the school, or her parents, or Brentwood, or the friends she was finding here. Was it possible that Nicky's fall had simply been an accident and not linked to her guilt?

She wanted to believe it wasn't linked, but would she just be fooling herself? How could she know? She came to the camellias and saw that many of the hard green balls had begun to open and spread what had been tightly furled blossoms. Why couldn't she be like them? Her emotions had begun to open since being here, especially after Scott had said that they belonged together.

How could she go back to being a hard cold knot again when all she wanted was to continue blossoming?

Into her consciousness came the image of a full and perfect

red camellia blossom surrounded by fresh green leaves. It existed in a realm of peace and certainty, and was edged with light Jenny couldn't discern yet knew was there.

She didn't know how long the image stayed with her. What she did know was that it took her inner turmoil away and left her with the knowledge that Nicky's fall had nothing to do with her. It was purely accidental.

When she went in the house for supper, she felt as if a mountain had gone from her back. She played with Nicky in a lighthearted way that had him giddy with delight.

"Why don't we try calling Dr. Phillips a little earlier this evening? Maybe we'll catch him at home." She dialed the number and it was answered on the first ring. She handed the phone to Nicky.

"Dr. Phillips, this is Nicky." Jenny could only guess at Scott's end of the conversation, but she knew Nicky was brief and direct on the phone.

"We've called you every night because I want to see you. Mom said you came to the hospital but I was asleep.

"I have a cast on my left arm.

"Okay." He handed the phone to Jenny.

"Hi, Scott."

"Jenny! You don't know how good it is to hear from you and Nicky."

"He's been very persistent about calling every night, but I knew you were involved with family. Did Richard and Cynthia get here?"

"Yes. Lots to tell you about them, and Mikey, too. When can we get together?"

"Can Nicky and I come to your house tomorrow morning?"

"That would be wonderful. Is ten o'clock too early?"

"Not at all. We'll be there."

"Great. Let me say goodnight to Nicky, please." She handed the phone to Nicky, who'd been listening to his mother.

"Okay. Goodnight." He hung up the phone.

"I've never been to his house, Mom. Have you?"

"No, I haven't. It'll be something new for both of us. You can take him some of your cookies from cousins Lucinda and Leona."

Jenny spent a long time looking out her dormer window that night. She was too excited to go to sleep and went over the various apologies she had to give Scott first thing. When she finally went to bed she was anxious for daylight to come.

She followed Scott's directions and rolled into the visitor's spot at his apartment complex precisely at ten o'clock on Saturday morning. He was outside waiting for them and opened the passenger door where Nicky sat.

He unfastened the seatbelt and lifted Nicky straight into his arms. Nicky put his right arm around Scott and nestled his face against Scott's neck. Scott tightened his embrace as Nicky began to sniffle.

"I wanted to see you," he said.

"I'm sorry I wasn't there, because I wanted to see you, too," Scott said.

"I fell and hurt myself," Nicky said between sniffles.

"I know but you're better now, aren't you?" He stroked Nicky's back.

"They put a cast on my arm. See?"

"I see. Can I put my name on it?"

"Yes."

Scott sat him on the trunk of the car, wiped his face with a handkerchief, dropped a kiss on the boy's head and set him on his feet.

"Let's go get your mom." Scott held Nicky's hand as they went to the driver's side and opened the door. Jenny was dabbing at her eyes, trying to stop the tears from flowing.

"What's the matter, Mom?" Nicky asked.

"I think your mom needs a hug, don't you?" Scott said. He gently pulled her out of the seat and put one arm around her and the other around Nicky, who put his good arm around Jenny.

Scott showed them around the complex and all the rooms in his own apartment. He sat on the couch and put out his arm for Nicky, who leaned against him. After awhile Nicky climbed into Scott's lap and fell asleep.

By unspoken agreement they said nothing about Nicky or their own affairs. Scott told Jenny about Richard and Cynthia, Alnetta and Roy, while she told him about cousins Lucinda and Leona.

Nicky began to stir and rub his eyes. He sat up. "I'm hungry," he said.

"Then it's time to go have lunch somewhere," Scott said. "What would you like to have that you know your mom will say yes to?"

"Pizza, Mom?" Nicky looked hopefully at Jenny.

"Fine."

"After lunch we might try the park for awhile. Okay?" It was the only way to keep Nicky with them and still give them an opportunity to talk, Scott thought.

"No swings yet, but you can handle the carousel, Nicky, can't you?" Jenny asked, certain he would say yes and thus give them time to talk.

"Yes, and some other stuff that doesn't need two hands," Nicky agreed.

When they got to the park Jenny was glad to see there

were enough other children on the playground to keep Nicky interested. She and Scott sat where he could see them from the carousel.

Now she could make her apology. "Scott, I am sorrier than I can say for the unkind way I treated you at the hospital. I knew it was wrong while I said what I said, but I was so confused and afraid I wasn't thinking straight. Can you forgive me, please?"

"Of course, Jenny. I realized you were under some kind of pressure, but I won't deny that I was hurt because it was so unexpected."

"I've been miserable ever since. The other thing is that I gave no thought to how Nicky might feel, until he said that he thought you liked us but you didn't come to the hospital. I hadn't even told him you'd been there, so then every day he said he wanted to see you. You probably felt the same way. Can you forgive me for that selfishness, too?"

"I already have."

There was another aspect to this that she wanted Scott to understand.

"There's one more thing about Nicky, Scott. He has never reacted to any man like he did with you today. I knew he liked you from the first time he saw you here in the park, and that he's always called you his friend. But when you picked him up out of the car and held him, I saw that you mean a lot more to him than just a friend and that he truly did need you to comfort him in a way that I couldn't. He can't put it in words, but I see how he has clung to you all day." She blinked rapidly to keep the tears away.

"Do you want me to tell you what it is, Jenny?" He glanced over at Nicky on the carousel. "I love him as if he were my own little boy, and I think he feels that from me.

What's happening between us today is reassurance that all is well. We both needed it." How would she react to that bit of truth? he wondered.

She seemed surprised, and as the implications of it hit her, she blushed. "I didn't know you felt that way," she murmured.

"I told you Mikey stayed with me, so we had a lot of time to talk. He saw the sadness I was trying to hide and knew it had to do with you. I told him what had happened. He thought about it, then said that only fear could have made you say what you said. I've been pondering this for days. What were you afraid of, Jenny? Obviously it had to do with Nicky, but how?"

Only the peace that had come to her yesterday with the image of the camellia made it possible for her to explain to Scott the basis of that fear.

"So Mikey was right," Scott said. "The fear is gone now?"

Now that the separation between them was over, she wanted to tell him of the lovely image that had come to her. She laid her hand on his as she described what had happened. In his rapt attention and steady gaze, an idea came to her. "What were you doing yesterday afternoon?"

"Sitting under a tree praying for you, my darling Jenny. Praying that God would take away your distress and give you peace of mind. When you called me last night I knew the prayer had been answered." Even though they were in a public place, he couldn't resist kissing the palm of her hand.

"Do you do that often, Scott?"

"What? You mean pray?"

She nodded her head. She hadn't known he had the faith to call upon.

"No, but I was able to because of some insight I got through Mikey. He said it was for the three of us: himself, you, and me."

"Something to do with Adam," she said and Scott noted

that this was the first time that he could remember Jenny saying her brother's name.

"Yes. We'll talk about it another time when it's just the two of us. Okay?"

"Okay." She touched his hand again. "Thank you for the prayer."

On the way back to the car Nicky held Scott's hand tightly, and when they got back to his apartment, Scott put the boy in his mother's car. He fastened the seatbelt, then squatted down to be on eye level with Nicky.

"Nicky, thanks for coming to see me. That's number one. Number two is I want you to call me another name."

Nicky was surprised. "Why?"

"Because Dr. Phillips is like my business, a name for people who don't know me very well. I want you to call me Dr. Scott because that's my first name and only people who are close to me can call me that."

Nicky broke out in a big smile. "Okay, Dr. Scott."

"Number three is very important, Nicky. You're almost seven and old enough that you have to think of your mom and grandparents and me before you do silly things like climbing trees you know you're not supposed to climb. You make us all worry and be afraid for you. Your mom especially doesn't need that kind of worry. You understand?"

Nicky's face was sober. "Yes," he said.

"Shake on it?" Scott extended his hand and shook Nicky's hand, then, unable to resist, enveloped him in a bear hug before closing the door.

On the driver's side he kissed Jenny's cheek. "Thanks for coming. I'll call you tomorrow."

He stood in the driveway, watching until he couldn't see the car anymore.

Chapter 26

Scott returned to school rested and refreshed. A priority on his list of projects was Billy Cross, the boy Dave said was being bullied by two sixth graders. Scott needed to see this for himself, so he kept a sharp eye on Billy, whom he knew. Monday in the cafeteria he saw two boys knock Billy's tray out of his hand onto the floor and walk away laughing. The biggest boy looked as if he should be in high school. Scott could understand how his size alone was intimidating. The other boy was wiry and fast with a sullen expression. No wonder the other students stayed out of their way and didn't run to assist Billy.

School records identified the big boy as George Hall, nearly fourteen and still in Springview because of being held back twice. His friend was Matt Bryant, twelve. Both files carried complaints from teachers about the boys creating disturbances in the classroom, in the hall, and on the playground.

On Wednesday Scott was returning from the Activity Room,

turning over the amazing things he'd seen and heard as a result of Lynn's talent in letting students find their niche and developing it. The bell rang and students began to fill the hall. Scott looked for Billy, and saw him coming out of a science classroom. Behind him was George Hall, who pushed Billy so hard he fell flat on his face. His heavy bookbag bounced on his back as George and Matt walked over him, sneering.

"Help Billy up," Scott ordered to the surprise of George and Matt, who hadn't seen the principal among the students. Sheepishly, the boys obeyed.

"Billy, are you all right?" Scott asked.

"Yes, sir," Billy said, head down in embarrassment.

"I want you to stop by the nurse's office just in case."

Billy took this bookbag and went in the direction of the nurse's office while Scott shepherded George and Matt to his office, sat them down and closed the door.

He opened a drawer, pulled out two forms, and filled them out without saying a word to George and Matt, who fidgeted in their chairs.

When he was through, he laid down his pen and looked at them. "I have just written out your suspension forms. You will be escorted off this campus in a few minutes and you are not to set foot on it again until Monday when class begins. You both have been observed bullying students, especially Billy Cross. You know that is against the rules here at Springview. This time you are being suspended for the rest of the week. If you continue doing it, your penalty will be much more severe. Do you understand me?"

He looked coldly and sternly at each of the boys, knowing they would take any lesser attitude as a sign of weakness.

They mumbled a yes.

He called Dave. "Mr. Young, would you please come to my

office and escort George Hall and Matt Bryant off campus immediately? Thank you."

He could count on Dave to handle this better than anyone else, and was thankful when he appeared at the door and took the boys away. Scott sincerely hoped this episode would put a stop to bullying at Springview, since George and Matt were its prime practitioners. Once the word got around it should have a good effect.

On the heels of making what he hoped would be a dent in the bullying problem, Scott took a call from a Mrs. Evans who identified herself as the secretary of an organization called Better Brentwood Schools.

"We hear there are interesting things going on in Springview this year, Dr. Phillips, and we would like to pay you a visit if that's all right with you."

"I'd be happy for you to visit us, Mrs. Evans. When would you like to come?"

After some consultation the visit was scheduled for the following Tuesday from ten until eleven-thirty in the morning with light refreshments at the end.

When Dave came in to report seeing George and Matt off, Scott told him about the call. "Do you know this organization?"

"It's fairly new, about three years old, I believe. What's interesting is that it is not political, it's interracial, and they try to be quite objective because they really want better schools here."

"Who's in it?"

"Retired educators, housewives, people with legal and business backgrounds, male and female."

"What do they do, give you a report card?"

"You could call it that. They publish a summary evaluation of each school they visit and it's generally well-received because they have no ax to grind."

"I'd better alert Sam so at least everything will be clean. No litter on the grounds. I will be curious to read their evaluation."

He passed the information on to Ed Boyd, then went to Jenny's office. She invited him in, motioned him to sit, and finished her call to Lynn.

"I came to tell you we're being visited by a VIP organization next Tuesday at ten in the morning. You and Ed and I'll have to plan."

"That sounds exciting and challenging. Who is it?"

He gave her the information he'd received from Dave and waited to hear her reaction. The abundance of her ideas always pleased him.

"This could work to our advantage, as long as they find more positives than negatives," Jenny said. "I can think of one way to ensure that happens."

"And that is?"

"I don't know how many people are coming, but after a little tour, we could invite each person to sit in a classroom to observe a regular lesson. Our students and teachers are the best advertisement Springview has."

"We could do that easily. The other thing that happened today is we suspended the two boys who were bullying Billy Cross."

Jenny listened soberly to the account. "Do you think that's the end of it?"

"I don't know, but I hope so."

"George is pretty frightening. I'd bet anything he gets beaten on at home."

"He may be, but that doesn't mean we can ignore it."

"I understand that. The cycle has to be broken and perhaps this will help. I'll go check on Billy, see that he's okay."

It was getting dark earlier and earlier, Scott mused, as the first week in December came to an end. He'd arrived home the last day of August and here it was the first week in December already. In terms of work it seemed he'd been here twice as long as that.

When it came to his relationship with Jenny, the time varied according to how they were getting along. Right now it was flowing swiftly and smoothly. He was looking forward to spending time with her this weekend if all worked well.

He made spaghetti and meatballs for dinner and ate it while watching the local and national news on television. He was getting up to put the dishes in the dishwasher when the phone rang.

"Dr. Phillips, this is Sergeant Hampton. You have a student at your school named Billy Cross?"

"Yes. What about him?" Scott had a sinking feeling in his stomach.

"He got beaten up and is in the hospital. We asked him who did this but he asked for you. Can you come right away? He's in emergency."

"I'll be right there."

He called Jenny. She needed to be there also, because Billy trusted her and she'd be helpful with the family. A brief call assured him she'd be waiting for him, and in another twenty minutes they were at the hospital.

Sergeant Hampton introduced them to Billy's parents, a bewildered woman who was crying on the shoulder of a tight-jawed man. "Who would do this to our Billy?" the woman moaned.

"We're going to find out, Mrs. Cross. We think his school principal might help."

The boy on the bed was scarcely recognizable. Both eyes were swollen, his mouth was cut and swollen, and there was something wrong with his right jaw. Before Scott could see any other injuries, the nurse said, "Talk to him now, because we've got to give him something for his pain, and then he won't be able to talk."

Scott bent down to Billy's ear. "Billy, this is Dr. Phillips. Who did this to you?"

Billy's lips barely moved but he was able to make the names loud enough to be heard. "They warned me not to talk but it was George and Matt. Don't let them get Aaron."

The nurse emptied her needle into Billy's arm. "He'll soon be asleep and won't feel the pain," she assured Mrs. Cross.

"What other injuries does he have?" Scott asked.

"Dr. Shelby will be with you as soon as he can to talk with you about Billy. You can all wait in his office. Let me show you where it is."

She led them down the hall to an office that seemed like it wouldn't hold the five adults plus two children, but the sergeant helped her bring in more chairs and they all squeezed in.

The five-year-old girl was Billy's sister, and the eight-year-old boy was his cousin, Aaron. Since Billy warned them not to let George and Matt get Aaron, it was clear that Aaron had been an eyewitness to the attack.

Scott said, "Aaron, can you tell us what happened?"

Aaron looked at Mrs. Cross, who nodded her head.

"Billy and me went to the store for Aunty. It was dark, but we go there all the time. The parking lot was crowded, and when we came out Billy was a little ahead of me. People came in front of me and I couldn't find him, so I started looking between the cars. I still couldn't find him, and I began to get scared. I heard some noise, and it was coming from behind the dumpster. I peeped around it and saw George and Matt beating Billy. Then they kicked him real hard a coupla times. I knew they'd do the same to me if they saw me so I hid until

ey were gone. Then I ran into the store and told the security
an to call the police."

"You know for sure it was George and Matt, even though
was dark?"

Aaron shrugged. "Everyone in the neighborhood knows
corge and Matt and try to stay away from them. They're
d news."

"But why did they pick on Billy? He never bothers
yone," Mrs. Cross said, wiping her eyes.

"Did he ever complain at home about them bothering him
school?" Jenny asked, directing her question at both parents.

"Once he asked if I could take him to school so he
uldn't have to ride the school bus, but I have to be at
ork very early so I couldn't. I asked if there was trouble
the bus, but he said no. He keeps a lot to himself," Mr.
oss said.

"These two boys have been bullying him for quite a
ile. It was reported to me but I did nothing about it until
could see it for myself which I did several times. On
ednesday they pushed him so hard he fell flat on his face
the hall. I saw that, so I suspended George and Matt that
y and told them they weren't allowed back at school
til Monday."

"If you hadn't suspended them, my boy wouldn't be laying
ere all beaten and bruised," Mrs. Cross said accusingly.

"Perhaps not, Mrs. Cross. But if I'd allowed it to go on, it
ll might have come to this, because they were getting worse
the time. They've scared other students and we can't have
at at the school. You can't have bullies running the school.
u have to put a stop to it. We are very sorry about Billy,
cause he was in no way at fault. He's the kind of student
want to have at Springview, and I know the police will do

all they can to see to it that George and Matt pay for what the did to Billy." He looked at the sergeant, who had been listen ing quietly while writing in his notebook.

"Knowing the names of the people who did this is the mo important thing, and having the testimony of Dr. Phillips an Aaron and the security guard at the store who called us give us an airtight case," Sergeant Hampton said.

The door opened and a middle-aged man with glasses an a chart in his hand strode in. "I'm Dr. Shelby," he announce "Who are Billy's parents?" He shook their hands. "I'm sorr about your boy," he said. After other introductions were made he perched on the corner of his desk and looked at the char

"I can't give you the entire picture of what might be wron with Billy. We all can see that he suffered blows to the hea and face. He was also kicked, and has bruises all over. W can't tell you yet what internal injuries he might have unt we do extensive tests. What he has on his side for recovery youth and general good health. Sergeant, you'll have a fu report as soon as I can get it done."

"His eyes look so bad, Doctor. Are they going to be a right?" Mr. Cross asked.

"We can't tell until some of the swelling goes down."

"Are his ribs cracked?" Scott asked.

"Yes," the doctor said. "You'll hear from me," he said, an left the room as quickly as he'd entered it.

"Is there anything we can do for you, Mr. and Mrs. Cross? Jenny asked.

"I guess not," Mrs. Cross said wearily. "I just hope he' get well."

"I'm sure he will. When he gets well enough to begin worry about his lessons, I want you to know that we'll see it that he has a tutor to help him."

"That'll be good, because he likes to get good grades," Mrs. ross said.

"Does Aaron live with you?"

"Yes, and you don't need to worry. We'll take good care f him." Jenny saw Mr. Cross get tight-jawed again.

On the way home, Jenny wondered if the police would be able find George and Matt. "They might be hiding somewhere."

"Maybe not. They probably think their warning to Billy ould keep him from telling since he's never told before. I ope it all goes swiftly, because I intend to have an all-school eeting Monday morning about the entire affair."

"Good. Everyone needs to know exactly what happened. will be a warning to other bullies, and it will keep the mors down. Maybe we could have the students write notes Billy, in keeping with the school as a family idea."

"That kind of support would certainly make Billy and his mily feel better. We just have to pray he won't suffer any ermanent damage from this."

That triggered another thought in Scott's mind. "Can we pend some time together tomorrow, Jenny. Just us?"

"Let me see what Dad and Mom are doing and I'll give you call. Would the afternoon be okay?"

"Afternoon would be fine. Thanks for being with me night. Your presence made it easier for me."

At her doorstep, he cupped her face, kissed her cheeks, then issed her lips with a deep-felt tenderness. "My darling nny," he murmured, then kissed her again before turning, oing down the steps, and driving away.

Chapter 27

Jenny awakened to bright sunshine and blue skies. When she opened her window and stuck her head out, the brisk wind had a definite chill to it. That was as it should be for December, and a far cry from what she would have experienced had she still been in Chicago. She'd be sure to dress warmly for the afternoon.

She was anxious for what the day would bring. Mom and Dad were taking Nicky to the country with them this afternoon, but before that, Scott was coming early to visit with Nicky. The bond between the two of them still wasn't something she took for granted. It rested in the back of her mind along with facets of her relationship with Scott such as his praying for her at the time she was trying to find answers.

She couldn't put it all together—there were too many different pieces—but maybe after this afternoon with Scott, some of them would fall into place. She hoped so. She wanted to eel a change from where she'd stood all these years, and she wanted a step forward from where she stood with dear Scott.

The morning went by quickly, and when she opened the door to Scott, he had some unexpected news. "Sergeant Hampton called this morning to tell us they picked up Matt and George without any problem, except that George's father was so belligerent they almost had to arrest him."

"Hi, Dr. Scott." Nicky came running from another room.

Scott bent over, gave Nicky a brief hug, then looked at his cast. "You don't have space for any more names. Been busy at school this week, haven't you?"

"All the kids wanted to sign it. Can you come outside with me? I want to show you a new trick on my bike." The new trick had a high likelihood of another injury which, of course, Nicky hadn't thought about. Scott reminded him gently of the bargain they'd made.

"I forgot," Nicky said.

"That's okay, you'll remember next time. Let's work with this trick to make it safer."

When Jenny and her parents came out later, Nicky proudly displayed his new skill. "I won't hurt myself," he said.

"It's almost time for you to go with Grandma and Grandad," Jenny said. "Come get cleaned up."

"The two of you get along really well," Jenny's dad observed as they watched the women shepherd Nicky into the house.

Scott was glad to have the opportunity to respond to the implied question. "I told Jenny last week that I love Nicky as if he were my own little boy, and I think he feels it and responds to it. I hope that meets with your approval, sir."

"I've known you all of your life and you've known Jenny all of hers. That ought to count for something. He's a fine boy, Scott. Take good care of him." He extended his hand, and

Jenny, happening to glance out the window, wondered what the handshake was about. She'd have to remember to ask Dad.

"Where are we going?" she asked as she stepped into the Lexus.

"I'll give you three guesses," he smiled.

"What do I get if I guess correctly on the first try? You know I'm a good guesser." Her eyes sparkled, and Scott grinned in response.

"You're good, but you have to make your first guess in the next ten minutes."

"That's no fair," she pouted.

"All's fair in love and war," he sang.

"We're going to the picnic place," she announced triumphantly a few minutes later.

"How'd you guess?"

"I just knew. My womanly intuition," she teased. "So what do I get?"

"First choice from the goodie bag in the back seat."

When they arrived, Scott brought out two heavy blankets to sit on and two to wrap around them if they needed them as shelter from the wind.

"Do you feel too cold to sit?" Scott asked. "We can take a walk or we can just sit in the car."

"Let's walk a little. It's so peaceful and quiet," she said.

"Darling Jenny, I brought you here so we could have this peace and quiet in which to talk about Adam. Adam is always between us, and always will be if we don't come to some understanding. It only takes one person to reach out and try to bring an estrangement to an end, and I'm willing to be that person because I've never gotten over the way you cut me out of your life that day Adam drowned." He took her gloved hand n his as if he needed the physical contact to get him through his recital.

"You wouldn't let me see you, even though I sent a note. You wouldn't speak to me at the funeral, when you were the only person I wanted to talk to because I thought you, of all people, would understand how I felt. You wouldn't let me see you after the funeral, and then you went to San Jose. The accident turned my life upside down, and your refusal to see me or talk to me confirmed what I feared—that you hated me for not saving Adam. Was I right?"

"I hated us both," Jenny said through her tears, "but I hated myself most of all. I held us both responsible, but mostly me, because Mom had told me to check on him. But I waited because I didn't want to leave you with Tiffany. I was jealous and so I let my little brother drown."

Her tears became sobs, and the sobs became so strong that Scott pulled her down to his lap and wrapped his arms around her. He cradled her, and rocked her, as she cried as if her heart were breaking. He said nothing, just wiped his own tears and let her cry until she couldn't cry any more.

"Let's go back to the tree, where we can sit and be warm and drink the hot tea I brought," Scott said.

As soon as the heated beverage had soothed her throat, Jenny said, "That's the guilt I have carried all my life. I know I'm unworthy of forgiveness and that's why I lost my faith." She looked at Scott with haunted eyes. "You may as well know the worst. I was attracted to Doug because he reminded me of you, and I thought I could steal some happiness, therefore I deliberately didn't tell him about Adam. So when he was killed in some unnecessary accident shortly after Nicky was born, that's when I knew I hadn't been forgiven and happiness was not for me. I put all my attention on Nicky and working with young children to try to make up for Adam."

"It's the same with me," Scott said. "I couldn't save Adam so I chose a career of saving other children, especially the ones at risk, and I've put all of my energy into it, hoping to leave the past behind me. And hoping to find my self-worth again. The guilt makes me keep pushing, especially when I see kids hurt or abused, like Billy. I haven't married, although I am lonely, because I could never find another Jenny." They sipped from the thermos and Scott opened a package of the cookies Nicky had given him.

"Did you try church?" Jenny asked, biting off a corner of cookie.

"Occasionally, but without success. You?"

"The same. I took Nicky once after we got here and the minister talked about God casting out people who had transgressed. It scared me and I didn't go back."

"We need to talk about Mikey, Jenny. In your years away when you were trying to deal with your guilt, did you ever think of Mikey and what he was going through?" Scott said.

"I took a lot of psychology courses and learned about survivor's guilt, but I have to confess I couldn't handle Mikey's in addition to yours and mine."

"It started with him right away, because a few kids at school knew what happened and accused him of letting his friend drown. His school years were terrible, and he began to act out by cutting classes, then dropping out, running away, and getting into drugs. None of us could help him, although we all tried."

"How awful, Scott. I didn't know."

"He told me that sometimes he had terrifying visions of Adam."

"I had them, too, of you and Adam. Even since I've been here, but I couldn't tell you."

"I wish you had. Sharing takes away half the pain. Will you tell me if you have another?" He hoped she'd say yes, because it'd mean a willingness to trust him to a further degree than she had before.

"I promise," she said. "Go on about Mikey."

"He went from bad to worse, until one day a voice told him that if he wanted to be free of the pain and guilt he had to let it go. He took himself to a guy at a rehab clinic who'd said he'd help Mikey when he was ready to be helped. Mikey told me that's when his healing began."

"I'm so glad for him," Jenny said.

"He had this message for you and for me, Jenny. We have to let it go. No one else can do it for us. Each of us has to decide to let it go."

Jenny's weary sigh seemed to come from the bottom of her feet. "Exactly how does one come to that decision?"

"We're all different, and we have to come to it however we can."

"Have you been able to let it go, Scott?" She'd been trying to rid herself of this burden for years, but without success.

"What Mikey pointed out to me was that I'd paid over and over through my work for anything that happened at the pond that day. Jenny, you know we haven't considered that Adam might well have been drowned even before we were supposed to check on him and Mikey. You and I assumed the responsibility for his drowning, and it might not have been ours to assume in the first place. Have you ever thought about it that way?" She looked so pale and listless. His hope had been that their no-holds-barred conversation about Adam would give her the release that had happened with her crying. The next step was to have her understand Mikey's experience and embrace it with the expectation that it could work for her. That wasn't happening.

"Mom said something like that, and that maybe we were only supposed to have him for that span of time. I couldn't accept that knowing how she and Dad had wanted a son and how special Adam turned out to be."

"But it might be true, Jenny. It would be a way for you to let it go."

"That's true," she said.

"Jenny, look at me." His suddenly firm voice made her turn to him in surprise.

He took her hands in his. "Don't you want a future for you and me and Nicky?" His eyes burned into hers.

Jenny was shaken. Where had that sudden passion come from, when they'd been talking about Adam?

Scott squeezed her hands. "Do you, Jenny?"

"You and me and Nicky together? Of course," she said.

"Thank God! You had me scared there for a moment." Scott leaned forward to embrace her. "Kiss me, Jenny."

She put her arms around his neck and kissed him.

"You're the only woman in the world for me, Jenny, and I'm not willing to wait any more years until we can be together. We have to work hard at this Adam business until we both have let it go completely. Otherwise it will always be a ghost between us. I think we should start going to church together and let's see what we can find there to heal us. Okay?"

"I'd like that," she said, feeling an infusion of energy from his declaration and the kiss. "Nicky will be ecstatic. He loves to go to his class every Sunday."

On the way home, Jenny recalled that she'd set out hoping to discover ways to advance in her relationship with Scott. She thought the hardest part had been done when she'd told Scott how she felt about Adam. The resultant sobs had been like expelling poison from an old festering wound.

Now if she could find the way to let it go emotionally and mentally, her faith could be restored and she could look forward to a new and healthy future.

Scott spent the evening with his parents. They had some food, talked about Thanksgiving, and Elly said Richard had called once since then, plus Cynthia had sent a lovely thank you letter. "I don't think it'll be too long before they get engaged," she said.

"I thought they'd announce it before they left," Scott said.

"I had the impression they might be thinking of locating here," Dad said. "They spent a lot of time sightseeing.

"Come into the library, Scott," his dad went on, "I want to show you what I've done."

On the walls, Scott saw the treasures of his dad's map collection, some of the ancient world, and some of the modern world. They were handsomely mounted and arranged in chronological sequence.

"It's been years since I've seen some of these, Dad. They're an impressive addition to the room." He looked at each one then sat opposite his dad.

"It was easy to do after you and Rich did the books—that was the difficult part. Have a seat."

"You're looking a hundred percent better than you did then. I was watching you move around earlier, and you are like your old self."

"I do feel good, thanks to your mom and the doctor. I don't mess around with what I'm supposed to eat and drink. I take exercise and get enough sleep. What I brought you in here for is to find out how things are going with you, Scott. You're not up to your usual standard."

Scott couldn't remember when his dad had approached him this way. He was sitting in his lounge chair, clad in gray slacks and a heavy gray sweater, his hands relaxed as he focused his warm gaze on Scott.

Before Scott could get himself together to answer, his dad asked, "Is it the job or is it Jenny?"

"Both," Scott answered. He found himself talking about some of the issues at school and how much he wanted the permanent position. He touched on the problems he and Jenny had just tried to deal with. As he heard his words spilling out, he couldn't believe he was talking so intimately with his dad and feeling increasingly comfortable in doing so. There was none of the holding back he'd always felt from Dad before, but a meeting of the minds that made it easy for him to open his heart.

When he was through, his dad said, "I've been thinking about you these past few weeks, Scott. I'm afraid I might have given you the impression that I was not in favor of what you chose to do. If that is so, I'm sorry. You made the right choice for you, and from what I've been hearing and reading about Springview, Joe Alston made the best move in getting you. I'm proud of your integrity and your intellectual skills. You're using them in the right career, and I think you'll get the job."

"That means a lot to me, Dad." It was hard for Scott to get the words out, but he felt his dad understood.

"When you first came back, and then Jenny came, I told your mother that all that old business about Adam had to be talked about, because it's caused so much pain for our two families. I'm glad to know you've had the courage to open it up. Stick with it, son. We're behind you all the way."

He stood up. "That's what I wanted to tell you, Scott, and now I'm going to bed."

Scott couldn't resist putting his arm around his dad's shoulder in a hug as he told him goodnight.

In church the next morning, with Nicky sitting between him and Jenny, he said an earnest prayer of gratitude for the reconciliation between him and his dad. It was a confirmation that he and Jenny were on the right track.

Jenny kept her mind and heart open to receive whatever positive message that might come during the service. When the choir sang the refrain, "He'll forgive our transgressions, and remember them no more," she bowed her head in acquiescence. If only she could now hold on to that!

Chapter 28

The halls of Springview were noisy and buzzing as students and staff left their usual class schedule to assemble in the gym, where the maintenance crew had been busy setting up chairs. The principal had called this special meeting, but no one seemed to know what it was about.

When all had gathered, Scott came in and stood on the improvised stage, where a microphone had been placed.

"Good morning," he said, and waited while the last whisper stilled. "You have heard me say that I see this school as a family. We work together, we help each other. When something good happens, we are all happy. When something bad happens, we all feel it.

"Last week something bad happened. I'm going to tell you exactly what happened so everyone knows the same story, just like I let you all know when we had the break-in."

As he related the story, beginning with the reason for

George's and Matt's suspension and ending with their arrest, it seemed to him the room held its collective breath. He paused and people breathed again, coughed, shuffled in their seats. Then he resumed.

"Now all of you know the entire story. I also want all of you to think about it. You know bullying is against the rules here in Springview. George and Matt wanted to bully their way through school. You see what happened. There are a few more of you in this room who are trying the same thing off and on. I want to warn you here and now—no bullying is permitted at Springview. You will be caught and penalized. Sometimes there's a fine line between the teasing that goes on and bullying. If anyone doesn't understand the difference, ask a teacher or ask me.

"We don't know how long Billy Cross will be out of school, but I'm sure he'd feel really good to hear from his classmates. I'll be going to see him and I'll be happy to deliver whatever you write.

"This meeting is adjourned." He stepped down and left the room. He had deliberately chosen to end it that way, no questions to be answered. He hoped it would enhance the seriousness of the event for which the meeting had been called.

As he walked to the office with Jenny, she commended him on the way he'd handled the meeting.

"I was thinking of going to see Billy this evening," she said.

"I had the same idea. The doctor should have more to tell us now."

It was a different Billy they saw sitting up in bed and talking to his family. The swelling had largely disappeared from his eyes and the cut on his mouth had healed. His dislocated jaw had been set and was obviously still giving him trouble, because he was trying to talk out of the left side of his mouth.

His eyes lit up when he saw Scott and Jenny. He smiled as they asked him how he felt. "Better," he said.

"He's coming along," his mother said, "but he's not out of trouble yet." Her eyes filled with tears and Mr. Cross explained. "Doc says they still can't tell what damage has been done to the right eye, and he has internal bruising that has to heal, so he won't be coming home any time soon."

"Mr. Cross, I hope you won't mind me asking you if there's insurance to cover this," Jenny said.

"There's some, but I don't think enough, especially if they have to operate on his eye and that's worrying me," Mr. Cross said.

"The church mentioned setting up a fund," his wife said.

"That'd be great, because everyone could contribute," Jenny remarked. Mrs. Cross remembered how such a fund had raised several thousand dollars a few years ago because it had widespread publicity.

"Have any of the TV channels been here?" Jenny asked.

"The police said they didn't want any publicity yet. They'll let us know when it's okay," Mr. Cross answered.

"When the story does get out the fund will grow. I don't think you'll have to worry about it," Scott said.

On the way back he asked Jenny, "Why wouldn't Hampton let the TV in?"

"I don't know the legal aspects dealing with the youth of the three boys, but maybe that's why. Or perhaps there's more to this than we know and they don't want to go public with it yet," Scott mused.

"That sounds mystifying. More like what?"

"I'm not sure, but that's what's in my mind."

Before she got out of the car, Jenny asked Scott, "How're you getting along with Mikey's idea?"

"I'm almost there, Jenny. I had a wonderful evening with Dad aturday. We talked about the job, and you and me. He said hen we both got back here, he knew the business about Adam d to be dealt with because it had come between the two milies, and he was happy you and I were now opening it up."

"You don't feel any separation now between you and him?"

"It's all gone. He even apologized if he'd made me feel he dn't appreciate the work I've been doing."

"Scott, I'm so happy for you!" She kissed him on both cheeks.

"That conversation came out of the blue and I took it as con- mation that letting go is the right thing to do. How about you?"

"No more bad dreams, and I look forward to each day now. an see a goal I've never seen before, and that's a step forward."

He hugged her tight and kissed her hard. "I wish you could ake yourself go faster, darling Jenny. The more I see you, lonelier I get for you."

"I know. But like Mikey said, I have to be able to let it all . I'm trying, Scott. Truly I am."

Later, as she looked out of her window, she knew that part the problem was that in the daytime she and Scott were em- oyees at the same business and had to act that way. As soon school was out they saw each other or talked on the phone sweethearts. Which was her identity?

It might be easy for Scott, but it was difficult for her. Some- es she almost wished she hadn't been sent on this job, yet loved the school and she loved being home with her ents and having them with Nicky.

Still, she was in a better place than she'd ever been before 1 for that she was thankful. Nothing stood between them v. She and Scott could say the name Adam with freedom, 1 that was a tremendous step forward.

The next day was gray and cool, but inside Springview all

was warm and welcoming, when the ten members of t
Better Brentwood Schools were ushered in. Mrs. Evans w
a tall, well-built woman who seemed to be in her forties, we
coiffed, well-dressed, and gracious as she introduced peop
to each other.

Jenny thought Scott was at his best as he welcomed t
group and led the tour, pointing out the now famous wall t
students had painted, the library, described the Harve
Festival, the rise in grades, the concept of the school as
family and some of its implications. The people were pleas
to be offered the opportunity to visit classrooms, then r
assembled in the Brentwood Room, where they were serv
fruit, cheese, cookies and beverages.

Questions were asked about the break-in, the fight in t
girls restroom, absenteeism, teacher ratio per students and d
he think the level of difficulty of the classwork was sufficie
to prepare the students for the higher level?

Scott found the questions well thought-out and given r
spectfully. Many notes were taken, and the group spoke e
thusiastically of being able to see the classrooms for ther
selves.

"I'd like to invite you back next week for a special proje
Mrs. Cannon has been working on as educational consulta
Would you explain it, please, Mrs. Cannon?"

"It's a program designed to stimulate students to talk mo
and to think creatively. We think that a better command of t
spoken language will enable them to do better on tests. T
program is called 'It's My Turn' because the students get
talk to the adults instead of the other way around. They p
on plays, tell stories, act out poems, sing, design their ow
costumes and set up the stage for their skits. Most of t
students never had a chance to speak to an audience the

eren't familiar with. They increase their vocabularies and gin to recognize grammatical mistakes. I'm sure you'll be rprised and entertained by what you'll see."

"May we bring other people?" a gentleman asked.

"Please do," Jenny replied.

"We've certainly enjoyed this visit, Dr. Phillips, Mr. Boyd d Mrs. Cannon," Mrs. Evans said. "I think a number of us ill be here next week also."

"I think that went very well," Ed Boyd said later. "You made at program sound so good, Jenny, I think we ought to invite e school board, the superintendent, and the mayor, Scott."

"Is it really that good, Jenny?" Scott asked.

"It will be by next week, I can guarantee it," she announced.

"It would certainly put a feather in our cap, so let's do it!"

Chapter 29

The approaching Christmas season was already in the a[ir]
Scott noted as he left his apartment for work the next mornin[g]
He'd been so consumed with his own affairs he hadn't thoug[ht]
about it, but it was the second week in December and all th[e]
businesses he passed wore red and green decorations. He'[d]
have to start thinking of gifts, always a problem with hi[m]
Then he grinned. This year he'd have Jenny to consult abo[ut]
things for his family. He'd ask her to go with him this weeken[d]
before it got crazy at the malls.

He'd been at work only an hour when his secretary an[-]
nounced that a TV channel had come to interview him abo[ut]
Billy Cross. His first thought was that the police had give[n]
the go-ahead for their own reasons. He kept his descriptio[n]
brief and succinct. That afternoon another channel inte[r-]
viewed him, then the newspaper came and did a lengthy i[n]

terview, not just about Billy, but about bullying and its prevalence as a problem for school administrators.

"The lid is off, and I want us to follow up the stories to be sure they are accurate. Also they may have new information from the police that we don't know about yet," he told Ed and Jenny.

Both TV channels did good stories on Billy Cross, beginning with pictures of him in the hospital, a comment from Dr. Shelby, his parents, and ending with Scott. No mention was made of Aaron. The biggest story was in the paper. The reporter had been very thorough, stating research on the problem of bullying, its presence in some local schools and tying it in with Billy Cross as a prime example, and of the principal of Springview as an illustration of how it should be handled. He quoted the police as stating that for now the alleged perpetrators were being charged with aggravated assault.

It seemed that everyone in school had seen one or the other of the TV channels, and students who hadn't yet written to Billy now wanted to do so. Scott had sent a memo around that he'd deliver letters on Saturday and by the end of school on Friday, teachers brought him boxes and bags and baskets of mail for Billy. The carriers were decorated with cartoons, bows, and even balloons.

"Aren't these kids great? They are so creative," he told Ed and Jenny.

"They are. Just wait until you see their performance on Wednesday." Jenny's smile was dazzling, and even though it was caused by her belief in her students, Scott's heart responded to it. What a superb woman she was, and how he yearned for the day when her belief in him would be that strong.

Billy's room was crowded with visitors when Scott and Jenny got there Saturday afternoon. Among them was one of the TV channels. Scott suspected that a hospital staff person had told them this student's mail was being delivered.

"What about his lessons?" Mrs. Cross asked Jenny quietly.

"I've arranged for his tutor to come every day next week. She'll bring the ones he's missed and help him keep up with any assignment he'll have before school is closed for the Christmas holidays."

"How do you feel he's doing, Mrs. Cross?" She asked the question as mother to mother, knowing Mrs. Cross would understand.

"He's worried about the operation the doctor says he'll need on his eye, of course. My Billy is very strong inside, but I think this has shaken him up. Him and his dad and I do a lot of praying together, and that helps. They have a counselor who talks to him every day for a little while and he seems to like that."

"He is, as you say, very strong inside. At school he would never complain about what George and Matt did. When he got home did he talk about it?"

"He's always kept a lot in himself, although he's very friendly. Maybe the counseling will get him to open up some."

As they left, Mr. Cross stepped outside with them. "My wife and I want you both to know we appreciate all you've done for our Billy," he said offering a handshake to each of them.

"At Springview we like to protect our students and we're very sorry this ever had to happen," Scott said.

"Well, we pray it's all going to turn out all right in the long run," Mr. Cross said and returned to the room.

Jenny told Scott what Mr. Cross had said, and they agreed that counseling was necessary.

"I'd never seen Billy excited before. Did you see his face when I gave him his mail?" Scott asked.

"You're right. He looked as if he'd found the end of the

rainbow. I don't suppose it every occurred to him that he's very likable."

"By the time he gets through reading all that mail, he should have some idea."

The rest of their time together they spoke no more of anything connected with Springview and concentrated on strolling through the mall buying gifts for Scott's family. They had dinner at an Italian restaurant and relaxed. Then they bought gifts for Jenny's family.

Jenny knew she'd never forget these hours with Scott as long as she lived. Magic dust had been sprinkled everywhere, a magic made up of the Christmas decorations, the carols that filled the air, the beautiful lights streaming from lampposts, the gaiety of the people as they laughed and chatted, their delight when they found just the right gift. There was a fragrance drifting in and out of the stores. A sidewalk vendor was selling small cups of chocolate. Scott bought two, and they sat on a bench, sipping the delicious concoction. It was smooth and deep in flavor.

Scott turned to her, his eyes as deep and rich with feeling as the beverage. "Happy?" he murmured.

"So happy I could fly," she whispered back, her eyes locked with his. When they walked, their steps matched perfectly. They were so in tune they paused instinctively at the same place to look for or to purchase a gift. They held hands, and when their hands were too full of packages, they still managed to touch each other.

There was an electric excitement running through Jenny at just being with Scott. She knew he felt it, too, by the secret glances they passed back and forth, the way they would be at a counter and would move closer together even when there was space around them. The bond between

them was tightening, drawing them closer and closer, whil
their unspoken communication told of their longing t
become one.

Scott pulled the Lexus into her driveway and shut off th
motor. They needed no words, as they embraced and kisse
again and again. The tension was too tight for casual con
versation.

Scott carried her load of gifts for her as she opened he
front door.

"I'll call you," he said, and was gone.

In church the next day, Jenny pondered the minister'
sermon that mistakes or transgressions, small and large, an
universal, because humans are not perfect. To hold on t
them, as she had held on to her guilt, is to stunt one's spir
itual growth. She could certainly testify to that. To ge
beyond them, one has to ask for forgiveness. She understoo
that part now.

But how to feel worthy enough to ask for forgiveness? Sh
still had to figure that out.

At school she worked with Lynn Bartlett and several othe
teachers on the initial production of It's My Turn. It had bee
decided that Amanda would act as the Mistress of Cere
monies, welcoming the guests and explaining the progran
Two other students had tried out, but Amanda's personalit
and ease outshone them. Rhonda was practicing how to b
stage manager and had learned what all the performers wer
supposed to do. She had several students as assistants.

By Wednesday, the auditorium was frantically busy wit
sets being put up, costumes being tried on in the two tin
dressing rooms, electrical switches being tested for lights an
keyboards, and stage props being identified and put in the ap

opriate places. Everyone was nervous, including Jenny who cted calm in order to keep the students calm.

At six-thirty p.m. the audience began to file in. The two ont rows had been ribboned off for special guests, and they, o, began to come in. Scott welcomed each one personally, d had special students at the door to usher the superinten- nt, the mayor, the school board and the Better Brentwood ommittee to their seats.

The program was to begin at seven. Jenny was frantic. manda hadn't arrived. Everyone else was backstage. She sked people if they'd seen her. No one had. What was she to o? She hadn't arranged for a backup. Scott would never rgive her! With all these important people in the front to be itness to this failure, after being invited to see success!

Her cell phone rang. "Mrs. Cannon, this is Amanda."

"I can't hear you. Speak louder."

"Can you come get me? I'm at the J&S Store. You know here that is?"

"No, tell me."

"It's by the railroad tracks at Ninth St."

"I'll be right there."

She hurriedly told Lynn where she was going. "This will ke about fifteen minutes. Can you arrange for the musical roup to play while I'm gone? Don't announce any change the program. Just lower the lights and put them on."

Jenny found herself praying that her car would run, there'd e no traffic problem, that Amanda would be all right when e got to the store. When she found the store, Amanda and nother girl were waiting and ran to the car. When Amanda egan talking, Jenny said, "Wait, Amanda. Tell me all that ter. We've got to get back to the school."

She parked the car and the three hurried to the stage door. It was seven-fifteen. Jenny checked Amanda to see that she looke as she should, then gave Lynn the signal to take the band off

Amanda stepped out with a spotlight on her. The studen began to applaud. With natural poise, Amanda waited a momer then began her welcome and the explanation of It's My Turn.

Jenny and Lynn stood to the side, offstage, where the could watch each act. The theme of the evening was Schoo Daze. Jenny knew it was hackneyed, but the students didn' and they put all their ideas into what school meant to ther They were comic, touching, poignant, occasionally brillian and the audience loved it.

Jenny thought Amanda was particularly dramatic becau of nearly missing this big opportunity. She made improvise comments between acts, and when it was over, she intre duced each performer and then had all the students who ha helped behind stage come out and take a bow.

The student audience stood up, shouted, and whistled the appreciation. Jenny was tickled to see the special guests joi the standing ovation. She took Lynn by the hand and insiste that she come to meet them.

Congratulations were passed around freely.

"Who would've thought those kids had so much talent! the superintendent remarked.

"We might not have discovered it had it not been for M Bartlett here," Jenny said.

Mrs. Evans immediately began asking Lynn questions.

"I've never seen anything like this at Springview," Jc Alston commented.

"It certainly is a change," said another school board membe

"I'm sorry Larry Gordon wasn't here to see the program Scott remarked to Joe Alston. Larry was the only member c the board absent.

"I am too. I expected him, so something must've come up.
But the rest of us will give him a full report." He winked at Scott.

When the auditorium was empty and Scott had thanked the
excited and proud students, he asked Jenny to come to his
office before she went home.

"When the show didn't start on time I went backstage but
couldn't find you, Jenny. Then Lynn Bartlett said you had
gone to get Amanda. What happened?"

Jenny had hoped he wouldn't find out about this, and she
hadn't known he'd been backstage looking for her. She took
a deep breath.

"Amanda wasn't here a few minutes before seven, and I
was very worried. Then she called me on my cell phone to
ask could I come get her at J&S Store, so I went, picked up
her and another girl, and got back here at seven-fifteen. I'd
told Lynn to put the band on until I got back. They filled in,
so I think—as far as the audience knew, we started on time."

"What was Amanda's story?"

"It wasn't a story, Scott," she protested. "She and her
cousin were on their way when the cousin's boyfriend, with
whom she'd broken up, came after them. They ran and got
inside the store. That's where she called me from and asked
could I pick them up."

"You didn't think to tell me?"

"Not with you sitting beside the superintendent. Plus, every
minute counted. I needed to get her and get back here as soon
as possible."

"Where is this store?"

She'd been hoping he wouldn't ask. "Over by the railroad
tracks." Once again she had acted impulsively and emotionally, thinking only of Amanda and of the program. She hadn't
stopped to consider what might have happened on the way

back there or back, nor how the situation might have been solved some other way. It had turned out okay, but she knew Scott wasn't thinking of that.

Scott sighed. "If you had followed policy, Jenny, you would have told me and I'd have had Dave Young get Amanda. You wouldn't have had to leave your post, and if something had happened with the ex-boyfriend or at the store by the railroad tracks, Dave would have been much more able to protect the girls than you. Do you see how I'm thinking?"

"Yes, I see." She felt chastened because he was right. She and Amanda had been lucky this evening. But her choice of action had not been wise. She could see that clearly now.

"The show was excellent and I thank you for your hard work. However, I truly hope you'll manage to think more about our policy and procedures, Jenny. If you're ready to leave, I'll escort you to your car."

Chapter 30

Jenny didn't know how long it had been raining but the streets were slick when she got in her car to drive home.

"Be careful," Scott said as he closed her door and watched her drive out of the staff parking lot.

The pleasure of the evening had vanished. All she could think about was how her actions had disappointed Scott. She had bragged about how successful the evening would be, had the arrogance to guarantee it! Then in her heedlessness, had spoiled it for him.

She blinked her eyes to control the tears, but they kept coming, blurring her vision as she peered through the windshield and heard the swish of the wipers. They weren't very good and she kept putting off getting new ones.

Why couldn't she curb her impulsiveness, especially when it came to school affairs? This wasn't the first time it had happened, but it was the first time Scott had been so severe with her. She'd been corrected by her boss and justly so. It had hurt, because professionally she had great admiration for Scott as principal. As educational consultant it was up to her to perform on the same level he did, not on a level that fell so short that he had to call her attention to it.

She had seen in his eyes that she had let him down. He'd expected better of her and she hadn't followed through.

The pain of that realization brought a new burst of tears as she came to a part of the road that was unfamiliar to her. She turned on her brights and saw she'd taken the wrong turn a mile or so back. This road was more rural but she could get home from here.

Her thoughts returned to Scott. She hadn't even told him she was sorry. Maybe he didn't want to hear that anyway. She'd said it before. Yet look how she'd done the same thing tonight.

Suddenly the lights of a speeding car appeared in her rearview mirror, blinding her. The driver passed her on the inside lane, causing her to swerve to the outside. Her wheels didn't hold to the slick road and she went down the embankment, the car picking up speed as it reached the bottom and crashed into denseness.

Instinct had her turning off the ignition before she hit her head on the steering wheel and blanked out.

"The superintendent told me he was very impressed with this school," Ed told Scott as he was getting ready to leave. "I thought the program went off very well. How about you?"

"Much better than I ever thought it would be," Scott agreed.

"See you tomorrow." Ed picked up his briefcase and went out of the door as Dave came in.

"I was just checking around. Rain's coming down pretty hard. Jenny's already gone?"

"Yeah. Sit a moment, Dave. You know a store by the tracks called J&S?"

"Sure. Pretty rough. Lots of characters tend to hang out there. Why?"

"Jenny went there this evening to pick up Amanda." He told the whole story as he'd heard it from Jenny. He rolled a pen in his fingers and moved around in his chair.

"Why didn't she tell you, and I'd have gone to get her? That's no place for Jenny and those school girls, especially after dark! Jenny acts first and thinks later," Dave said angrily.

"Exactly what I told her. I came down on her hard, but all I could think about was what might have happened because she didn't follow policy and inform me. Why do you think the girls were in that place?"

"A lot of our students live in that neighborhood, Scott. Rents are low and it's what they can afford. That's why Springview is so good for them, now that you and Ed and Jenny are here. It's a good environment for them."

"I hope so," Scott said wearily. "Thanks for coming by. See you tomorrow."

It was getting late, but Scott was still not inclined to go home. He felt restless and uneasy. He was sorry to have spoken to Jenny as he had, but it was imperative that she learn to respect school policy, otherwise he wouldn't be able to give her the excellent evaluation she needed at the end of the year.

He cleaned up his desk, and finally turned out the light and went home. Maybe when he got there he'd call Jenny to see how she was feeling.

Why is it so dark? Jenny wondered as she opened her eyes. She always had a dim lamp in the corner of her room in case

Nicky woke up and came up the steps. She tried to move, and moaned from the pain in her head and neck.

Memory came back slowly. The car sliding off the road and down a hill. She had to see where she was. She made herself lift her head and felt something sticky run down her face. She rubbed it with her finger and smelled it. Blood. She must have cut her forehead.

She could hear the rain, but she couldn't see anything. She had to get out of the car and up the road. Nicky would wake up in the morning and she had to be home. She had no idea what time it was, but she knew she couldn't sit here the rest of the night.

Cell phone. That's what they were for. Hers was in her bag. Where was it? Turn on the lights and see. The key was in the ignition. She turned it. Nothing happened. She tried it again. Nothing. Okay. She'd find the bag anyway. She took off her seatbelt and felt in the passenger seat. No bag. It must have fallen to the floor.

All the moving was making her dizzy, but she had to get the cell. She held onto the steering wheel with her left hand and bent over as far as she could, pushing her cold fingers around until they fastened on her bag.

She sat up slowly and opened the bag. When her fingers grasped the cell phone a spurt of triumph went through her. Now everything would be all right.

She pushed the on button. No light. Maybe she was touching the wrong button, since she couldn't see in the dark. She took her time and pushed a button again. She knew it was the correct one, but she counted just in case. It had to work. She'd just used it a few hours ago to talk to Amanda.

Then she remembered. She'd had to tell Amanda to speak up. The battery was low then, and she hadn't thought about

just stuck it back in her bag and took off to get Amanda. It
eded recharging, and the battery in the car wasn't even
rning over.

*Nicky. I have to get home for Nicky. I have to open the
or and get out.* She pushed on the door but it didn't
dge. She pushed some more, then she pounded, then in
speration she tried to throw herself against it, and all
nt blank again.

Scott was home and in his pajamas, but he wasn't ready
sleep. It was late, but he had to speak to Jenny even if he
ke her up.

He dialed her number. No answer. He dialed it again and
it ring ten times. Still no answer. She'd left Springview
re than an hour ago. Where was she on such a rainy night?
ertainly wasn't like her to go visiting. She would have gone
aight home. He dialed her cell. No answer.

Something was wrong. He dressed quickly and went back
the school then took the route she would have taken. He
ove carefully, looking right and left, searching for any sign
an accident, but saw nothing. So maybe she was safely
me after all. He'd just check to see that her car was in the
veway and he'd talk to her tomorrow.

When he arrived at the house and there was no sign of her
, terror struck him. *Oh, Jenny, what has happened? Where
you? Show me where you are so I can come to get you.
ar God, please help her. I beg of you, protect her and tell
where to find her.*

Scott was calling her. She couldn't see him in the dark,
she heard him asking where she was so he could come
get her.

My car went down into the woods. I took a wrong turn. She heard him say something else but couldn't make out what it was.

The next time she woke up, she saw Adam. He was happy and smiling at her.

"Let me go, Jenny," he said.

She tried to go to him, but he disappeared, leaving her in a shaft of light. The light surrounded her and in it she understood that the forgiveness she sought had always been available from the lord of loving kindness. Faith and answer to prayer had never been inaccessible nor denied. It was her own stubbornness that was the problem. She had refused to sever the guilt.

The light moved through her, invading all her being, until she felt cleansed, filled with gratitude, warmth, and peace.

The next time she opened her eyes, it was to see a blaze of lights and men cutting their way through deep thickets to get to her car.

Someone was carrying her, and it wasn't Scott, but he was holding her hand even though it was covered by a blanket. She smiled and drifted off again.

The sun was shining when she awakened the next time. The first person she saw was Scott. He looked unshaven and sleepless.

He bent down to her. She touched his cheek. "You've been keeping vigil," she whispered.

"Yes. I couldn't bear to leave you." His eyes were moist. "Now that I've seen you awake, I can go get cleaned up. Your mom and dad are here."

"How are you?" Mom asked. She kissed her and smoothed her hair back.

"I'm not sure," Jenny said. "I think I'm sore all over and must look a mess. I know I felt blood on my face."

"You might have a little scar on your forehead, and a bruise here and there, but mostly you were in shock. That's why you're here."

"How'd you know where to find me?"

"You can thank Scott for that," Dad replied. "He woke us up to say you'd left the school a long time ago, but you didn't answer your phone so he came to see if your car was here. He said he was going to look for you. I came, too, and he said you'd taken a wrong turn coming home and your car had gone off the road into the woods. I knew the turn he was talking about, so we followed that road and saw the skid marks."

"I couldn't figure out what was holding the car so tight that I couldn't open the door," Jenny said.

"Everything was wet, and when your car started down the hill, it picked up momentum and wedged you tight into a patch of thick shrubbery, bines, and saplings. It took several of us to cut through it to reach you."

"Where's Nicky?"

"We sent him on to school with the promise that we'd bring him to see you this afternoon if you're still here," Mom said.

"The car?"

"Don't know yet. Lots of damage to the front of it, of course. When we found the place, Scott left me up on the road to call the ambulance and he went down to find you. How did he know where to look for you, Jenny?"

Dad and Mom were looking at her gravely. She didn't know if they'd believe her, but she'd tell them just what happened.

"I was slipping in and out of consciousness. One time I heard Scott call me. He asked me where I was so he could come get me. I said I took a wrong turn and my car was in the woods, then I blanked out again."

While she was telling, she decided to let them know what

else had happened. She held out a hand to each of them. "I want you to know the other wonderful visitor I had. I saw Adam. He was smiling and he was happy. I tried to follow him but I couldn't."

"You know he's all right now," Mom said.

"Do you feel better about him?" Dad asked.

"I do." In the glance her parents exchanged Jenny realized how worried they must have been about her. "Thanks for being patient with me," she said.

"We knew that sooner or later you'd find your way back," Dad said.

"Patience is what being parents is all about, as you well know," Mom said, smiling.

It wasn't only for parents, Jenny mused after she was alone. It was a quality she was going to have to practice. Patience to think through her actions before undertaking them and patience as a replacement for the trait of stubbornness that was a part of her character, and that she hadn't realized until last night.

Chapter 31

"I don't think you should be going back to work so soon," Mom said as Jenny came slowly down the stairs on Friday.

"I'm really okay, Mom. Might be moving a little slowly for me, but the doctor said I'm healthy."

"You've still got the cut on your forehead."

"I know, but I'm not vain. That miracle tape the doctor used that pulls it together so I don't have to get stitches is doing fine. Mom, it's the last day before Christmas holidays, and I really do want to see everyone."

"I know I'm just being a worrywart, honey. You'll be comfortable in that rental car, won't you?"

"I will, and I'll see you later," Jenny said.

Being cared for as she had been since the accident was a blessing for which she was thankful, but it was great to be out in the open again and to be going to Springview.

The news of the accident had spread in the mysterious way

of the grapevine, and she was besieged by staff who saw her and wanted to know the details. They hadn't expected to see her until after Christmas. Even Scott and Ed were surprised.

"I didn't know you were coming in today," Scott said when she went to his office. "Are you well enough? Here, sit down." He put her in the chair near his desk.

"I wanted to see everyone," she said, "and I needed to ask you a policy question. I want to give Lynn and Gladys an appreciation gift. Is that appropriate?"

He glanced at her to see if she was serious. "There is no written policy about gifts between people of equal status. When it comes to gifts or favors between staff and students, that's a different matter for obvious reasons. Did you receive the policy manual when you arrived?"

"Yes, I think so. I need to read it again. Scott, I'm sorry about not consulting you Wednesday night. I acted without thinking it through, and I realize how unprofessional that was."

"I didn't mean to speak to you so severely."

She interrupted him. "You were right to do so, and maybe that's what I needed to make me see where I've been wrong. I just hated disappointing you," she said, trying to maintain an objective attitude.

A single knock on the door was followed by Ed. "Sorry to interrupt, but Sergeant Hampton is here and wants to speak to the three of us."

"Bring him in," Scott said, and pulled up two more chairs.

"We have surprising information about your break-in which will be all over the news, but I wanted to tell you privately first," the sergeant said.

Scott, Ed, and Jenny glanced at each other. "How did you find it out?" Scott asked, expressing their thoughts.

"Through interrogating the boys who assaulted Billy Cross."

"They were involved in the break-in too?" Jenny asked. It didn't seem likely because they would have bragged about it and it would have come to light.

"Not directly, no," Hampton said. "It was when they began to realize the legal seriousness of what they'd done to Billy. The assault was one thing, but when the possible long-term damage to his eye was brought into the picture, George Hall lost his bullish attitude and became a scared boy. He wanted to do anything he could to lessen the severity of his sentence, and asked would it help if he gave us information on the break-in. We said it would be taken into consideration if it could be proven to be true. Matt Bryant said it was true because he knew all about it as well."

"Was it someone here at the school?" Scott asked. The police officer's deliberate recital was keeping them all in suspense.

"No, but it was someone whose name first came up around here." He turned to Jenny. "Do you recall when I asked you if the three girls you interrogated gave you a name, and you said no?"

"That's right. They didn't know anyone specific. But there was a boy who was in the same grade as one of their older siblings who was always in trouble." Jenny thought hard. "Someone with an odd name, like Rocco. No, it was Jojo." She looked at Hampton with wide eyes. "That's who it turned out to be?" she said disbelievingly.

"What was his connection to George and Matt?" Ed asked.

"He is George's first cousin."

"There's more to it than pure vandalism, I know," Scott said. "Why did he do it? There must have been someone else involved."

"You're right, Dr. Phillips. Here's the other part of the story. Jojo had graduated from bullishness at school, to petty larceny, car hijacking, and other small crimes. He operated out of Columbia and got a reputation as a person you could hire for small stuff. A man hired him to break into this school and leave no trace. He paid him half the money up front. Jojo did a good job. We didn't have a clue, as you know. When he went to the man for the other half of the fee, the man said he didn't have it just then. He's been putting Jojo off ever since. Jojo knows he has the money."

It was like looking at a suspenseful movie, Scott thought. Your mind races ahead to identify the mastermind behind the crime. That's what his mind was doing, but surely it was too farfetched to be true.

"When Jojo is in town, he hangs out at George's house. He's George's idol, so Jojo often tells him what he's been hired to do. It puffs him up in his young cousin's eyes. Lately he's been making threats about the local guy who owes him money. So George, to save his own neck, gives us the name of the man who paid Jojo to vandalize Springview." Hampton might be deliberate and official, Jenny thought, but he knew how to build up to a climax.

"Mr. Lawrence T. Gordon," he announced, looking particularly at Scott to see his reaction.

I was right, Scott thought.

"I can't believe it," Jenny said. She glanced at Scott. He believed it.

"How did he think he could get away with that?" Ed asked.

"Apparently he didn't give Jojo enough credit. Gordon thought Jojo was truly dumb and would be scared to put his word against that of a banker. But Jojo uses the latest electronic gadgets. Loves them. Has a mini-recorder he always wears for what he calls his business transactions and a camera. He gave us the evidence."

"Jojo owned up to it?" Jenny asked.

"Like George, he figured cooperating with the police ould reduce his offense. Also he was happy to pull the rug ut from someone who thought he was such a big shot, yet as too mean to pay what he owed Jojo."

"What was Gordon's motive?" Scott asked. "Did he say?"

"On advice of counsel he's not saying anything. Remember hen I asked you if you had any enemies, and you said no?"

Scott nodded his head.

Sergeant Hampton looked at him. "You were wrong."

Chapter 32

"He's going to stonewall as long as possible, Scott. Then he'll quietly resign from the school board for some phony reason," Dave said when Scott told him of Hampton's disclosure.

"Aren't you surprised, Dave? High school is one thing, but we're all grown men now. Why would he endanger his whole career and standing in the community by hiring a known petty criminal to pull a mean trick like this? I don't understand his thinking."

"You don't think like that, Scott. You're always trying to pull the good out of your students, show them their potential. Larry Gordon doesn't see that much good in people. He just sees what he wants and will use anyone to get it. He wanted you out and Bruce in, and set about to make it happen. Incidentally, I just found out the other day that one of the teachers who's complaining about the new policies is Larry's cousin.

He's a fourth-grade teacher, Sherman Boone. You'll need to keep an eye on him."

"I know Boone. I don't think he'll be any trouble. What I want most is to put all of this behind me so I can concentrate on what I came here to do."

The next day, the TV channels and the paper were filled with the story. Scott was thankful it was Saturday and no one from the media could get to him in his office.

Over the lunch table with his parents, his dad spoke of other men he'd known like Larry Gordon in his law practice. "Their arrogance makes them contemptuous of others and of anything that stands in the way of what they've convinced themselves is rightly theirs."

"I'm sorry for his wife. I've met her and she doesn't seem to be that way," his mom said.

"He probably has her under his thumb," Dad said. "We'll just have to wait and see how it all plays out. But I'm thankful it's no longer a concern for you, Scott."

"Amen to that," Scott said.

What was of concern to him now was Jenny. There was something different about her since the accident but he hadn't had an opportunity to spend enough time with her to define it precisely. It seemed to be an underlying calmness, almost a serenity. Could it be that she had been able to make the final step and let go of her burden?

He hadn't seen Nicky for a few days, so maybe he'd just nosey by the house right now and see him. And Jenny.

They were both in the yard when he pulled into the driveway.

"Hi, Dr. Scott. I haven't seen you for a long time." Nicky flung himself against Scott's legs. "Can I have a ride on your shoulders?" he asked.

"Wait a minute, I have to say hello to your mom first."

Scott walked over to Jenny who was sitting on the steps and smiling at him.

"Hey." He sat beside her and put his arm around her shoulders.

"Hey." Her eyes were clear and filled with warmth.

"How are you, Jenny?"

"Wonderful. You?"

"The same, now that I'm here with you. It seems I need to ask you a policy question about riding on shoulders." A smile quirked the corner of his mouth.

"It depends on who the shoulders belong to." Her face was sober but there was a gleam in her eyes.

"They belong to me."

"The manual says permission is granted."

The message in her eyes was so forceful and deep it took the breath out of Scott.

"Jenny?" he whispered.

"As soon as the ride on shoulders is over, I want you to take me someplace, Scott. I'll go ask Mom to look after Nicky."

"Why can't I go?" Nicky asked.

"Not this time, but maybe the next." Jenny's position was clear.

Scott took Nicky several times around the yard, all of the time wondering if this was when Jenny was ready to go to the pond. He thought so, he hoped so. When she came back out with a warm jacket on and he looked in her face, he knew it was so and his heart started beating wildly.

When they were both in the car he said, "Don't tell me. I know where we're going."

He drove slowly and carefully with one hand, the other holding hers. He parked the Lexus and they walked hand in hand through the mostly bare trees to the pond. The air was cool and the sun broke through clouds now and then.

"I have so much to tell you, dearest Scott, and this is the
ace to say it because this is the place where things went
rong between us. I found out things I hadn't known the
ght of the accident."

This wasn't what Scott had expected. "How do you mean?"

"I drifted in and out of consciousness. One time when I
me to, it was because you were calling me. You heard me
swer, didn't you?"

"Yes, thank God. I heard you and I saw you in the car sur-
ounded by brush. I was so scared, Jenny." He brought her to
im and held her tight.

"I knew you'd find me," she said.

She stepped back so she could see his face while remain-
g in the security of his arms.

"The next time I woke up I saw Adam."

An expression of wonder came over Scott's face. "You
w Adam." His voice was hushed.

"He smiled at me and he was happy. He told me to let him
o. When he went away I tried to follow him, but I was sur-
ounded by light."

She paused, and such peace came over her that Scott knew
e was reliving the experience.

"There was no voice, Scott, but I was left with the knowl-
dge that faith and prayer and forgiveness had always been
vailable to me. The problem was me and my stubbornness.
wouldn't let go of the guilt."

"Oh, Jenny" was all he could say.

"It seemed like the light was all in me and through me so
at I felt cleansed and grateful in ways I can't describe, and
was at peace."

They stood in silence assimilating what Jenny had ex-
erienced.

Then she said, "I told Mom and Dad I'd seen Adam and that he was happy and smiling. But I wanted to tell you all of it, and I needed to tell you here. I'm ready to let it go, just as Mikey said. Are you?"

"Yes. My last bit of reserve was tied up in waiting for you." Scott faced the pond. "I let it go."

Jenny faced the pond and opened her arms. "I let it go. Goodbye, Adam."

Scott turned to Jenny. He cupped her face tenderly in his hands, his eyes burning into hers. "I love you, Jenny Mayes Cannon, with all of my heart and soul. I have loved you all of my life. No one has ever been as much a part of me as you."

Jenny touched his face, her eyes brimming with love. "I love you, Scott Phillips, with all my heart and soul. No one has ever meant to me what you have ever since I was a child. You have always been a part of me. Always." She stood on her toes to kiss him. "Thank you for waiting for me."

"I had no choice." He hugged her so tightly she could barely breathe, but it was all right, she thought, because from now on they would breathe as one.

"Will you marry me, my darling Jenny?" he asked when they came up for air from a long kiss.

"Of course," she sighed happily. "It's in the policy manual."

Epilogue

On this final Saturday in May, it seemed that all the elements had conspired to make her wedding day perfect, Jenny thought as she stood in the bridal room of the church, basking in the touches to her veil, makeup and gown that Mom, Helena and Alnetta were making.

The sky was a heavenly blue decorated with fluffy white clouds. Through the screened window, a balmy breeze caressed her. She could hear birds trilling their songs among the leafy trees surrounding the churchyard.

The white roses of her bridal bouquet filled the room with their fragrance. She smiled as she remembered the florist's bewilderment when Jenny had insisted on the inclusion of a camellia in the center of the bouquet.

"I know it's unusual, but it has a special meaning for me," Jenny had told her.

Her inner self, tightly entwined around guilt, had gradually loosened like a camellia bud, and now, with new understanding and love, was in full bloom.

"Katy, please stand still while I fix your hair," Patty said. "You're not going to be much of a flower girl if you keep pulling at your curls."

"Alicia, come here and let me tie your sash again," Cynthia said.

"Am I going to be a flower girl when you and Uncle Richie get married next month?" Alicia asked, her cheeks flushed with excitement.

"Yes, you will, because I have only one niece the right age."

"Have you and Richie decided on a house yet?" Alnetta asked, adjusting the small train on Jenny's gown.

"Not yet, but at least we know it'll be right here in Brentwood."

"What about you and Scott, Jenny? A house, or will you stay in his apartment?" Alnetta had arrived this morning and was busy catching up on the news.

"The apartment, but we'll start looking for a house when we get back from London." Jenny looked at her hair critically. "Helena, I think the veil needs to be farther back. I don't want it over my face at all because I want to see everybody."

Mom, smoothing the neckline of Jenny's gown, told Alnetta, "We're all so proud of Scott. The school board couldn't wait to offer him the contract for principal. Did they even have any other candidates, Jenny?"

"There were three others, but Scott was head and shoulders above them in achievement. In this one year the test scores have already gone up."

"Will you be working with him next year?" Alnetta checked herself in the mirror thinking how glad she was to

ave slimmed down following the birth of her son, especially
s she was the matron of honor.

"We decided that I should work at home on the research
ve already done for the doctorate and wait to see which uni-
ersity will accept me, Chicago or Duke." Jenny refreshed her
pstick. She was ready to go.

"Duke is just a few hours away in North Carolina. Wouldn't
ou prefer that?" Cynthia asked. She felt so close to these
omen who, in a month's time, would be related to her.

"We'll be happy with either one. Patty, check outside and
e how much longer we have to wait."

Patty came back in, eyes shining with excitement. "The
urch is packed, Jenny, and the organist gave me the signal,
let's get in line."

Mom had to go out first to be escorted to her seat.

As Jenny waited at the back of the line, she stood on her
es to catch a glimpse of Scott, handsome in his tux, coming
wait for her, accompanied by his dad who he'd asked to be
s best man.

Scott seemed to be looking up the aisle trying to see her.
trio of butterflies fluttered their gossamer wings inside her
omach. Soon she and Scott would be married!

The music began. Nicky, in a miniature tux, went steadily
wn the aisle bearing the rings on a satin pillow. He was
llowed by Alicia and Katy, scattering rose petals and looking
orable in their full-skirted white dresses with rose sashes.

Alnetta, matron of honor, was next in an elegant column
cream silk selected by Helena. Each woman wore the dress
a shade that suited her coloring and personality.

Cynthia, in pale rose, was next, escorted by Richie; then
tty, in robin's-egg blue with Mikey; and last, Helena, in
ender with Dave Young.

Jenny felt her father step in place to escort her down the aisle. He took her hand and placed it on his arm.

"Jenny, my beloved daughter, I want you to know Scott was always my choice for you."

"I'm so glad, Daddy." She squeezed his arm.

The organist sounded the opening notes of the wedding march. The congregation came to its feet and turned toward them as she and her dad walked in slow rhythm down the long aisle.

She looked from side to side, seeing so many old friends as well as the ones she'd made since returning home. Tiffany, in a striking hat, gave her a tiny wave. Maybe now that Scott was definitely unavailable, Tiffany would marry Roger. The first pews were filled with family, hers and Scott's. What a joyous day! She couldn't help smiling and nodding to people. There were cousins Lucinda and Leona. They'd postponed one of their trips to be here, and she was grateful.

They came to the front where Scott and his dad stood. She felt the intensity of Scott's gaze, and turned her face to look at him.

"Dearly beloved, we are gathered here," the minister began.

Jenny heard the familiar words with one part of her mind, but the other part of her being was in communion with Scott. They were meant to be together from the very beginning, but circumstance and their own imperfect selves had delayed their destiny.

They repeated their vows clearly, unhesitatingly. When Scott said, "With this ring I thee wed," and she did the same, Jenny thought her heart would burst with happiness.

The minister pronounced them husband and wife, and told Scott, "You may kiss your bride."

"My darling Jenny, my wife," he whispered as he kissed

r with passionate tenderness. Jenny gave him a lifetime of
omise as she returned the kiss.

The grace of God had brought them to this day despite
emselves. It had worked miracles, and, as they walked back
wn the aisle with Nicky between them and people applaud-
g, Jenny vowed that no matter what they might have to go
rough in the future, their faith and their love would grow in
rength and endure.